DEATH AT THE WYCHBOURNE FOLLIES

Recent Titles by Amy Myers from Severn House

The Nell Drury Mysteries

DANCING WITH DEATH
DEATH AT THE WYCHBOURNE FOLLIES

The Jack Colby, Car Detective, Series

CLASSIC IN THE BARN
CLASSIC CALLS THE SHOTS
CLASSIC IN THE CLOUDS
CLASSIC MISTAKE
CLASSIC IN THE PITS
CLASSIC CASHES IN
CLASSIC IN THE DOCK
CLASSIC AT BAY

The Marsh and Daughter Mysteries

THE WICKENHAM MURDERS
MURDER IN FRIDAY STREET
MURDER IN HELL'S CORNER
MURDER AND THE GOLDEN GOBLET
MURDER IN THE MIST
MURDER TAKES THE STAGE
MURDER ON THE OLD ROAD
MURDER IN ABBOT'S FOLLY

DEATH AT THE WYCHBOURNE FOLLIES

Amy Myers

This first world edition published 2018
in Great Britain and 2019 in the USA by
SEVERN HOUSE PUBLISHERS LTD of
Eardley House, 4 Uxbridge Street, London W8 7SY.
Trade paperback edition first published
in Great Britain and the USA 2019 by
SEVERN HOUSE PUBLISHERS LTD.

British Library Cataloguing in Publication Data
A CIP catalogue record for this title is available from the British Library.

ISBN-13: 978-0-7278-8850-1 (cased)
ISBN-13: 978-1-84751-974-0 (trade paper)
ISBN-13: 978-1-4483-0183-6 (e-book)

All Severn House titles are printed on acid-free paper.

Severn House Publishers support the Forest Stewardship Council™ [FSC™],
the leading international forest certification organisation.
All our titles that are printed on FSC certified paper carry the FSC logo.

Typeset by Palimpsest Book Production Ltd.,
Falkirk, Stirlingshire, Scotland.
Printed and bound in Great Britain by
TJ International, Padstow, Cornwall.

AUTHOR'S NOTE

The county of Kent boasts many splendid ancient houses, castles and stately homes. Wychbourne Court is one of the latter and located between the famous Knole and Ightham Mote and not far from Anne Boleyn's Hever Castle. Unlike them, Wychbourne Court and its occupants, local residents and guests are fictitious. London's Gaiety Theatre, spoken of so fondly in this novel, is also factual, as was the Guv'nor. The Gaiety finally closed its doors just before the Second World War. The actors who appeared there in this novel are also fictitious, as are the other characters.

Wychbourne Court didn't materialize all by itself; it had tremendous help both from my agent, Sara Keane of Keane Kataria, and from my publishers, Severn House – Kate Lyall Grant and her incomparable team, including Sara Porter, copy-editor Emma Grundy Haigh and Piers Tilbury have expertly magicked *Death at the Wychbourne Follies* and its predecessor, *Dancing with Death*, into being. To all of them my deep gratitude.

WYCHBOURNE COURT

Members of the Ansley Family appearing in Death at the Wychbourne Follies

Lord (Gerald) Ansley, 8th Marquess Ansley
Lady (Gertrude) Ansley, Marchioness Ansley
Lord Richard Ansley, one of their three sons
Lady Helen Ansley, their elder daughter
Lady Sophy Ansley, their younger daughter
Lady Clarice Ansley, sister to Lord Ansley

The Upper Servants

Nell Drury, chef
Frederick Peters, butler
Florence Fielding, housekeeper
Mr Briggs, Lord Ansley's valet
Jenny Smith, Lady Ansley's maid

Guests, other residents and visitors

Arthur Fontenoy, former lover of the 7th Marquess
Rex Beringer, guest
Lady (Katie) Kencroft, guest
Lord (Charles) Kencroft, guest
Lynette Reynolds, guest
Neville Heydock, guest
Alice Maxwell, guest
Tobias St John Rocke, guest

and

Inspector Alexander Melbray of Scotland Yard

ONE

'Follies!' A snort from Mrs Fielding.

Nell Drury struggled to hold back a giggle. The housekeeper's disapproval was only to be expected, but as chef Nell could beg to differ.

'Crackling crumpets,' she whipped back, 'why shouldn't they put on a show for fun? The Ansleys can beat the Ziegfeld Follies any day of the week.'

'Pierrots indeed. Fancy her ladyship dressed up like a clown like those we see at the seaside. It isn't right.'

'It's for good causes,' Nell said brightly. She knew the only reason Lord Ansley had reluctantly agreed to his offspring's demands was that the money raised would be given to war charities. In this year of 1926, the war had been over for seven years, but how did one calculate 'over'? The surviving men and women had come back to their homes physically but many were still stuck in 1918, some with physical injuries, others with mental wounds and all with scars that they struggled to deal with.

Mrs Fielding stood up, thus tacitly declaring the gathering at an end. '*And* it's beginning to snow,' she added darkly, ignoring Nell's point.

Nell peered through the windows of the butler's room, still affectionately known as Pug's Parlour, where she and the other upper servants of the Kentish stately home of Wychbourne Court had gathered for a brief lunch. To her surprise, Mrs Fielding was right. Snowflakes were indeed drifting past the window and settling on the kitchen yard outside. The first this month, though as it was only mid-January there was plenty of time for more. In a few hours, the guests would be arriving, and this threat from the weather wasn't a good omen for the smooth passage of the weekend ahead – or for the Wychbourne Follies.

'You mark my words, nothing good will come of it.' Mrs Fielding gave a final sniff and marched out in a swirl of her old-fashioned bombazine skirts. Mr Peters, the butler, shot a compassionate look at Nell as he followed the housekeeper out. He'd no choice, as his *tendresse* for Mrs Fielding was now an open secret. That just left Lord Ansley's valet, Mr Briggs, as Lady Ansley was awaiting the arrival of a new lady's maid. Mr Briggs, Lord Ansley's valet, was as usual in a world of his own, with a happy smile on his lips. He had been shell-shocked during the war, and now had his own way of dealing with life.

Privately, Nell too had her doubts about the Follies, but she dismissed them. Her job as chef was to get moving with such a splendid dinner this evening that it would ensure that the path to the Follies and the weekend was a smooth one. A welcoming dinner that included sea bass in champagne sauce, followed by pheasant and then apples with cream of kirsch could not fail to please the guests who would be joining them this Thursday to stay until Sunday. Why shouldn't everything go smoothly anyway? Snow outside, the warmth and comfort of Wychbourne Court inside, and her cooking – what more could anyone ask?

These were the 1920s; the war was behind them and despite the problems it had bequeathed, a brave new world was springing up all over the place – and so were ideas in her mind. Cooking was an art, the kitchen was her studio and her job was to see that the dishes she produced lived up to that. Gone were the heavy meals of the past, gone were the restrictions of wartime rationing. Coming in their place was the excitement of rediscovering scents and spices of the past and adding them to the glories of exotic new flavours and dishes from far afield. And Wychbourne Court, with its own herb and vegetable gardens, together with its orchard, was a paradise for Nell to fulfil her dreams of creating her very own cuisine. Away with doubts and worries. All would go well this weekend.

Gertrude, Lady Ansley, however, was still battling with her doubts. Until this change of plan for the Follies had been sprung on her by her children, it had seemed such a pleasant idea to hold a reunion of her former Gaiety Theatre friends at Wychbourne Court together with an impromptu performance in the ballroom. She had seen little of them since her marriage over thirty years ago to dear Gerald, 8th Marquess Ansley, and very occasionally she still hankered after those old exciting days on the stage. Her career there had been short but successful thanks to her role in *The Flower Shop Girl.*

'Did you find those old postcards, Helen?' she asked her elder daughter anxiously. The cards of her friends and herself in their Gaiety years had sold in their thousands, but a new generation occupied the London stage now. Displaying the old cards would bring pleasure to her former friends, and indeed herself, for memorabilia of those times were usually consigned to the Velvet Room. Here she could relax from her duties as the Marchioness Ansley and dwell briefly in the past.

Helen yawned, adjusting her elegant pose on the chaise longue. If only the fashion for Eton crops would pass, Gertrude lamented, so that her daughter's golden hair could once again soften her classically beautiful face, but Helen was adamant on remaining à la mode. 'All on display in the Great Hall,' Helen reassured her. 'Peters is looking after it. That annoying little man's helping him.'

'Mr Trotter means well, Helen,' Gertrude said placatingly, 'and it keeps your aunt busy.'

That was an understatement. Gerald's sister Clarice, who lived with them, was *always* busy where the ghosts of Wychbourne Court were concerned. She was dedicated to their welfare – as Clarice put it – and had arranged for Mr Timothy Trotter, a well-known spirit photographer, to spend a few days at Wychbourne. Naturally, being Clarice, she had not remembered to mention this either to her or to the servants. Yesterday Peters had to make urgent arrangements for a dark room to be set up and equipped, which had involved her son Richard motoring to Sevenoaks for chemicals, plates and other strange objects. Mr Trotter had anxiously assured them all that he was bringing his own enlarger and he would be of no trouble at all – which of course ensured he was the opposite, as he fussed around.

Gertrude reverted to her principal worry. 'Did you arrange for the posters and programmes too?' It was a pity that her younger daughter, Sophy, was so busy with the local Labour Party that she couldn't have given this task to her. Helen was a darling, but unpredictable and easily bored. That was the burden beautiful women carried, Gertrude thought. They had too much attention paid to them and could not see the right path for all the tinsel lying along their way. If only Helen would marry that nice Rex Beringer.

'Done,' Helen answered languidly. 'We've spread them among the breakfast room, the library and the bedrooms. But have you done the dirty deed yet?'

Gertrude blenched at this turn of the tables. 'Not yet,' she said defiantly. 'I thought I'd tell them during dinner.'

'Tell them *after* dinner. Then that stuffy Hubert Jarrett will be full of port.'

Gertrude sighed. This weekend had originally been planned merely as a reunion and somehow she hadn't plucked up the courage to tell her guests that the Follies, which had begun as such a jolly idea for their own amusement, had somehow turned, courtesy of Richard, into a fully-fledged performance to be held in Wychbourne village at the Coach and Horses inn. Furthermore, the purchase of tickets would be open to the villagers and of course the Wychbourne Court servants. All in a good cause, Richard had assured her jauntily, and after all it was a splendid notion to give the proceeds to charity. Nevertheless, Gertrude shivered at the thought of what might go wrong. Suppose that troublemaker Jethro James bought a ticket?

Gertrude clutched at Helen's solution. 'Very well,' she said meekly.

'And, Mother,' Helen said in alarm, 'you did tell Neville Heydock that Lynette Reynolds will be coming?'

'Well, no,' Gertrude admitted. Lynette, true to form, had at first refused the invitation only to change her mind at the very last moment. Although her present husband would not be attending, Lynette would.

'Neville Heydock is still a dish, even if he is an oldie.' Helen giggled. 'I can't wait to see his face when he sees her.'

Gertrude was too busy imagining his former wife's expression to reply at once. It hadn't even occurred to her that there might be trouble. Lynette was always so emotional, and even though she'd obviously married again that whole episode over the divorce from Neville and the subsequent hushed rumours had been so unpleasant that she wouldn't want to be reminded of it.

Could anything else go wrong? Nothing surely. There was Alice Maxwell of course. She was another Hubert Jarrett in her own way, taking her career (and women's suffrage) very seriously indeed. Gertrude had heard that both of them were hoping for elevation in their status, Hubert for a knighthood and Alice to become a Dame of the British Empire. That was very unlikely, in Gertrude's opinion, given how long even Henry Irving and Ellen Terry had had to wait for such recognition. Of course in their cases, whispers of an unconventional life had delayed their prospects and that certainly couldn't be said of either Hubert or Alice, who both had the strictest moral principles. But what would they say when they found out about the plans for the Follies? Come to that, what would they say to one another? Helen had passed on the current gossip that the two were not on speaking terms far too late for Gertrude to change her invitation list.

Apart from Gerald, only two people saved Gertrude from complete despair. One was the invaluable Nell. She was a brilliant chef and would ensure that dinners and luncheons would be magnificent and she was a trusty companion in arms in times of trouble. Nell would be watching on her behalf for warning signs.

Her other saviour would be her guest Tobias. He will calm things down, Gertrude thought thankfully. Tobias St John Rocke, the comforter at the Gaiety Theatre, the keeper of secrets, on whose shoulder they had all wept from time to time. The peacemaker, the purveyor of common sense, would be here.

In a calm sea, everyone is a pilot, so the proverb went. A stormy one demanded swift action, though. Nell drew a deep breath. Blithering beans, the clock was ticking away fast. One of her under-chefs was weeping, the other one was sulking, Mrs Fielding was gloating, Mrs Squires, her plain cook, was grimly minding her own business, the scullery maids were hovering in terror waiting for their instructions and everyone else was speedily inventing missions other than in the kitchen. Nell had just been informed that the chestnut purée for the pheasant had been thrown away, admittedly in error. She gritted her teeth. Blame could be apportioned later if appropriate, but what was needed now was a solution.

'Right,' she said briskly. 'Jumping jellies, what are you all waiting for? Roast and glaze more chestnuts *now.* Use them as garnish. Make a Madeira sauce for the pheasant. And don't look at me like lobsters pleading to go home. Snap to it.'

They snapped. She could see by Michel's expression that he was the culprit, but she knew he wouldn't do it again. Incident over. Order began to reassert itself. Kitchens were express trains to wonderful destinations. It didn't take much to knock them off the rails, and it didn't take much to push them back if you knew what you were doing. After a happy year as chef at Wychbourne Court and her earlier six years' training under Monsieur Escoffier at London's Carlton Hotel, Nell was well aware of that. The occasional bad egg popped up, but that was to be expected. Only not this weekend, she hoped.

As she finished her inspection of the almond soup (under-chef Kitty's speciality), Nell saw Mr Peters coming through the doorway. What did he want? Mr Peters wasn't a tall man, but he brought his own air of authority with him, although before he came to Wychbourne he had no training as a butler. He had been the batman to Lord Noel, the Ansleys' son who had died at the Battle of Ypres. Kenelm, their eldest son, was in the Colonial Service and living abroad, and Richard was the youngest at twenty-six this year.

Mr Peters' mission proved to be straightforward, thankfully.

'Tea may be served, Mrs Fielding. The last guest has arrived in the drawing room,' he announced.

The guests' accompanying servants had already been shown to their rooms in the servants' wing. Thank goodness there were only the three of them, Nell thought. They could be more troublesome than the guests themselves. One of them was valet to the diplomat Lord Kencroft, another was a formidable lady called Doris Paget, dresser to the famous actress Miss Maxwell and the third was Mr Heydock's gentleman's gentleman, Mr Winter, a veritable Jeeves, so Nell had heard, who accompanied him everywhere. All of them seemed trouble-free, according to Mrs Fielding.

Nell was glad that tea was the housekeeper's province, not hers. Mr Peters had made the announcement sound like the trump of doom, which Nell devoutly hoped it wasn't.

'Is Mr Heydock here then?' Kitty asked eagerly. 'I'd love

to see him.' The highlight of the autumn had been her visit to Drury Lane theatre to see *Rose Marie*, the romantic operetta set in the Canadian Rockies.

'I saw a picture of Lady Kencroft in the *Illustrated London News*. Lady Sophy showed it to me,' said one of the kitchen maids. 'She was with Rudolph Valentino. He's making another film about the Sheikh.' Valentino, for all his good looks, wasn't Nell's cup of tea, but he seemed to be the idol of every woman she met.

'I doubt if she's bringing Rudolph to Wychbourne,' Nell said crisply. 'You'll have to make do with Neville Heydock.' At least he was fun. He'd appeared in many comedies and musical plays as he had a remarkable singing voice. He could knock spots off most leading men even though he was no youngster. She'd seen him at a play at the Albion in London's Strand and couldn't wait to see him here at Wychbourne. 'He'll be performing in the Follies here on Saturday.'

'Perhaps he'll sing "Rose Marie, I Love You",' Kitty said eagerly.

'Saturday's my evening off.' Mrs Squires made a rare contribution to the conversation. 'I thought I'd go with my friend Ethel.' Unlike many of the Wychbourne servants who lived in the east wing, as Nell did herself, Mrs Squires' home was in the village.

'There's a late supper to be served after the performance,' Mrs Fielding commented darkly. 'That means you won't be going, Kitty,' she added with noticeable satisfaction. Because they were members of Nell's staff as chef, Kitty and Michel did not come under her jurisdiction, a permanent source of frustration to the housekeeper.

'Some of us might be able to go to the performance,' Nell put in.

'Not those of us who know their duty, Miss Drury.'

Nell did not take the bait. She was a high-ranking chef – and Lady Ansley had asked her to go to the performance. For some reason that Nell had not yet grasped, her ladyship was worried about what might happen – and that worried Nell. She loved Wychbourne and felt part of it, which meant doing what she could to help in times of trouble. And those came from time to time. That was hardly surprising as there had been Ansleys at

Wychbourne since before the Norman Conquest; the original farmhouse had long since become this splendid red-brick mansion with two eighteenth-century wings added to all the earlier centuries' handiwork.

Nell concentrated on the task in hand: dinner preparations. The sea bass with champagne sauce, which had been a favourite recipe of the famous Carême, chef to the Prince Regent, required attention. The pheasant – now with Madeira sauce – was under control, as were the apples and syllabubs. Syllabubs were the famous Dr Johnson's favourite, she remembered, and a wonderful standby. Order began to reassert itself. Kitchens were like recipes, she thought. You didn't have to follow every detail, but you did have to know what you were doing.

She was dimly aware that in the background the conversation about the Follies on Saturday was still in progress, but then her attention was seized by Muriel, one of the scullery maids, who was bringing in the fish kettle and steamer. She had stopped for a brief chat with the kitchen maids, and Nell could hear what it was about.

'Lady Sophy said her ladyship and all her old friends are going to dress up like Pierrots and do a dance,' Muriel was saying.

Nell groaned to herself. Lady Sophy was apt to chatter rather too much about the family plans – it all came of her political beliefs that family and servants should all be one big happy family. So they were, but that didn't mean that every member of it wanted every other member to know what was going on or that some members couldn't employ others to carry out their wishes. Moreover, whatever Lady Ansley's fears were, they weren't going to be helped by discussion here.

Nell knew very well that it had been Lord Richard's idea to hold the performance in the Coach and Horses and that Lady Ansley was scared stiff about how her guests would take the news. Even though most of them were active on the stage they might well have opinions on whether appearing in the Follies was advisable, now that the venue had been changed to the Coach and Horses. The guests would still be expecting their impromptu revels to be held in the Wychbourne Court ballroom with a jolly audience of themselves and a few friends, but for the more austere among them it might be quite another for the family to be selling tickets in a public house. Lord Richard, Lady Helen and Lady Sophy had acted with the best of intentions, but sometimes those paved the road to disaster.

Here were the people she had known and loved, Gertrude thought, looking round the dinner table somewhat reassured. There were other guests here too, of course. Clarice was looking after Mr Trotter, who appeared somewhat overwhelmed, judging by the anxious way he was looking from one to the other of the assembled company. Rex Beringer as usual had eyes only for Helen who, together with Richard and Sophy, was on her best behaviour. Gertrude had feared that they would plunge all too quickly into discussions about the Follies, but instead – *apparently* with genuine interest – they were questioning her Gaiety guests about their memories of Edwardian times.

There were seven guests from her Gaiety days. Some she had not seen since her own days on stage; others she had met ten years ago at George Edwardes' funeral – the Guv'nor as he was known. He had been the long-term manager of the Gaiety and Daly's theatres; his name would be forever linked with the Gaiety Girls with whom he had brought music, comedy and drama together.

Once upon a time she had poured her heart out to darling Katie with her bouncing brown curls and generous heart; the dramatic and impulsive Lynette had cheered her darkest hours; Constance with her serious dark eyes had been the distributor of wisdom; and Alice had been the one to take missions on board, daring to defy even the Guv'nor on occasion.

They had all fallen for Neville Heydock, with his handsome looks, impeccable stylishness and magnificent tenor voice. Kind too, she remembered. No wonder Lynette had been head over heels in love with him. Gertrude had seen his expression however when he set eyes on her here; Lynette had merely thought it amusing, to Gertrude's relief. Hubert, Constance's husband, looked as noble and sombre in appearance as his majestic renderings of tragic and dramatic prose and poetry demanded. And yet she remembered him as a rather sullen young recruit in the chorus who couldn't say boo to a goose and was lucky to be given any solo lines at all.

And then Gertrude's eye fell on Tobias, her erstwhile rock, with gratitude. There he was, just as chubby and cheerful as ever, the well-remembered pacifier. He had taken on the task of entertaining Constance, who was even laughing, unlike her usual calm and quiet self. Tobias had always taken character parts, famous for his old uncle in *Waltzing in Summer*, the peasant in *The Count of Rosenbourg* and the jovial baker in *The Flower Shop Girl*.

They all looked much the same, albeit a little greyer, a little plumper, a little more serious. Both tea and the reception in the Great Hall before dinner had gone well. Katie, here with her husband, Charles, the diplomat Lord Kencroft, had been the sparkling, bubbly self that Gertrude remembered so well. Neville seemed to be chatting happily enough to Lynette; Constance's self-opinionated husband, Hubert, was even talking to his arch enemy, Alice Maxwell, who like Tobias had never married. Alice had always been so serious, so dedicated to her career, and like Hubert had moved from musical comedy to drama.

Gertrude relaxed. What had she been worrying about? Their time together at the Gaiety hadn't been all roses of course. There had been dark spots, but that was all in the past. Once the gentlemen had taken their port and joined the ladies in the drawing room, all she had to do was to mention casually where the Follies would take place. Yes, all had gone well so far, as Nell's cuisine was having its usual effect; the pheasants with the interesting sauce had been outstanding.

Then Gertrude heard the unwelcome word that she had counted on introducing at a later stage.

'Follies,' Lynette remarked. 'Such a clever idea, Gertrude.'

Gertrude did her best to smile with pleasure. 'It was Richard's idea. He and his sisters are all eager to follow in my footsteps – so they pretend – and have a gaiety theatre of our own this weekend. Do you remember—?'

'What exactly is expected of us?' Hubert broke in, perhaps not hearing or perhaps not caring what Gertrude was saying. He was gazing at his syllabub as though it were a bitter enemy, she thought, trying to control her rising panic.

She saw poor Constance freeze. How could she have married him? She so sweet and he so arrogant. Gertrude did her best. 'Richard has planned most of the revue, I believe, with sketches and songs, and he and my daughters have concocted a most humorous skit on a pantomime. He is hoping that you're willing to take part in the Follies, with your special talents, and of course he would be most honoured if you could render one of your masterly performances, Hubert.'

'A speech?' Hubert queried, as though he had never been asked for such a favour before. '"To Be or Not to Be", perhaps?'

'Splendid,' said Gertrude faintly, wondering how many Wychbourne villagers would appreciate the finer points of Hamlet's soliloquy.

Alice Maxwell stiffened at her rival being thus singled out, and quickly entered the discussion. 'I plan to present Yasmin's speech from Flecker's *Hassan*, followed by my famous rendering from *Medea.*'

'Excellent!' Gertrude tried to sound overwhelmed with gratitude, as though ancient Greek poetic drama about vengeful women who slaughtered their own children was exactly what she had hoped for.

Tobias must have picked up her dismay and promptly became the peacemaker she remembered so well. 'I'll do whatever you want, Gertrude. You know that. Always obey the director, eh? After all, we're all friends.'

'Darling, hardly *friends*,' Lynette murmured. 'But a pantomime and Follies sound just right for the Coach and Horses audience. They'll love it.'

Gertrude caught her breath in horror. Not now. Oh, please, not now.

'What Coach and Horses audience? I understood it was just one performance here in the ballroom,' Hubert barked.

'Good gracious. Haven't you explained, Gertrude dear?' Lynette said innocently. 'We're to perform in the village pub, Hubert. Won't that be spiffing, my dears?'

There was a silence. 'A *public house*?' Hubert looked stunned.

Gertrude trembled. What now. Speak out? Gerald was usually on hand to help, but in this he was powerless. But help came. Not from Gerald, not from Tobias, but from – extraordinarily – Peters.

'Coffee, your ladyship,' he announced blandly, 'is served in the drawing room.'

Gertrude clutched at this unexpected release. She had given no such signal to him as yet, but oh how grateful she was. She rose to her feet. 'Ladies, shall we adjourn?'

Nell, tucked out of the sight in the serving room, relaxed a little as the ladies left for the adjoining drawing room at the rear of Wychbourne Court. Mr Peters had been reluctant to break standard convention which required him to wait until her ladyship had given him the signal, but Nell had managed to convince him that now was the moment. By the time the gentlemen reached the drawing room after their port, Mr Jarrett would with any luck have forgotten his concern over the Follies' venue. She watched as the ladies swept out in their evening dresses with their long trains. Lady Helen's elegant blue chiffon dress was of course daringly short in front, though at the back it conventionally approached the floor. Lady Clarice seemed reluctant to leave Mr Trotter behind, but Mr Rocke seemed to be looking after him. Lady Sophy – typically – managed to pass by the serving room door and whip it open.

'Well done, Nell,' she whispered demurely, then swept on in her sister's wake. As she was much shorter than Lady Helen and sturdier in build, Lady Sophy was well accustomed to ceding the limelight to her sister and it troubled her not a whit. Nell longed to follow them as a fly on the drawing room wall, as there might be trouble brewing. Lady Ansley had looked very upset at the dinner table and there might be something Nell could do. Could she serve coffee herself instead of leaving it to the still-room maid? Why not? She was suitably dressed in her black chiffon afternoon dress and for a mere fly on the wall that would pass. By hearing what went on, she might be able to tell whether her ladyship's fears were justified.

The coffee was helping, Gertrude thought gratefully, as the gentlemen at last came through the door from the dining room. The ladies had long returned from brief retirements upstairs and the port would surely have worked its magic with the gentlemen. Even Mr Trotter had a smile on his face, and Gerald didn't look in the least worried. Mr Trotter had entered flanked by Tobias on one side and Gerald on the other, who had clearly spotted his lack of ease. Her husband's consideration in such matters always moved her.

'With such temptation awaiting us here,' Tobias declared, 'I'm glad I forewent my second glass of port. By George, that 1912 is splendid, Gerald.'

'You certainly admired plenty of it, Toby,' Neville said lightly.

'It's about time there was another such stunning vintage,' Gerald remarked and Gertrude relaxed. Gerald could be relied on to dispel any threatening clouds.

She relaxed too soon. 'This public house suggestion, Gertrude,' Hubert began.

She found new strength. 'An *inn*,' she said firmly. 'It has an excellent hall used for inquests and council meetings.'

'Nevertheless, the revue you have in mind is open for all comers, I presume?'

'The ticket revenue will go to war charities,' Gerald said pleasantly.

In vain. 'I prefer to support them in different ways,' Hubert said stiffly. 'I am not at all well. My art draws all my strength. It demands a proper stage and an audience appreciative of my work. I do not perform in public houses.'

'Shakespeare did,' Alice retorted.

'So he did,' Tobias beamed, coming to Gertrude's rescue. 'I fancy playing Sir Toby Belch on Saturday, Come, Hubert, it's an honour to perform at Wychbourne.'

Gertrude's hopes sank again as Hubert swept on as though Tobias had never spoken. 'I gather from Constance,' he continued loftily, 'that there is a plan for us to dress as Pierrots. I cannot permit that. I maintain high standards and am not willing to prance around in a clown's costume nor to permit my wife to don the frilly white frocks that I understand fulfil the same purpose for ladies.'

'But Hubert—' Constance began imploringly.

'Enough.' His hand was lifted.

'You always were a pompous bore, Hubert,' Neville said amicably. 'A clown yourself, in a way.'

'Consider your words more carefully, Mr Heydock,' Hubert flared up. 'We are speaking before ladies, or I would reply more forcefully to your comments.'

A momentary dead silence was followed by an uproar as everybody tried to speak – and then shout – together. The noise grew and Gertrude could take no more. Anything, *anything* to end this nightmare. Even the sight of Nell in the doorway brought no comfort. There was nothing she could do, or anyone come to that.

The subject had to be changed immediately. This had been meant as a pleasant reunion, Gertrude mourned. They had been such happy days, hadn't they? Change the subject, change the subject. *Now.* One memory came back to her, an unhappy one. It had lain buried for thirty years, but what harm could there be now in raising it?

Even as she thought that, she heard her own voice saying desperately what she had never dared to ask before.

'What *did* happen to Mary Ann?'

TWO

Tobias saved her in the strained silence that followed. Startled faces, even scared, as Gertrude saw them turn to Tobias.

'Alas, Gertrude, we never knew the full story behind that,' he said sombrely. 'Of course, you did not know Mary Ann yourself, because she had left us before you replaced her in *The Flower Shop Girl*. Life in the theatre moves so fast that we leave much behind and never realize it. Such a pleasure that you have created this splendid opportunity for us to meet once more. Tell me, Gertrude, will you be singing "Song of My Heart" in Saturday's Follies? And are we to have the pleasure of your playing Princess Beauty in Lord Richard's pantomime?'

'I cede that palm to Helen, but thank you, Tobias.' It was heartfelt. Gertrude's eyes were filling with tears of relief and the attention moved away from her as Tobias steered the subject away from the taboo subject of Mary Ann Darling. True, no one had actually declared it taboo, but that was always the impression Gertrude had received when, as an eager young actress, she had first appeared at the Gaiety in 1893. Seeing Mary Ann's photograph among the postcards displayed in the Great Hall must have lodged her in her mind.

Now she disciplined herself to show no outward signs of emotion – not even when she looked in vain to Gerald for his usual nod of support. He wasn't even looking at her or at Constance with whom he was sitting. It almost seemed as though he too were part of a story from which she was excluded. No, surely that was too fanciful. After all, neither Mr Trotter nor her children seemed to be sensing that the subject of Mary Ann was marshy ground on which to tread. That terrible moment had passed – or had it?

She realized that Katie was glancing at her in anxiety. 'You must sing "Song of My Heart" on Saturday, Gertrude,' her friend said warmly. 'Isn't that a wonderful idea, everybody?'

The prompt chorus of agreement was all it took to convince Gertrude that there was indeed a story of which she was ignorant and with which so many here were well acquainted.

Not all, though. Gertrude's heart sank. Of all times, Mr Trotter chose this moment to speak.

'Who was the Mary Ann you mentioned?' he asked eagerly.

Thankfully Tobias stepped in once more. 'Mary Ann Darling was a dearly loved friend who left us at all too early an age.'

Mr Trotter was not to be deterred. 'I think I remember that name now. Wasn't there a girl of that name who disappeared?' Not discouraged by the lack of response, he added, 'In the nineties, I was addicted at age ten to Sherlock Holmes and avidly followed the doings of Scotland Yard in the search for her. I even became a bit of a sleuth myself, convinced that she had been murdered and I alone could solve the case.' He gave a nervous laugh, then quickly stopped, as no one followed suit.

'Murdered, Mr Trotter?' Gertrude repeated in horror, as she registered not only that Peters but Nell was quickly moving among them offering more coffee. Never had she been more thankful to see them. Peters had an uncanny knack of judging correctly when to intervene. Even so, nothing was going to rescue this evening from disaster.

Perhaps she was wrong for Tobias broke the silence, replying, 'Good gracious, Mr Trotter. Such melodrama. I do believe that Mary Ann was in fear of someone and that therefore murder might have been mooted as a possibility but it went no further?' He glanced round the table but still no one spoke.

At last Charles Kencroft commented, 'Suicide was also talked of at the time but that hardly seemed likely unless it followed a lover's quarrel. Her private life was not known to us but there were no indications that she was engaged to be married.'

'I read in the newspapers that a body was found in the river a year or two later and identified,' Tobias said. 'The cause of death was unknown and in any case by that time public interest had died down. The last I saw of poor Mary Ann was as she left the theatre for Romano's. Such fun she must have had there and so sad what followed.'

Gertrude felt the situation slipping away from her once more as silence fell, and she had to discipline herself to fight back tears again. Alice was looking bleak, Constance upset, Katie bewildered, and even Lynette was silenced. Charles Kencroft too remained quiet. Gertrude barely knew him anyway. Never a thespian himself, he had, like Gerald, been one of the stage-door 'johnnies' at the Gaiety before she had joined the cast of *The Flower Shop Girl* and later he had married Katie.

Tobias smoothly picked up the conversation again. 'Should we not discuss Saturday's performance of follies present? Talk of distressing follies past can be postponed, especially as not everyone present here tonight recalls Mary Ann. Memories of so long ago can be unreliable, and why should we raise such matters now? Sleeping dogs, my dear friends, sleeping dogs.'

The conversation swiftly moved to a different topic after that, and Gertrude could see her guests were relaxing. She still trembled, though – chiefly because Gerald had remained silent. And he must have met Mary Ann.

Nell usually enjoyed these precious moments in the Cooking Pot, her nickname for the small chef's room where she studied the recipes and menus and prepared her working schedules. Here it was that her dreams to create her own cuisine spurred her through the routine paperwork. They were more than just dreams. She was going to make them come true. In her cuisine, all five senses would play their roles and thanks to Wychbourne she could immerse herself in their glories whenever she liked. Sight, for instance: she had only to stroll through Mr Fairweather's gardens to see fruit and vegetables in abundance. Smell: was there anything to compare with the smells arising from a well-run kitchen? Sound: the bees humming on the flowers or the clattering of pots that signalled a dish in the making. Touch: the soft down of the first peach of the season. And taste: the epitome of them all.

Usually the Cooking Pot provided ample scope for her to take her plans onward. Not this Friday morning, however, with the events of last night still racing through her mind. The guests had at first seemed a fascinating group of actors and actresses. Alice Maxwell's tall, stately figure was familiar to Nell from her stage appearances, as were the pompous Hubert Jarrett and of course Neville Heydock. She'd even seen Tobias St John

Rocke once, a short plump man with eyes that darted everywhere. The lively Lynette Reynolds was new to her and was someone to be wary of, Nell thought, in contrast to the calm Constance Jarrett. Then the pleasant evening had deteriorated into something quite different. It had meant little to Nell, but its effect on Lady Ansley had been obvious.

A knock at the door interrupted her, just as she'd picked up Mrs Leyel's inspiring *The Gentle Art of Cookery* to check a recipe. Rose water? Did she have any? Nell made a quick mental note to have a word with Mr Fairweather when summer came.

'My dear Nell, pray forgive my intrusion at such a busy time.' Arthur Fontenoy swept off his hat as he appeared in the doorway.

'Always a pleasure, Arthur.' Nell meant it and hastened to move her pile of recipe notebooks from the only other chair.

Now in his seventies, the dapper Mr Fontenoy, or Arthur as he had insisted on her calling him, had been the loving friend of Lord Ansley's late father, Hugo, the seventh marquess, and Arthur now lived in Wychbourne Court Cottage on the estate. Unfortunately, this was close to the Dower House where Lord Ansley's mother still reigned supreme. It was unlikely in Nell's view that the dowager and Arthur would have been chums, even without the exacerbation of Gerald's father's will, which bequeathed a handsome legacy to whichever of them survived the other. Whereas Arthur was remarkably good-natured about Lady Enid, as the dowager wished to be addressed, she did not extend this courtesy to him.

'I heard from Clarice of Peters' appearance last evening at such a convenient moment and it did not surprise me, Nell,' Arthur began. 'Nor your own presence there and later in the drawing room. You have a remarkable talent for sensing such times. However, Clarice also tells me that dear Gertrude is still most upset.'

Nell's heart sank. That was why she hadn't yet had Lady Ansley's usual summons to discuss the menu. 'Is it the Coach and Horses problem or this possibly murdered lady?'

'Chiefly the latter, I suspect. I gather that Gertrude did not know Mary Ann, but most of the guests appear to have done so. There are frequent tales of people who have disappeared into thin air or mysteriously self-combust and usually there is some simple explanation. Sometimes one fails to emerge, though, as in the case of Mary Ann. Even though a body was identified later the story of her disappearance still has the power to fascinate. The word "murder", which entered the conversation last evening despite Mr Rocke's vain attempt to quash such a notion, was distressing. It is certainly why Gertrude is distressed.'

'Even though she did not know this Mary Ann Darling? Did *you* know her, Arthur?'

'I met her and remember seeing her on stage in the early nineties. She was delightful – not that my private preference lies in the direction of young ladies or indeed any ladies. She was nevertheless quite beautiful and carried charm and modesty with it. She had an innocence – or so it appeared to the audience – that was refreshing after the growing trend for knowingness in music hall artistes and burlesque.'

'I wasn't born until 1896, but I expect I saw old postcard portraits of her, like those displayed in the Great Hall,' Nell said, scouring her memory. 'What do *you* think happened to her? *Was* she murdered? From what I heard last night, there seemed some doubt.'

'On that I am, as Shakespeare expressed it, a blank. I know the story only as far as Mary Ann's disappearance. However, I do know that Miss Darling had a great many suitors and at least one far less welcome admirer threatening her in letters, following her around and pestering her at the stage door. And one night after a performance of *The Flower Shop Girl* she vanished.'

'You'll have to be more exact than that, Arthur. In a puff of smoke?'

'After the performance, if I recall correctly. She dined at the famous Romano's restaurant with someone whose identity was never made clear, and then took a cab rather than her escort's carriage to her home. When the cabbie pulled up, his cab was empty.'

'Didn't he hear anything?' This sounded loopy. How could he not?

'As far as I recall, no. No body was found until much later, and it's hard to see what could have happened to result in that empty cab – one did not leap down from moving horse-driven cabs in full evening dress. Mary Ann, however, had been in fear of someone, so I was told, and the gossip was that she had either been abducted or killed.'

'Murder *is* a possibility then.' Nell shuddered. 'You said she had received threats, and the River Thames is close to the Gaiety Theatre and Romano's. A lot of women have been found drowned there.' She thought for a moment. 'Was the cab one of the old growlers?'

'That I cannot confirm. I see your point, however. It was unlikely to be a hansom because even though it would have been dark, it would be difficult to descend without the driver noticing, especially as the cab would have been moving slowly. However, as far as the general public were concerned, she had just disappeared. Details of that cab journey were not disclosed at the time. I only knew the information I have given you because – I confess in strictest confidence – Lord Ansley's father, my beloved Hugo, who died shortly before Gerald met Gertrude, had been aware of his son's attachment to the Gaiety for some time before Gerald met Gertrude there. Hugo was eager to know the reason for Gerald's fascination with the Gaiety and as I was for obvious reasons unknown to Gerald at that time, I was able to visit the theatre frequently. Being deemed a safe escort for young ladies, I frequently dined at Romano's, and indeed I became acquainted with Mr Edwardes himself.'

'Do you think that anyone at the theatre would have known about Mary Ann's visit to Romano's that night and about the cab?'

'Undoubtedly. From Mr George Edwardes himself down to the stage hands. In addition, Romano's would have been full of dining Gaiety Girls who could have seen her depart and with whom; the doorkeeper too would have known. Word spreads quickly in theatreland.' He paused. 'Which follows that Wychbourne's present guests would probably have known. Even though I wasn't at the Gaiety the evening Mary Ann vanished, it did occur to me that their reactions in the days after her disappearance were just a little underplayed for such a prominent member of the cast.'

'Perhaps just an awkwardness that will have blown over now,' Nell said hopefully.

'I trust so. We shall discover in due course, as rehearsals for the Follies revue are taking place in the Wychbourne ballroom this afternoon and the performance itself at the Coach and Horses on Saturday – snow permitting, of course.'

Nell had only made one dash outside this morning as far as the kitchen yard and seen a thick blanket of snow, with more drifting softly and inexorably down.

And that, she thought, might lead to trouble. Wychbourne was a large house but if the house party was snowbound, relationships might be strained. Unlike Christmas puddings, stirring up old mysteries might not make for a smooth mixture.

'And, Nell, I should mention that there are further delights planned for this evening.'

'I have a feeling I'm not going to like this,' she said with foreboding, as Arthur was looking mischievous.

'Oh, come now, who could resist? Our Mr Trotter, for our entertainment, has offered his professional services – with Lady Clarice's enthusiastic approval – of a session after dinner tonight to photograph the guests and to capture on the plates any spirits who might be honouring them with their presence. I gather he is well known for such portraits. He will develop them tomorrow in his hastily established darkroom here, and if the ghosts have no objection will print them with his enlarger and display them to us before the weekend is over.'

Nell laughed. 'Gibbering jellyfish, Arthur, I'll say this for Lady Clarice. She's never daunted. Is this Mr Trotter a genuine medium?'

'He seems to be. Unlike Mr William Hope, whom Harry Price so famously unmasked recently, our Mr Trotter is under no such investigation by the Society of Psychical Research.'

'Why are you telling me all this, Arthur?' she asked cautiously. 'I hope Lady Clarice doesn't see me as part of this great entertainment.'

'Not to my knowledge. But I wanted you to be aware of, shall we say, increasing tension – that even your exquisite cuisine might not be able to calm.'

When the belated summons came to join Lady Ansley in her Velvet Room, Nell saw all too clearly just how upset she was. Nell had taken special pains with the dinner menu in particular:

scallops cooked in the French way with bacon, parsley and white wine, followed by Aylesbury duck, and Boodles' orange fool, a firm favourite. Just as well in the circumstances, she thought.

'I'm glad it's a very special dinner this evening, Nell,' Lady Ansley said, laying down the menu. Nell suspected she hadn't even read it. 'Our friends will be tired after the rehearsal this afternoon.' Nell could see it was an effort for her to smile. 'We'll have dancing afterwards. That will cheer everyone up.' Lady Ansley suddenly looked dismayed. 'But that spirit photography proposal. Really, it's too bad. Mr Trotter seems eager that our guests are photographed in the rooms that Clarice assures me are haunted by Wychbourne ghosts. I'm not at all clear why our guests should feel any affinity with *our* ghosts, but Clarice seems to hope they will encourage our guests' ancestors or any other spirits roving around to join them. I shall ensure that our guests don't feel obliged to attend, but what else can we do to entertain them? Mr James has naturally called off the shoot for this morning, as the snow is really quite thick. Gerald at least is pleased at the cancellation – he cannot abide shooting, but the gentlemen expect it. What can we offer instead? Cards? Board games? Hide and seek?'

'Perhaps not. The housemaids and chambermaids will still be working.' Nell pictured Mrs Fielding's face if her beloved routine was disrupted by hide-and-seeking guests. 'Why not build a snowman or have a snow fight?'

She had suggested it as a half-hearted joke but Lady Ansley seized on it with relief.

'What fun. I'd like that.' Then her face fell. 'I don't see Hubert Jarrett or Alice Maxwell playing in the snow, much as I'd like to toss a very big snowball straight into Hubert's face. Nell, I know that you will have your hands full with dinner preparations this afternoon, but I would be so grateful if you could oversee tea. It will have to be brought to the ballroom because we shall be in the midst of the rehearsal. I'm sure Mrs Fielding would appreciate it if you're present.'

Mrs Fielding undoubtedly would not, but she would have to put up with it, Nell thought, speedily rearranging her schedule in her mind. 'Of course.' She hesitated, wondering if she should speak or not. Yes. 'Are you worried about the Follies, Lady Ansley?' she asked.

Lady Ansley grimaced. 'Yes,' she admitted. 'Our three musketeers, as Gerald calls our supposedly adult children, are trying to make the revue a success – even Helen is doing her best. Richard of course is driving them mad with his usual impetuousness and Helen is obediently obeying. Sophy, who is usually the one with the common sense, has been taking a back seat because she's so busy elsewhere, but now she's taking much more interest. I'm hoping the snow may prevent her waving flags for the Labour Party, and that she'll pitch in to help backstage. Rex is here for the weekend, of course – such a nice man.'

Nell agreed. Rex Beringer adored Helen who merely took him for granted, and he was therefore often an ally of Sophy's. Indeed, it often occurred to her that Rex and Sophy would make a far better match than Rex and Helen.

'Nevertheless,' Lady Ansley continued, 'I'm afraid . . .'

'Of what, Lady Ansley?' Nell asked.

'I don't know, Nell. If only I did.'

Greatly perturbed, Nell returned to the servants' east wing. It couldn't just be the Follies or ghostly gathering that was troubling Lady Ansley. It had to be Mary Ann Darling. That gave her an idea. Instead of taking the back stairs to the east wing, she took the grand staircase down and through the Great Hall, curious to see the postcards and posters exhibited there of the Gaiety days.

There they all were in their former glory: not only the guests here at Wychbourne this weekend but Gertie Millar, Nellie Farren, the great Forbes-Robertson, Seymour Hicks, his wife, Ellaline, and dozens more, some of whom she did not recognize. But one of the postcards stood out: that of Mary Ann Darling. Nell studied it curiously. She was indeed beautiful – but then all the Gaiety Girls were, so what was so special about Mary Ann? She couldn't decide at first, but eventually concluded that it was the fact that she didn't look aware of her own beauty, that she was not challenging the viewer to admire it as so many of the other Gaiety Girls were doing in this array of postcards. Nell thought she would like to have known Mary Ann Darling.

* * *

'You make a wonderful monster, Rex.' Helen giggled.

Sophy agreed. She liked Rex Beringer a lot, even if their politics differed – he never understood her reasoning on socialism – but her sister didn't seem to care too hoots about him. Nevertheless, Helen expected him to dance attendance on her as though it was her due. That was the trouble with being beautiful, Sophy supposed. She herself had never had that problem and was glad she was herself and not Helen.

Even though he was busy at work, Rex had come down specially from London for this extended weekend as they had asked him to help with the Follies. He was such an easy-going man that she thought he'd be a dreadful actor but had turned out to be first class – if you could call prancing around on a stage wearing a mock monster's head acting. He was playing the beast in the half-hour pantomime, which they had planned for the second half of the revue, *Princess Beauty and the Beastly Rotter.*

At the moment Richard was lounging on the sofa in the Blue Drawing Room, where they had elected to run through the plans for the pantomime before the afternoon rehearsal. A *prehearsal*, he'd called it, and was even enthusiastic about it. That was good, because he wasn't very enthusiastic about anything nowadays, Sophy thought. His love life was amiss of course. He hadn't fallen in love with anyone for at least a month, and the weekend guests hardly provided any suitable candidates.

'Thank you, my Beauty,' Rex shouted at Helen through the monster's head, while performing another swagger round the room. He was a slightly built man, which made it even odder, Sophy thought, to see him with this huge thing over his head.

'The first scene in the Matrimonial Agency for Beasts then,' Richard decreed, hauling himself off the sofa to take his place as the agency clerk taking the Beast's details for a future wife. Helen of course was the disdaining beauty and Richard the clerk. Sophy had been consigned with her full permission to the role of Ugly Sister, who rather fancied marrying the Beastly Rotter. Unfortunately, the Beastly Rotter didn't want her. He was set on the Beauty.

'I want a wife!' the Beast howled obediently.

Clerk Richard looked bored. 'Whose wife do you want? Ho, ho, ho,' he added.

'It won't be me.' Helen teetered on to join them in her strapped high-heeled shoes.

'Oh yes, it will,' the Beast proclaimed loudly in true pantomime style.

'Oh no, it won't,' Helen snapped back.

'What about me?' Sophy asked plaintively on cue.

The Beastly Rotter turned a scornful eye on her. 'You're the Ugly Sister. I don't want you.'

Stupid words, but only words, Sophy thought, with a rare pang. Was that how he really thought of her, or was it just the play? As if he read her thoughts, Rex swept off the monster's head and winked at her.

'Fortunately, I've got a Mary Ann Darling on the books,' quoth Clerk Richard.

'Don't you dare use that in the show, Richard.' Sophy was appalled at this mischief-making. 'Mother's so upset already.'

Richard shrugged. 'Probably because of that new lady's maid who's arriving today. Anyway, it was only a joke.'

'No,' Sophy said firmly. 'There's something odd about this whole thing – the way they were talking in the drawing room about that girl last night. It's not a joke at all.'

'I agree,' Rex said seriously. 'I remember my mother talking about her. She was the Mary Pickford of the stage, all girly blonde and big blue eyes. Not as beautiful as you, Helen,' he added quickly, at which Helen smiled and Sophy cringed.

'Anything in this murder idea?' Richard asked with more interest.

'How would I know?' Rex replied. 'I was only a babe in arms when she popped off.'

'Maybe that Guv'nor of the Gaiety bumped her off?' Richard threw out with renewed zest. 'I say, could someone here this weekend have done her in?'

Sophy was even more appalled. 'We had enough talk about murder last year. The parents couldn't take any more, so don't you dare raise the subject.'

Richard shrugged. 'All right, I'll drop that line. But don't forget fairy tales are full of crime, people planning murders. Fee-fi-fo-fum and all that. Wicked witches.'

'Well, let's give ours a happy ending,' Sophy said firmly.

'Remember that the Beastly Rotter turns out to be a handsome prince in disguise so forget wicked witches.'

'That's wizard,' Rex capped neatly.

Neville Heydock tweaked his tie and prepared to make his appearance in the ballroom for the rehearsal. Not too bad, he told the mirror. His 'Jeeves', as he jokingly called Ronald Winter, wouldn't be at his side but Neville needed reassurance *now.* For years he had wanted to attend a Wychbourne Court weekend party. Being a star of the musical comedy stage and every girl's favourite dish was one thing but being invited here was the crowning social glory as far as he was concerned. If only they knew . . . He had thought there was no problem until last night, even with Tobias here. But then to his horror he had seen Lynette of all people descending the stairs yesterday evening, flaunting herself as usual in floating chiffon and diamonds. He should have expected it, but he hadn't. At least the claws hadn't emerged yet – perhaps she had too much to lose now that she had married again. And on top of all that, there was Mary Ann. Why, for Pete's sake, had Gertrude brought that up?

'What a surprise,' Lynette had said on seeing him, eyes glinting. 'Darling, so lovely to see you again.'

'And here we are to be on the same stage together. I'll be singing just for you, honey-baby,' he had responded in relief. Still no claws. He relaxed too soon.

'A touch of Gershwin perhaps? "The Man I *Don't* Love" from *Lady Be Good*?'

'Splendid,' he had rejoined with as much nonchalance as he could gather. 'But I'd prefer "It Had to be You".' Weak, but it would pass, and at least she hadn't put the cat among the pigeons yet, despite this talk of the old days and Mary Ann.

That had been last night, though. Now during this damned rehearsal he had to carry his performance through. Look suave, keep a stiff upper lip and all that.

Hubert Jarrett was also making his way to the ballroom with great reluctance. Rehearsal, indeed. As though he needed to rehearse his greatest speech. *His*, not Shakespeare's. It was the interpretation that lifted the speech beyond the mundane. Moreover, he was going to be reminded of days he preferred to forget. He had thought that time far behind him, and that he was therefore reasonably safe. He'd married Constance in a hurry, left the Gaiety and had a far more successful career on the *real* stage, which would shortly, he was convinced, result in a knighthood. He had wanted to decline the invitation for this weekend, but Constance had set her heart on attending and he had for once bowed to her wish, in view of the fact that their hosts were the Marquess and Marchioness Ansley and one of the guests was Lord Kencroft. Their patronage would surely advance his knighthood.

And then Gertrude of all people had mentioned Mary Ann – and it had afterwards become apparent that his past *was* still remembered by at least one person.

At Hubert's side, Constance smiled up at him. 'You look splendid, Hubert. You will be the most impressive person in the Follies.'

'Thank you, my dear.' He had no doubt she was right, but he remembered what he had to tell her. 'I have reassured Gertrude that I will play in this revue, but I have explained to her again that I naturally cannot agree to either myself or you appearing in the final chorus line in a Pierrot costume.'

'Nevertheless, I shall do so, Hubert.'

He felt this quiet response – the first time she had ever defied him – like a blow on the face. But he said no more. He could not afford to with Tobias Rocke here, the keeper of secrets. Even his arch-rival, that misfit Alice Maxwell, was present. She had only played minor roles at the Gaiety when he had first met her, as indeed had he, but now she had aspired to *his* world; she had already followed in Sarah Bernhardt's footsteps and played Hamlet. *His* part. That was merely at a minor theatre and not to be compared with his own achievements, but nevertheless she had managed to have infuriatingly good reviews. Just because she was a woman of course, not because of any great talent. Something must be done.

It had not occurred to him earlier that there might be drawbacks to this weekend, but now he felt as though a sword of Damocles might fall at any moment.

* * *

'Tobias.' Alice Maxwell found him in the drawing room. 'Good, I'm glad you're alone. I'd like to talk to you before the rehearsal.'

Tobias beamed, rising from his chair. He liked a good tussle, especially when he had the upper hand, and Alice was an excellent sparring partner. She had always been an overpowering presence, though she was amiable enough. In the old days, she had led suffragette marches, and he had been surprised that she didn't take advantage of the new laws and stand for parliament herself. As it was, she still graced the stage, although dominated might be more accurate. Impressive, though. Her Medea was spot on, waving the knife she'd just used to kill her children. Pity that Sybil Thorndike had nabbed the role of Joan of Arc in the Shaw play; the rhetoric would have suited Alice down to the ground.

'My dear Alice, if only I could linger, but I simply can't,' Tobias told her. 'I promised Gertrude I would escort her to the ballroom for the rehearsal. She is upset, poor lady, at having mentioned the unmentionable last night. And here I am, minutes late already. Shall we have our little chat later?'

Alice remained where she was. The lady wasn't used to being thwarted, but Tobias was sure that she would agree with him. After all, she was hoping to follow in Ellen Terry's footsteps and become a dame.

'Such fun we shall have,' he assured her as he departed. 'All friends together again.'

Alice was far from sure about that. Coming here had been a mistake. It brought back memories, revived old scores and, worst of all, fears.

Tobias enjoyed walking up the grand staircase to meet Gertrude. It was indeed pleasant to be at Wychbourne for this reunion. Just like the old days, when he first acquired the reputation as keeper of secrets at the Gaiety. He deserved it. He had almost forgotten some of those secrets in the meantime, but it was surprising how they came back once faced with those he had comforted so many years ago. Mary Ann Darling was very dangerous territory, of course, but after all this time it could be tackled if he trod carefully.

'Dear Tobias,' Gertrude greeted him with relief as he entered the Velvet Room. 'You are still the great comforter.'

'You shouldn't have mentioned Mary Ann, my dear Gertrude,' Tobias said mildly.

'I know,' she said ruefully, 'but I did.'

'It's no great matter. It will soon be forgotten.'

Gertrude looked at him in surprise. 'But that terrible thought – *murder* – how could our guests forget that?'

'It will be briefly discussed and then forgotten. Taking it further would demand new gossip if not evidence and there has been none of either. Poor Mary Ann. It was over thirty years ago that she disappeared and somehow met her death. She stirred great passions.'

'Who dined with her that night, Tobias?' Gertrude asked abruptly.

'Don't you know, my dear? Then it is not for me to say.'

'Everyone who dined at Romano's would have known,' she pleaded.

'That is unlikely if Mary Ann and her escort had a private room. And I believe they did.'

'So you do know more about it, Tobias,' she said sharply.

He shook his head. 'Gertrude, I plead with you. Old tensions are being stirred all too vigorously. Should we not cancel tomorrow's performance in the Coach and Horses? After all, the weather is inclement. The snow is still falling.'

'How can we do that?' she asked in desperation.

'I will go down to the ballroom but you talk to Gerald, Gertrude. *Now.* I saw him in the steward's room.'

'Was it such a bad idea to agree to these Follies, Gerald?' Gertrude could see from his face what her husband's answer would be. Not only the Follies were on her mind. The new lady's maid had arrived from London and looked – well, altogether a handful, as her mother might have said.

Gerald looked grave. 'Not the Follies themselves. But you could not have known,' he said.

'About Mary Ann Darling?' she asked fearfully. 'You must have met her?'

'I did. I admired her on stage and I met her in my days as a masher at your stage door. She was very beautiful.'

Gertrude's fear grew. She had taken over Mary Ann's part in

the play. Is that why Gerald had married her? Not for herself, but because she reminded him of Mary Ann? Mary Ann had light coloured hair judging by the postcards, whereas Gertrude's was brown, but even so . . .

'Do *you* know what happened to her?' she blurted out.

Gerald showed a rare sign of anger. 'If I did, I would have given such information to the police.'

'Of course you would. I know that,' she faltered. 'Tobias thinks we should cancel the Follies.'

He calmed down. 'Cancel? What nonsense. Come, Gertrude, let us face those lions in our den, shall we?' He embraced her and all was well.

She took his arm and together they walked through to the ballroom. 'Let's put on the Follies and be damned,' he whispered to her as they entered.

Flaming flamingos, what was going on? Nell wondered. Mrs Fielding had looked pleased to see her when she reported to the still room to help with serving the tea, whereas she normally guarded her precious domain with fierce determination.

It transpired that two events had brought about Nell's sudden popularity. First, Miss Paget was proving a force to be reckoned with, as there seemed to be some dispute over whether or not the Earl Grey tea served to Miss Maxwell was the genuine Jacksons of Piccadilly blend or not. Secondly, the excitement of the arrival of Miss Jenny Smith, Lady Ansley's new lady's maid. Because of the heavy snowfall, she had arrived courtesy of one of the Home Farm wagons, but instead of reporting to Mrs Fielding at the east wing door she had marched breezily through the Wychbourne Court front door and insisted Mr Peters take her to see Lady Ansley on the grounds that it was her she was working for, not the housekeeper.

'That's a splendid-looking chocolate cake,' Nell said to Mrs Fielding warmly as they set off for the ballroom and was rewarded by seeing her doing her best to suppress her pleasure. Nell's attention was thereafter divided between serving tea, sandwiches and cakes at the rear of the ballroom and watching what was happening on stage. Absent-mindedly she took one of the cucumber sandwiches herself, as she watched, and then felt like

Algernon in *The Importance of Being Earnest*, who scoffed them all himself. Mr Jarrett would certainly think that disrespectful, as he was rendering his speech from *Hamlet* at the time. This was followed by Alice Maxwell's orations, but then at last came the comedy.

It was hard to believe that these were the same people who had been so vehemently attacking each other last night, Nell thought, and yet here they were working together in apparent harmony. She wasn't the only person to be watching the rehearsal in the background.

'Miss Drury, I wonder if I might ask you a favour,' came a timid voice at her side.

It was Mr Trotter, his trembling hands almost plucking at her sleeve. He didn't seem to require an answer to this for he rushed straight on: 'Lady Clarice has suggested I speak to you about my little gathering this evening. We shall meet in the Yellow Drawing Room after dinner.'

What on earth was this about? Belatedly, Nell remembered what Arthur Fontenoy had told her about the spirit-raising session. 'That's when you plan to photograph the ghosts?'

'I prefer the word spirits; it will by no means be a formal ghost tour. Lady Clarice mentioned there have been unfortunate events in former tours but my gathering will be no repetition of that.'

'That's a relief.' She managed to smile. She was cautious, though. The ghosts of Wychbourne Court were numerous according to Lady Clarice (and indeed many other people) but were far more sparing in their appearances thankfully. 'How can I help?' she asked.

'Quite simply, I wish to take your photograph in order to encourage the spirits.'

Here we go, Nell thought warily.

'You may have seen some of my work,' he continued. 'I was particularly proud of dear Doctor Griffith. A most successful session. At his side is the visible spirit of his departed wife. My other great success was the Grand Duchess Frederica, a White Russian exile, visited by her daughter who had lost her life in the Revolution.'

'Why ask me?' she asked cautiously.

'Lady Clarice believes you have psychic qualities and could assist in bringing forth some of the Wychbourne Court spirits by fixing your mind upon them.'

Nell was horrified. Psychic qualities? Her? 'What if nothing happens?' she asked, trying to keep calm, but conscious of the squeak in her voice.

'Then you will have a splendid photograph of yourself by one of England's great photographers, myself, and have lost nothing. Lady Clarice was most particular that I asked you.'

Nell surrendered, irritating though this self-important man was. After all, nothing could go wrong with merely having one's photograph taken.

Or could it? The dinner had gone well, but here she was, at a time when Nell would have preferred to crawl off to her bed, walking up the grand staircase with Lady Ansley and her guests towards the Yellow Drawing Room in the west wing. The electric lights were low and flickering, thanks to the Wychbourne generator's dislike of cold conditions, and created a suitable atmosphere for ghost – sorry, Nell corrected herself – *spirit* appearances. There were rumours that shortly Wychbourne village might be on the main electricity circuit and the Court's generators superseded. That couldn't come soon enough for Nell. The kitchen had two small electric stoves that were always at risk of the frequent generator breakdowns, and she had had so many soufflés and vegetable dishes ruined that a constant power supply would be bliss.

'I think a photograph of us all, Mr Trotter,' Lady Clarice declared, 'but in particular we must have one of the Gaiety ladies.'

'Certainly, Lady Clarice,' Mr Trotter declared. 'Are the barographs ready? Temperature is important.'

It appeared they were from Lady Clarice's vigorous nods. 'I should explain,' she said, 'that usually Mr Trotter is most successful with the spirits of those whom we have most loved, but he has kindly offered this evening to do his best to summon up the spirits of the Gaiety. So many of you will be thinking of those days that they will be persuaded to come. Miss Drury too is here with us, to contribute her own psychic gifts.'

Where the gulping goldfish did Lady Clarice get this daffy

idea? Nell wondered. It was harmless enough, she supposed, even if completely without foundation, so for Lady Clarice's sake she would go along with it. Concentrate on Wychbourne, she told herself. Her own ancestors would be completely lost in these surroundings. Think of spirits: apparently the Wychbourne ghosts were going to encourage them to appear. Right. She'd think of Calliope, the singing ghost, then of Adelaide, wife of the fourth marquess and she might give the doomed crusader, dear old Sir Thomas, a go too. And she'd put all this talk of the Gaiety and Mary Ann Darling out of her mind, at least temporarily.

'First,' Mr Trotter said, swelling with pride, 'we will visit the locations that the Wychbourne ghosts are accustomed to haunting so that they may begin to summon your friends from the Gaiety.'

Nell did her best, obediently following Mr Trotter and Lady Clarice as they led the group to the various haunting grounds of Calliope (who liked the west wing corridor), Adelaide (who liked one of the empty guest bedrooms), Violet – how could she have forgotten one of her favourite ghosts, dear, sweet Violet? Nell wondered. Ah well, too late to concentrate on her now.

So far the group had been relatively well behaved, but a few giggles were hastily being stifled by the time the group returned to the Yellow Drawing Room.

'And now, Mr Trotter,' Lady Clarice declared, 'we are ready for the Gaiety photograph.'

Afraid she might give way to a grin, Nell tried to concentrate on the Gaiety, while Lady Ansley, Lady Kencroft, Mrs Reynolds, Miss Maxwell, the Jarretts, Mr Heydock and Mr Rocke solemnly assembled on and around one of the large sofas.

'Gerald?' Lady Clarice summoned her brother sharply.

'Charles and I don't count,' Lord Ansley replied. 'We were mere mashers at the Gaiety door.'

'Do come, Gerald,' Lady Ansley pleaded.

She's scared, Nell realized with alarm. And it wasn't just Lady Ansley. Everyone here was on edge. Perhaps it was her imagination but in the gloom of the flickering lamps, with Mr Trotter endlessly fiddling with his camera amid total silence, it would be all too easy to believe that the spirits of the Gaiety were gathering.

THREE

And still the snow drifted relentlessly down. No good waiting any longer. It was Saturday morning, already ten o'clock and Nell had just returned from a discouraging word with Mr Fairweather about her planned celeriac niçoise for tonight. So that was off the menu. Ah well, she'd have to think of something else. *Pommes de terre Anas* with a dash of anchovy perhaps? Hardly surprisingly, the early morning deliveries of flowers and vegetables to the house had been badly affected by the weather, but a little persuasion had led to his yielding some chicory and asparagus from the heated forcing sheds.

All she had to do was discuss the menu changes with Lady Ansley and that shouldn't be difficult. Last night's spirit photography session had gone unexpectedly smoothly, as had even that last session in the Yellow Drawing Room. No ghosts had appeared, but Mr Trotter had been convinced that the Gaiety spirits were around them. No one had contradicted him.

The Follies this evening would present further challenges, though. Indeed, they had already begun. She had heard from Mr Peters that inconveniently the snow was not heavy enough to cancel the Follies, which meant that scenery, furniture and props were being conveyed to the Coach and Horses by Farmer Pearson's wagons and the old governess cart as most of the motor cars (including her own) and vans were refusing to start.

'At least horses don't get snowbound,' she'd commented.

'Shooting's been cancelled again,' Mr Peters had told her gloomily.

Another challenge. This one would lead once again to disgruntled gentlemen being baulked of their weekend pleasures, because there would be no shooting tomorrow either, as no shooting would take place on a Sunday.

When Nell arrived in the Velvet Room, she was relieved to find Lady Ansley looking more cheerful than she had expected.

'Were you happy with the rehearsal yesterday?' Nell asked,

once the menus for the high tea and the late supper were agreed. Nell hadn't been sure that the soup and light buffet for supper would meet with approval – no leeks, no spinach, Mr Fairweather had informed her grimly.

'Remarkably few hiccups, thankfully,' Lady Ansley replied, passing Nell's proposals without a murmur. 'Richard seemed happy with it anyway, although judging by what is going on with the scenery removal this morning, Sophy seems to be taking charge.'

From what Nell had seen of the rehearsal while serving the tea yesterday, the Follies would hardly qualify for the London Palladium, but it was certainly passable and she was looking forward to the evening ahead.

'I'm glad to say,' Lady Ansley continued, 'that Mr Jarrett has now agreed to perform at the Coach and Horses, and Mrs Jarrett and I are much relieved. Miss Maxwell too is content – and that is a triumph. Mrs Reynolds was not pleased about appearing with Mr Heydock on stage but has now dropped her objections; Mr Heydock has professed himself delighted. I admit that's surprising, but it suggests all will go smoothly.'

Nevertheless, Nell didn't miss the sudden anxious glance from Lady Ansley.

'And the spirit photographs?' she asked cautiously.

'Mr Trotter will have them ready late this afternoon. He is busy developing and printing them now. I do hope . . .' Lady Ansley paused. 'I have to confess, Nell, that I don't know *what* to hope. Should I hope that the photographs will reveal Wychbourne ghosts hovering over us, which will delight Lady Clarice but scare the more sceptical among us who have hitherto believed them to be mere legend? Or should I hope that no such ghosts will appear, in which case I fear Lady Clarice will be bitterly disappointed?'

Another pause, and then she added: 'And what if these photographs *do* reveal the Guv'nor or worse?'

Careful, Nell, she warned herself. The shadow of Mary Ann Darling might be hovering. 'We could hope for a few murky shadows that would please both,' she said cheerfully.

'You could perhaps put a name to such shadows, if need be.' Lady Ansley managed a laugh.

'An excellent idea,' Nell said gravely, hoping that had been a joke, as she wouldn't be present when they were looking at the photographs.

'And of course you must be present when Mr Trotter shows us the results this afternoon,' Lady Ansley said with a straight face.

Nell inwardly groaned. The less she saw of Mr Trotter the better. He seemed to be popping up everywhere, but at least he was a diversion, perhaps providing a calm before the storm. The sort of calm before the milk boils over? she wondered.

Back to her own domain, though. All seemed calm enough in the kitchen.

She and the other upper servants (to use the old parlance though they rarely used it nowadays) quite often took their lunch in the servants' hall together with the rest of the staff, instead of dining by themselves in the butler's pantry. Today there was a new member among them, Miss Jenny Smith, lady's maid for Lady Ansley (and Lady Helen on request). She had not appeared at breakfast or last evening, so Nell had been curious to meet her.

Miss Smith was from one of the London agencies, and proved an entirely different kettle of fish from her predecessor, Miss Checkham; she was lively, pretty and seemed to have an all too obvious mind of her own, judging by her domination of the scene when Nell arrived.

There was only one topic of conversation among the twenty or so gathered in the servants' hall: the Follies. The staff had been offered tickets for a shilling to their delight. Little wonder, Nell thought, as it was a chance to see the family for whom they worked – whom some of the servants never saw and the rest rarely. To see them cavorting on the stage was something not to be missed.

Mrs Squires was quietly gloating because as she had the evening off, she could easily attend. Kitty was not so fortunate as she and Michel would be responsible for the late supper. Kitty had been especially cross as not only would she miss hearing Neville Heydock sing but she now had a boyfriend in the village and *he* was going.

'Everyone's going but me,' she complained.

'What about you, Mr Briggs?' Mrs Fielding asked, but he shook his head vigorously.

'Don't you approve of such naughty goings-on?' Miss Smith giggled.

Nell was annoyed that no one had warned Miss Smith about Mr Briggs. As Lord Ansley's valet, he took his job very conscientiously, but that was the limit of his powers. He paid little attention to the world of today because it troubled him. His evening excursions to listen to the night-singing birds in the grounds and the far-off woods were the limit of his understanding.

He looked blank at Miss Smith's question, then crooned, 'Mademoiselle from Armenteers, parley-vous' over and over again.

Nell knew he was temporarily back on the Western Front; his head would still be full of the noise of guns and shells, side by side with the songs the troops sang on the march or at *estaminets* when the battalion was on relief.

'It's a sell-out tonight,' Nell intervened quickly, as he quietly continued, sometimes humming, sometimes singing. 'That means lots of money for the war charities.'

'Still doesn't seem right to me,' Mr Peters said. 'Every Tom, Dick and Harry coming to gawp at the family.'

'So what if it's a good show?' Nell replied.

'Lord Richard will have his work cut out,' he commented darkly. 'There's that Mary Ann Darling they're all upset about.'

Nell was taken aback. It wasn't like Mr Peters to pass on gossip from the main house. Times were changing, but not that fast. Bringing such a subject up now showed how shaken Mr Peters must have been by the uproar on Thursday.

Mrs Squires looked up from her apple crumble. She was a splendid plain cook but was never satisfied with her own work, although no breadcrumb would dare stroll out of place under her eagle eye.

'The lady that disappeared?' she queried. 'My friend Ethel knew her, the one that's coming with me tonight. She's Gentle John's wife, the one who does the tree felling on the estate. They live in one of his lordship's cottages in Mill Lane. Ethel was the lady's dresser at the old Gaiety long before she married John; she said Miss Darling was lovely. She'd float on to the stage like a princess in a fairy tale. And nice offstage too. You don't often find that, Ethel told me. All the gentlemen were after Miss Darling. Ethel was ever so upset when she disappeared;

she left the Gaiety then and never saw Miss Darling again. No one did.'

'Perhaps a wicked witch got her, if she was a princess,' one of the scullery maids said sombrely.

Some of these girls still half believed in witches and magic spells, Nell thought. Superstition was still rife in the village.

'More likely a loony,' Mrs Fielding commented. 'Wicked witches indeed.'

'Ethel told me once,' Mrs Squires continued doggedly, 'that Miss Darling hadn't been her usual self for some time.'

'Was she upset that evening?' Nell asked. Even though someone had told Arthur she had behaved normally, a reliable opinion such as Ethel's could be interesting.

'Oh, yes. She said she was going out to dinner when she changed after the performance. Lovely she looked that night for all she was so troubled, Ethel said. But excited too in a way.'

'Does your friend have any ideas about what happened to her?' Mrs Fielding asked.

Mrs Squires hesitated. 'Ethel always reckoned she was murdered,' she whispered.

Murdered? Nell looked at the faces round about her, some shocked, some just curious, some avid for the next juicy titbit. But she had to ask. 'Why was that, Mrs Squires?'

'Ethel says Miss Darling was a kind lady and she would have dropped a hint to somebody if she was going away of her own accord. Not a whisper from her though, so she must have been murdered.'

Nell had to force herself back to priorities. Even if Mary Ann's disappearance was important, it had nothing to do with the Wychbourne Follies. This was 1926, over thirty years since she had vanished. Mary Ann must wait.

'Will it be all right, Katie? I wish I'd never agreed to Richard's crazy suggestion,' Gertrude wailed. 'I don't feel in the least like climbing into that Pierrot costume and parading in front of everybody.' Faced with the approaching event, her earlier confidence was fading fast.

'Nonsense,' Katie Kencroft said firmly. 'Firstly, we've got rid of those awful short frilly frocks that female Pierrots often wear in favour of the costume the men wear and that's been adapted so we can just slip them over the top of our dresses. Secondly, it went well last night at the rehearsal. You said so yourself. And Charles said it was a screamer, and if my husband says that it really must be good.'

'That was with only us watching. Now we have to perform in front of an audience. A *public* one.'

'Which is there to enjoy what we're doing,' Katie pointed out. 'It will be a corker, especially with that clever pantomime your son has written. Your song will be the *pièce de résistance* – you still sing so splendidly. And Tobias agrees with me.'

'I don't believe either of you.'

'Tobias is a good judge. Don't you remember that time we were going to change the tempo of that song in the first act of *The Flower Shop Girl*, "Roses in the Snow" and we didn't listen to him? Tobias was right. It didn't work and Mr Edwardes was furious.'

Gertrude sighed. 'You're right, Katie.' She hesitated. Should she put her *real* fear into words? Katie was such a good friend once but that was a long time ago. Katie had married Charles Kencroft and she Gerald, and now they lived separate lives. She had only met her once or twice since. She had seen Katie in *Country Life* and Lynette in *Play Pictorial* but they were only photographs, not the girls she had known. Katie lived in the north of England now and although Gerald sometimes mentioned bumping into Lord Kencroft at Boodles, there had been no news of Katie. Now the petite, bouncing, beautiful Katie she remembered had grown into a comfortably gracious woman, but how had she changed in other ways?

Gertrude decided to speak out. What had she to lose? 'It's this Mary Ann Darling mystery that's worrying me.'

Katie grimaced. 'You made a blob there, Gertie, but how could you have known? It's a delicate subject, which is why we didn't talk about it at the time.'

'*Why* is it delicate?' Gertrude plunged on, determined to get to the bottom of this puzzle.

'I never knew. It was just a taboo subject, perhaps because we felt guilty that she seemed to have been in distress and we either didn't notice or did nothing about it. It was certainly an upsetting time for us with the police coming around and all the questions. We were all upset – Lynette partly because Neville wasn't with her that last evening and told the police he saw Mary Ann. Alice was beside herself when Mary Ann disappeared because they were good friends, Constance was cross because Hubert was mooning over Mary Ann and left Constance alone at Romano's, and Tobias went off his trolley when she vanished.'

'And you, Katie?' Gertrude dared to ask.

Katie hesitated. 'I'd always liked her, Gertie. But when you came, I was so glad. It broke the spell we all seemed to have been under since Mary Ann's disappearance and even for a while before that. And it wasn't a pleasant spell. But you were an outsider and brought a breath of fresh air. It meant I didn't have to think about Mary Ann.'

Gertrude was still mystified. 'Didn't you talk about her among yourselves? You must have known at least whom she dined with.'

'If so, I don't remember.' Katie glanced at her and obviously realized that she wasn't convinced. 'Tobias probably knows more about it,' she added defensively. 'He if anyone would have known any secret she had.'

'But if so he would have told the police. Mary Ann *disappeared.*'

'You're right. My guess is that Tobias kept his mouth shut – typical of him.'

'Even if she *was* murdered?'

'If the police had thought that we would all have been under suspicion, but I don't remember there being any suggestion of murder when they questioned us. But, Gertie,' she added, 'firstly, it's time we went to applaud that quaint Mr Trotter's photographic skills, and, secondly, we have to forget Mary Ann. We don't know where it might lead.'

'You're right, Katie,' Gertrude said. But what she was thinking was: where *might* it lead? Gerald had known the Gaiety before he met her.

Nell disciplined herself to take Mr Trotter seriously, but it was hard, with Lady Clarice beaming at his side and Mr Trotter preening himself like a film star. The photographs were spread out on a table in the Great Hall, developed and printed from the glass plates and each one snugly sitting in a cardboard frame.

By the time Nell arrived not only Lady Ansley and Lady Kencroft were there, but the other guests too, save for Mr Jarrett. Nor, she realized, was there any sign of Lord Ansley.

'How many spirits turned up, Trotter?' Mr Heydock asked – with scepticism written all over his face, Nell noted.

Lady Clarice gave Mr Trotter no time to answer for himself. 'Such magnificent results. Do look, Mr Heydock. There is no doubt everyone here agrees that we had the privilege of being visited by Adelaide last evening. That poor woman, married to the fourth marquess. Such a shame she lost her mind and thought she was Florence Nightingale. She became so insistent on curing the servants despite their not being ill. And the most peculiar remedies. I pondered on her sad story while the photograph was taken, and she *heard* me.'

Nell peered at the photograph Lady Clarice had been waving excitedly in the air. In it, Lady Clarice was sitting in one of the empty guest bedrooms with hands clasped in her lap. Behind her was the definite shape of a lady in mid-Victorian dress and hat. Not, as far as Nell could see, a nurse's uniform.

'I was not so fortunate.' Neville Heydock shook his head ruefully. 'Clearly Calliope's ghost took exception to my being in her presence, as I am a rival in her singing career.'

'I didn't strike lucky either,' Tobias Rocke said cheerfully. 'It's too bad. I popped down to the cellars hoping Jeremiah the smuggler would appear and offer me a slug of whisky.'

Lady Clarice looked at him disapprovingly, and then turned to Nell. 'I do believe we have you to thank, Miss Drury, with your special psychic gifts. The Gaiety photograph is a triumph. Do look.'

Take this seriously and live up to your apparent reputation for having an affinity with the supernatural, Nell told herself, as she obediently studied the photograph. It was, she agreed, very good. Sure enough in the top right-hand corner was an image of a young woman's face gazing down towards the group, a face that looked slightly familiar.

'We are honoured indeed,' Lady Clarice continued. 'I did not know her, but Lady Kencroft and Miss Maxwell have confirmed my hopes. That, Miss Drury, is the spirit of Mary Ann Darling.'

* * *

Still snowing. Nell donned her coat, hat and scarf, seized her torch and struggled into her wellington boots as she waited by the east wing door for Miss Smith and Muriel to arrive. This was real life, battling the elements, and at least she didn't have to dwell on the uncanny image of Mary Ann Darling that she had seen. Could the spirit of Mary Ann have been hovering? Somehow, having met Mr Trotter, Nell couldn't quite believe it.

Where were her fellow travellers? she thought impatiently. It was time to leave for the Coach and Horses. Moreover, she had a sneaking suspicion that Michel had forgotten the devilled salmon sandwiches for the late supper, and Kitty was not at her best either. Nell steeled herself. Tonight she was going to the Follies, snow or no snow, and had to ignore Kitty and Michel's woeful expressions at being left in charge.

'I'm here, Miss Drury.' Muriel, the young scullery maid who had been reluctant to take the enormous step of joining the Coach and Horses audience alone, scuttled towards her, already in her boots and throwing a scarf round her neck. It was hardly necessary as her cloche hat was so far over her ears that her tiny face and neck were almost buried in it.

'Let's go then. I don't think Miss Smith is coming,' Nell said crossly. She wasn't sure what to make of Miss Smith. She was certainly not in the same traditional mould of lady's maid as her predecessor, Miss Checkham. There'd be no 'knowing her place' for Miss Smith. She already spoke informally of 'Richard', omitting the title that was the accepted courtesy in the servants' wing. Miss Smith had certainly charmed most of the servants, though. Kitty was overawed and Michel was tickled pink at this exciting addition to the daily routine.

Nell strode along the drive in her boots with Muriel trotting in her footsteps, feeling like Good King Wenceslas plodding along with his page. Even the Wychbourne cat, Welly (short for Wellington because of his four white 'boots'), had disdained coming out into the snow today, despite his name. No help for it, though. With no motor cars functioning, all the wagons, carts and carriages had been snaffled after transporting props, scenery and costumes for conveying the family and guests and so walking was the only choice.

The hall was almost full when they arrived. Nell could see

Lord Ansley in the front row with his mother, the dowager Lady Enid, Lord Kencroft, the Reverend Higgins, vicar of St Edith's, Lady Clarice with Mr Trotter, Arthur Fontenoy – and, yes, Miss Smith. So how had she arrived? Not by walking, Nell thought.

'Where shall I sit, Miss Drury?' Muriel whispered.

'With me,' Nell replied. 'There's Mrs Squires and her friend. We'll join them.' She could see them in the middle rows; she recognized Gentle John with his wife, Ethel, whom she now realized was one of the two village laundresses.

'Won't they mind if I come too?' Muriel said awestruck.

'Of course not. This is a theatre. We can sit anywhere,' Nell said briskly, wondering whether this was as true in practice as in theory. This might be a show to raise money for the war charities, but the reason most of the village was gathering here was to see the Ansleys of Wychbourne Court and their famous guests. To the village, they were exotic creatures from another world, but Nell was thinking of them quite differently – as a group of people who seemed to be sharing a secret from long ago. Even so, she reprimanded herself, that wouldn't affect the Follies.

Just as they were about to take their places, however, Arthur Fontenoy came over to greet her. 'My dear Miss Drury, do pray join me. And your companion too, of course,' he added courteously.

Muriel turned bright red, but her shoulders grew straighter as she followed Nell and took her place with them in the front row.

'Only ten minutes to curtain up,' Arthur observed. 'What mysteries await us this evening, I wonder?'

Sophy Ansley was marshalling her strength. She was going to need it. Richard wasn't taking this evening seriously enough; his initial enthusiasm for the Follies had suddenly evaporated, thanks to his flirtation with Mother's new maid Jenny Smith, with whom he had driven off in the governess cart, leaving Sophy to walk. Luckily, as poor old Rex was bringing Helen in a wagon he had stopped for her. At least Miss Smith had expertly attended to Helen's hair and greasepaint before taking a seat in the audience. She'd offered to make up Sophy's face too, but Sophy had declined the honour. She had no intention of being under the bright lights for more than her brief appearance in the pantomime and Pierrot line-up. She'd be too busy organizing everyone else.

Helen was now prancing around as if she were at one of Ma Meyrick's nightclubs *and* being nice to Rex. Sophy knew only too well that this wouldn't last long. He never saw that his dream was only a bubble that would burst sooner or later. Except for him, the men Helen fell for were the opposite to Rex's role in tonight's *Beauty and Beast* pantomime; Helen's trophies were usually princes on the outside and beasts inside. At least, Sophy rejoiced, Rex had winked at her as Helen fussed around him. That was a good sign.

Sophy spotted a friend in the audience and was relieved that the Labour movement was represented. Wychbourne was a pocket of old England, but it was high time it realized there was a stark world outside where workers and workless alike struggled and starved. Meanwhile there was a show to put on. Well, no need to be nervous. Everything was in place, everyone was standing ready. Robert, the Wychbourne Court footman, was ready to draw back the curtain – hope it doesn't fall down, Sophy thought. Fingers crossed because only a flimsy temporary construction was holding it up. Their lampboy, Jimmy, had rigged up a limelight and sorted out the gaslighting. As for the guests, Sophy found it hard to think of them as being Mother's chums at a time when she was not much older than she herself was now. No Labour supporters among *them*, that was for sure.

When she had asked Hubert Jarrett whether he would make his exit through the audience, instead of down the back stairs by the stage, she had received a blank stare and a refusal. Miss Maxwell, however, had been reasonably gracious when Sophy had found her gazing at the 'stage' and 'scenery'. 'We are hardly taking the Golden Road to Samarkand in this public house,' she observed, 'but it is a worthy cause nevertheless. No doubt my speech from *Medea* will impress them.'

As for the other weirdies, Neville Heydock had put his arm round her. 'Dear Lady Sophy, what would we have done without you?'

She had firmly removed the arm, especially as his former wife had her sardonic eye on them.

'Typical,' Mrs Reynolds had declared. 'Ever the Lothario, aren't you, darling?'

By far the nicest of the bunch, Sophy thought, was Mr Tobias Rocke, a cuddly bear of a man who did his best to help and smooth things over. Even now, however, she could hear quarrelling from downstairs, where the costumes and props had been dumped.

'This is not what I am used to,' Mr Jarrett was complaining.

'Come now, Hubert,' Mr Rocke replied. 'We all have to mingle with the proletariat at some stage in our life.'

'I doubt whether you've ever practised what you preach, Tobias,' Miss Maxwell shot back at him.

'Do any of us, dear Alice?' he replied laughingly.

What with them and the calm, beautiful Mrs Jarrett floating silently through the days like the Lady of Shalott down the river, and the over-bubbly Lady Kencroft with her stiff and stately husband, this was a very strange collection, in Sophy's opinion. Fancy still arguing downstairs when the curtain would soon be rising. Of all things, she could even hear the dreaded name Mary Ann.

'Don't you remember, Hubert?' Mrs Jarrett was for once making her presence known. 'We didn't all dine at Romano's, but except for Gertrude we were all there at the theatre, even you, Charles, and you, Gerald.'

Her father was there? Sophy was taken aback. They must be talking about the night Mary Ann disappeared, so what had her father been doing there?

'Yes,' she heard Lady Kencroft reply. 'You were there, Charles, although we hardly knew each other then. We dined at Romano's too, though in separate groups. Were you there, Gerald?'

'I frequently went to the Gaiety and Romano's even before I met Gertrude,' her father replied stiffly.

Sophy shivered. She knew that tone in his voice. It meant that the subject was now closed. But that must have been over thirty years ago, she thought. How could anyone remember accurately what they were doing so long ago? So very long ago.

The smell of greasepaint. Memories flooded back to her. All she had to do was walk out on the stage and sing. Gertrude shivered in the makeshift wings that Rex and the Wychbourne Court footmen had created under Richard's direction, and wondered whether she would be able to take that first step on to the stage tonight. Her children were on the stage now, in the middle of a sketch. At least the audience was laughing. She remembered walking on to the Gaiety stage for the first time, aware that however warm and encouraging the audience was it would be comparing her with the lovely Mary Ann. Gertrude had studied her photograph time and time again, fearful that her own performance would be a poor second. At times she felt it would. At others not. She too had a gift, even if she didn't have golden hair and blue eyes.

Over thirty years ago she had taken that last deep breath and walked gracefully on to the Gaiety stage in her flower shop girl costume and heard herself singing 'Song of My Heart'. Now all these years later, Gertrude, Marchioness Ansley, took another deep breath, then patted the diamond brooch that Gerald had given her on their wedding day and which she always wore on difficult occasions. That done, she walked out gracefully on to the stage of the Coach and Horses Inn, with her daughter Helen looking up encouragingly from the piano, ready to accompany her for *her* song.

Neville Heydock came to the last verse of 'Rose Marie' with relief. Even with all the aplomb he had acquired from the Gaiety stage and afterwards, it had been hard. Luckily stage technique had come to his rescue, even with Lynette grinning sarcastically from the wings. What the blazes had possessed Gertrude to invite her?

It was all Mary Ann's fault. Lynette had been so jealous of her – without cause of course, and when he proposed to Lynette he had hoped their marriage would work. But it hadn't. And now this. Of all the ill luck to meet these particular members of the old crowd here, especially Lynette on the warpath. Pierrots indeed. He wondered if Lynette had the faintest idea how ridiculous she looked jumping up and down in that Pierrot costume, but then it occurred to him that he might look just the same. Ah, well. For old times' sake he could put up with it, even if some of those old times were far better forgotten.

He could see the pantomime was nearing its, frankly, tedious end, with Tobias on stage doing his usual comic stuff in drag as the Beast's mother.

'Good stuff!' he forced himself to say as Tobias came off stage.

Tobias beamed. 'Time for us Pierrots, Neville. I'll switch places with Lynette if you'd like to be with her.'

Pierrots were so funny at the seaside, but they didn't seem so at the Coach and Horses, Katie thought. This idea had been a mistake for all she had tried to reassure Gertie. Lined up here, with their bobbles, ruffs, caps, white suits and big buttons, pointed hats and big grins, her fellow Pierrots seemed to her almost ominous, threatening. Stupid, Katie told herself, it was just a chorus line in fancy dress. Even so, they did all look so *silly*.

Kick. 'Though it breaks our hearts to leave you, Goodbye Wychbourne Green,' Katie sang in unison with her friends, as the Pierrots linked arms. *Kick.* 'Goodbye, Wychbourne, we must leave you . . .' *Kick.* And the sooner the better, Katie thought. No, that's dreadful. Poor Gertie. We must tell her how much we're enjoying it. It's a great success, this reunion. And it *is*, isn't it? Tobias, Neville, Alice, Gertie, herself, Lynette, Constance . . . She wondered about her fellow smiling Pierrots. Nobody knew what anyone else was thinking – just as they hadn't thirty-odd years ago, when Mary Ann disappeared. They mouthed words and that was all. Whatever suspicions they all had, no one actually *knew*.

It was over. The final curtain had fallen and Nell leapt to her feet with the rest of the enthusiastic audience. Muriel was almost sobbing with excitement as she clapped away. When the applause died down and the national anthem was over, Nell left Muriel in Arthur's charge for the walk back to Wychbourne Court.

Nell had offered to help with a preliminary clear-up on the stage, so that the Ansleys could return for their late supper with their guests and forty minutes had passed by the time she could leave, the last to do so. The work had been much enlivened by the discovery that footman Robert had a good voice for bawdy music hall songs. She wondered what Mr Peters would have had to say about Robert's prowess for entertaining – he'd insisted they all linked arms while they rendered a rowdy unmusical version of 'Down at the Old Bull and Bush' on the stage. Mr Peters might have been amused, she thought, but for traditional butlers there was much of which to disapprove in this new world of flappers and fun.

Now she faced a long walk up the snowy drive as the wagons and carts had left. So had everyone else apparently. Mr Hardcastle had already closed because of the snow and there was no sign of anybody around. Snow was still falling although not so heavily, but apart from that and the wind stirring the bushes by the churchyard everything was still.

Nell was glad to reach Wychbourne Court though and to peel off her boots, coat and scarf. Then, highly pleased with the successful evening, she went straight to see how the late buffet was faring in the dining room. She expected to find a sulky Kitty and Michel there, together with a group of chattering, happy performers and admirers, but she was amazed to find the room deserted save for the Ansley family and Arthur. The buffet supper was relatively untouched, which explained why Kitty and Michel were looking even more martyred. It was only just before eleven o'clock and there was no sign of any of the guests.

Gurgling gurnards, she thought. What's going on here? Presumably either they had retired straight to their rooms or had had a quick supper already and were entertaining themselves elsewhere. What was more, she noticed that despite the success of the evening, Lady Ansley was still looking unhappy.

Seeing her, Lord Ansley beckoned her over.

'Ah, Miss Drury,' he greeted her anxiously, 'you saw no sign of a lost brooch at the Coach and Horses, I suppose?'

'It's my diamond brooch, Nell,' Lady Ansley broke in. 'The one with the sapphires. It must have fallen off in the wings or on stage when I was pulling costumes on and off.'

'I didn't see anything,' Nell said, appalled. 'But we've left the rest of the clearing up until tomorrow morning, so it might still be found. I'd be glad to go back now to look for it.' Her heart plummeted at the thought. 'Glad' was stretching it; 'willing with a sinking heart' would be more accurate.

'No, Miss Drury,' Lord Ansley said immediately. 'I shall go.'

'Two pairs of eyes are better than one,' Nell said stoutly, eyes pricking with tiredness. 'Mr Hardcastle has closed for the night.' She knew how much that brooch meant to Lady Ansley though, so she didn't want to risk it remaining there the following morning.

This time Lord Ansley did not demur. 'Thank you, Miss Drury. I'll telephone him and then we'll go down together. If you've no objection, it will be quicker to walk at this time of night than to summon a cart or carriage.'

Nell was grateful for his company. Even though the snow had stopped and with a torch to light the way in the darkness, it would not be a pleasant walk, not to mention the fact that it was freezing cold. Walking over the icy snow took all her energy and perhaps Lord Ansley felt the same for neither of them made any effort to talk. The charms of Good King Wenceslas were eluding her on this march. And Mr Hardcastle too, for when he opened the door he was clearly none too pleased.

'I'll unlock the rear door so you can take the back stairs to the stage and see yourselves out, your lordship,' he said pointedly.

The stage looked forlorn, with some of the scenery still in place and piles of costumes lying bundled up. The Pierrot costumes had merely been pulled off and thrown in a heap. Lord Ansley decided to hunt through the props in the storage room downstairs by the rear door, while Nell began checking through the pile of costumes on stage.

She had only just begun though when she heard shouting outside. Nothing unusual about that, but wasn't it odd for boozers to be mucking around on a snowy village green at this time of night? The church clock had just struck midnight and the pub had already been closed before she left at about twenty minutes to eleven. She peered out of a window, and in the light of the one gas lamp on this side of the green she could see someone waving his arms and running towards the pub, still shouting.

'Someone blotto probably,' Nell yelled down to Lord Ansley. Then hearing him heaving open the outside door, she ran over to the stairs and down to catch him up.

He turned back to her as the first blast of the cold night air hit her. 'Not drunk,' he said sharply. 'Hardcastle's opened up the front entrance to talk to him – the fellow seems to be pointing at the green over towards the church. Anything wrong?' he shouted out to the landlord.

''Tis a body, your lordship,' he shouted back. 'Dead, so Jethro says.'

'Stay here, Miss Drury,' Lord Ansley said grimly. 'I'll see what this is about.'

But Nell didn't stay there. A terrible fear came over her, a quite irrational one. After all, the body could be anyone's, a visitor or a villager who'd been in the audience at the Follies. She daren't think any further. Instead, in case she could help, she rushed after Lord Ansley. He and Jethro James – the chief poacher in the village – clad in cap and a heavy coat, began to run as best they could across the snow.

'Don't you go, miss,' Mr Hardcastle said, shivering at the pub front door. 'You stay here. I'll go.'

'We'll both go. Whoever it is might not be dead.' She began stumbling across the snow towards Lord Ansley and his companions, with Mr Hardcastle behind her. And then she could just about make out a shape lying on the snow.

Not just a shape. As she drew nearer, she could see something else by the body, despite the dim light. Something darkening the white snow – mud? earth? a coat? No, Nell felt her stomach heave. In the light of Lord Ansley's torch, she could see it was blood. A lot of blood, some in a pool, some just splatters across the snow. It belonged to the man lying there face down – only there might be no face, she realized with another lurch of her stomach. He was undoubtedly dead. A large stone lay to one side of him. A crumpled bloody object which could be his hat shielded whatever lay underneath. Nell had to fight to control her nausea. She should leave, she told herself, this could have nothing to do with Wychbourne Court. But she couldn't move and watched hypnotized as Lord Ansley and the two other men made the decision to turn over the body.

Tobias Rocke had not retired early with the other guests. He was dead. Horribly dead. The keeper of secrets had taken them to his grave.

FOUR

'We should take the gentleman into the pub, my lord. That's what the police said on the telephone. They'll be sending someone along in the morning, snow permitting.'

Frank Hardcastle's words faltered as he rejoined them after hurrying back to the Coach and Horses to make the telephone call. He must have seen the expression on Lord Ansley's face and realized that this was not acceptable.

'Wait here, if you would, Miss Drury,' Lord Ansley said quietly. 'And you too, Jethro. With your permission, Hardcastle, I'll use your telephone to speak to the police myself.'

Nell watched Lord Ansley stride away to the Coach and Horses, snow crunching under his feet. She was relieved that he had taken matters in hand. Frank Hardcastle meant well, but this was no accidental death; the head had been partly shattered by the blow and there was some kind of wound on the back too. She knew enough about what should be done in criminal investigations to be sure that moving poor Mr Rocke's body from the scene before the police arrived was not advisable. She shivered. On the other hand, waiting here in this appalling scene until the police arrived from Sevenoaks was a horrifying prospect. In this weather, their journey would not be easy or speedy.

She felt as frozen inside as outside. At least Mr Hardcastle was with her. She would not have wanted to remain here with Jethro. The wayward son of the gamekeeper, Harry James, Jethro had left home for the colonies, returned, served a sentence for theft, and was now an odd job man and itinerant farmhand – by day, that is. By night, he poached the game his father protected. Nell tried to feel sorry for him, because his father was a hard taskmaster, whose son had never lived up to his expectations. His poaching, of which his father was blissfully unaware thanks to Lord Ansley's discretion, was Jethro's revenge.

Nevertheless, he was a surly individual, his good looks marred by the scowl he perpetually wore.

Mr Hardcastle was a different kettle of fish, and even if he displayed no great cordiality towards Nell, he presented no threat. Competent as he was, though, and a good landlord, he didn't fit the popular image of a cheery innkeeper.

At last she could see Lord Ansley returning. It had seemed an interminable wait even though in fact only ten minutes or so had passed. 'They've now telegraphed the chief inspector; he'll be here as soon as possible given the snowy roads,' he told them briskly, 'and he'll be accompanied by the doctor and a photographer. His van should be able to cope if they come along the London Road and turn at Watt's Cross rather than relying on Bank Lane being passable. Meanwhile I suggest we take it in turns to retreat to your inn, Hardcastle, two by two. The embers of your fire are still very warm.'

'Won't be doing that,' Jethro snarled. 'I'm off.'

'You are not,' Lord Ansley informed him. 'You stay here with the rest of us.'

'Nothing to be done for a dead man.'

'He can be shown respect.'

This time Jethro wisely stayed silent.

'And before you and I leave here, Jethro, we need to consider one matter,' Lord Ansley continued. 'Has Mr Rocke been robbed? For your own sake, Mr Hardcastle and I need to be sure that that is not the case.'

'You accusing me of murder, your lordship?' Jethro snarled.

'On the contrary, by asking you to turn out your pockets and remove your hat and jacket I'm ensuring that the police can have no such suspicions.'

Jethro saw the sense of this, and sullenly did as requested, while Nell forced herself to kneel down at Tobias's side to check his watch was there.

'Leave that to me, Miss Drury,' Lord Ansley said to her quietly, and, nothing loath, Nell stood aside as they finished inspecting Jethro's pockets and then moved to look briefly at Mr Rocke's albert, watch, wallet and cufflinks. All in place.

For once Jethro was innocent, although with Mr Rocke lying face down his pockets would have been difficult to reach unless

Jethro had moved the body before they arrived, Nell reasoned. No, he would have blood on him if he'd done so, and in any case he would quickly have made his escape with any ill-gotten gains, not called for help. Nausea began to rise again, and she wondered how long she could keep it at bay.

Lord Ansley and a self-righteous Jethro departed, leaving Nell with Mr Hardcastle. He was his usual taciturn self, hunched up against the cold with his hands in his pockets for extra warmth. Nell decided to concentrate on what the police might be looking for when they arrived. Anything rather than let her eyes dwell on the pitiful sight of Mr Rocke's body with that awful stone lying close to it. And the blood. Look away. Think of something else. Pretend you're a policeman.

She seized on this idea and did her best. The snow's disturbed all around the body, she told herself, with no clear footprints in it. Their own trails of footprints to and from the Coach and Horses were still visible as it had stopped snowing, temporarily at least. There was also a set coming to this point from the far side of the green. Probably Jethro's? Other prints caught her attention, though. She could see sets leading from the churchyard gate across the narrow road that encircled the green and then some footprints returning. Looking at them closely she decided there were two sets coming towards them, not side by side, nor one precisely behind the other, but overtreading them in places. There were also what seemed to be splashes of blood. Her stomach lurched again. *Concentrate on the footsteps.* A single set led back to the gate.

With the help of the dim gaslight and her torch, she ventured over the ten feet or so to the roadway and then across it, without trampling on the existing footprints, glad to briefly leave that ghastly scene. As she peered over the fence by the open gate to the churchyard she saw that the sets of prints continued to the church porch, two towards her, one away. No signs of blood here though – or were there? Up nearer the porch there might be some, but she dared not risk going inside the churchyard to look more closely – and she didn't want to anyway.

Could that be where Mr Rocke had been killed while talking to someone? Had he walked away from the porch with a companion who then attacked him on the green? No, why would there be a wound in the back *and* that stone? Had he staggered away from a first attack inside or outside the church, trying to reach safety and been pursued, then attacked again once he reached the green? That would account for the wound in his back. No stone could do that though, and she'd seen no other signs of a weapon lying around.

Why would Mr Rocke have been in the church porch though? she wondered. If he'd come straight from the Coach and Horses, he would have to have been attacked at the latest very soon after it closed, not long after ten thirty. She had left at about ten forty. She'd seen nothing on her return to the Court, nor any sign of anyone on the village green. Or—

'Nell,' Lord Ansley called out to her. 'We're back. Your turn for the fire.'

Breakfast. Nell woke up with a start. Neither the birds nor the arrival of dawn had managed to wake her and it was past eight o'clock. Why had she overslept? Then she remembered, and the image of Mr Rocke's dead body was vividly and frighteningly with her. This was no ordinary Sunday. Thankfully, the family's breakfast was not her responsibility but her duties usually began early with deliveries and schedules to plan. Today there would be a horrifying difference.

The body would long since have been taken away by the police to the mortuary, and the porch of St Edith's church and those footprints would already have been trampled under many feet attending the Reverend Higgins' early service, she reasoned. The police had eventually arrived, although not for an hour and a half, by which time they were in no mood to listen to Nell's pleas about recording footprints in the snow, especially as not long afterwards it had begun to snow again. That evidence would have gone for good. Their chief and apparently only interest lay in Jethro because he had found the body; they remained suspicious even when another search of his pockets produced nothing. She and Lord Ansley had left as soon as they could, leaving the photographer still fiddling with his flash-lamp, feeding it with powder.

Now she must face the day and do what she could to help cope with the situation. Fleetingly her mind noted that the guests might have to stay at Wychbourne Court later than planned, which had been for departure that afternoon. That would mean adjusting menus and supplies. Very well, this wouldn't be the first time. Most of her mind though was preoccupied with the enormity of what had happened and what might happen now. There was no doubt that whether Jethro was the guilty party or not, this was murder, which meant that the Sevenoaks police were quite likely to call for the assistance of Scotland Yard, especially as Mr Rocke had been a guest at Wychbourne Court. That meant spectres from the past might arise. Forget that, Nell Drury, she ordered herself, and think of now.

The minute she entered the kitchen it was obvious the news had spread. Work had stopped and half a dozen pairs of eyes fastened on her.

'Is it true he had his throat cut with an axe?' Kitty asked, wide-eyed.

'He was banged over the head with a gravestone, I heard,' head footman Robert volunteered.

Nell took a deep breath. She had to deal with the mighty goddess Rumour who seldom had anything to do with the real truth. 'No,' she said calmly, 'it wasn't an axe and I saw no gravestones lying around on the green.'

'They're saying you found the body, Miss Drury,' Mrs Squires contributed, confirming Nell's fears. Early service at St Edith's had obviously set tongues wagging with a vengeance.

'No, Jethro James found the body.' Keep your voice calm, Nell told herself. 'Lord Ansley and I went back to the Coach and Horses to look for some jewellery that had gone missing, so that's why we were there.'

'Was the corpse all bloody?' Jimmy asked in an awed voice, having just joined the party.

Nell swallowed hard. To Jimmy, dead bodies merely summoned up Sherlock Holmes. 'There was a lot of blood around.' She had to control another retch as the memory of what she had seen rushed back again.

'I never liked that Jethro,' Mrs Squires observed. 'He's a real Peter-Grievous, that lad. Always whining about something. Creeps up behind you all slimy-like.'

Put a stop to this, Nell told herself, or Jethro will be pilloried as a murderer for evermore. 'Jethro just happened to be there as were Lord Ansley and I. Jethro found the body, and if he'd killed Mr Rocke he would have run away, not come to fetch us. Now, is breakfast over?' she asked in her best chef's voice.

Kitty and Michel snapped to attention. 'Yes, Miss Drury. Some took it in their rooms, others down here, but they're finished now. All talking about the murder of course.'

Of course. To Nell's relief Mr Peters came in. He would handle the situation better than she could manage this morning. 'His lordship's been talking to the police,' he announced calmly. 'And her ladyship's ready to see you, Miss Drury. The guests are gathered in the morning room.'

No prizes for what they would be talking about: why Mr Rocke was murdered; who could have wanted to kill him; how soon could they leave? Nell steeled herself. It was going to be a hard day.

'Of course, we have to stay here,' Katie said, looking round the assembled group. Her husband had asked her to explain what was going on to the other guests, while he talked to Lord Ansley. It wasn't easy. Hubert was looking even more poker-faced than usual, Constance scared, Neville bore his habitual 'what's all the fuss about?' expression, Lynette was endeavouring to look bored, and Alice bore the tragic look for which she was so famous on stage. At least Mr Trotter must have taken refuge with Lady Clarice or Arthur Fontenoy, otherwise he'd no doubt be hopping around trying to see if poor Tobias's spirit could be captured on camera.

Katie's task was made harder by the fact that she was so shocked and upset herself. Tobias had once played a big part in all their lives, and she was determined to help Gertrude at this terrible time by ensuring that they all behaved decently. Tobias had been one of them and they owed it to him to find out what had happened. It just didn't seem possible. At half past nine, Tobias had been cavorting around on the stage dressed as the Beast's Mother, Ermyntrude; twenty minutes later, he was prancing up and down in the Pierrot line; and an hour or so later he was dead, probably at the hands of someone leaving the pub sozzled.

Katie's words were in vain, because trouble began at once.

'The snow has abated and I shall leaving this afternoon with Constance,' Hubert declared. 'That is as we had planned. I am not in good health and simply cannot give a performance tomorrow evening after travelling half the day. I owe that to my public.'

'I prefer that we stay, Hubert,' Constance said firmly to Katie's amazement and judging by their expressions, she thought, to everyone else here, including Hubert.

'Today, Constance,' he decreed.

'Tomorrow would be more polite, Hubert.'

Oops! Time to intervene, Katie thought, seeing the expression on Hubert's face. 'Let me explain,' she said speedily. 'Our hosts have been obliged to ask us to remain in accordance with the police's wishes.'

A silence. 'The commissioner shall hear of this,' Hubert then replied in fury. 'Art is not to be seconded to the whims of the police force.'

'It will be an inconvenience to us all, Hubert,' Alice said gravely. 'But we artists are adaptable, are we not, Neville?'

'Certainly,' Neville agreed with pleasure, clearly delighted at seeing Hubert put in his place by his bête noire Alice. 'We all have our duties to bear in mind, but even though we have nothing to do with this tragedy, we must put our late friend first.'

'And friend he was indeed,' Katie declared. 'We knew and loved Tobias. He knew our secrets, he knew our strengths and our weaknesses. Of course we must stay until tomorrow.'

That silenced them. At first she was relieved, but – perhaps it was her imagination – she sensed they were holding back, unwilling to reveal their thoughts. It was only for a moment or two, though, and then everything seemed normal once more.

'That was years ago,' Lynette said airily, 'and we haven't met since. Any secrets we confided in Tobias are long past being so.'

'Are they?' Katie said soberly. 'Some secrets never die.'

'My goodness, Katie, that sounds almost as though you're threatening us,' Lynette drawled.

'How could I? I don't know your secrets,' Katie said crossly.

'If there *are* any,' Alice contributed.

'We all share one,' Neville pointed out, clearly enjoying this.

'Mary Ann Darling. I do wonder nevertheless whether it's the *same* secret about her that we share.'

'What on earth do you mean, Neville?' Katie asked uneasily. This conversation was entering dangerous territory.

'I understand, Neville,' Constance said eagerly. 'We've never really talked about that day and whether she was murdered like poor Tobias. So it could be a different secret for all of us. We all feared that she might have been, but we all kept silent. Why was that? Was *that* the secret?'

'My dear Constance, you are talking nonsense,' Hubert barked immediately.

Alice promptly begged to differ. 'I find Constance's suggestion most interesting.'

'Dearest Connie, you did make it sound like a very Grimm fairy tale.' Neville laughed lightly.

Constance took heart. 'I was just wondering,' she said firmly, 'whether that is why Tobias was murdered.'

Katie looked at her friends: was the sudden silence from blank incomprehension, or were they simply astounded?

Hubert was first to clear his throat and speak. 'You are not yourself today, Constance. Your comment implies that one of us could be responsible for Tobias's death, which you cannot surely have meant. No, no, Tobias was killed because he was out late at night; he must have been robbed or attacked by a drunken madman. His murder is nothing to do with us. That theory is more suited to the lurid novels you insist on reading, my dear. We can return home in perfect confidence as to the cause of Tobias's death.'

'Can we?' Lynette raised an eyebrow. 'That's claptrap. If we're playing detectives how can we be sure of that? We no longer *know* each other, nor can we be certain of what each of us was doing after the Follies ended last night. How therefore can we vouch for one another? For all we know, Tobias could have been as queer as a coot and picked up someone in the audience.'

'Of course he didn't,' Alice snapped. 'I'd no time for the man, but he wasn't that way inclined.'

'How can one tell? Out of our sight, he might have been a ladykiller – all too literally,' Lynette retorted. 'But then—'

'Inappropriate though your words are, Lynette,' Hubert

intervened coldly, 'I do recall that Tobias was infatuated with Miss Darling and therefore could well have known exactly what happened to her and why.'

'What a jester you are, Hubert,' Neville dropped into the horrified exclamations that followed. 'Just like my former wife, you like stirring up sleeping dogs who don't exist?'

'Of course. Such fun,' Lynette agreed. 'Shall we wake up those that do, darling?'

'Sophy?' Rex put his head round the door of the Blue Drawing Room.

'Oh, Rex, come in do. Save me from having to work out what the Follies cost to put on. I promised Father I'd do it. Fine performance that ends up in someone being killed.'

In spite of herself Sophy felt herself trembling, but she wasn't going to do so in front of Rex. She prided herself on not betraying such emotions, and after all they'd been through in the past, this awful murder was the last straw.

'I'll help you on the figures, but more urgently, Sophy, Helen needs you,' Rex said. 'She won't listen to me. She seems to have taken this death to heart. Hardly surprising. Even though she didn't know Tobias, it just shows that she's not fully recovered from that business last year.'

That was understandable, Sophy thought. The nightmare they'd been through with Charlie Parkyn-Wright last year had taken its toll and now they had another murder investigation to cope with.

'Can't you take her on a jolly?' she asked. 'Or take her photograph. Make use of that nice darkroom Richard set up.'

'Mr Trotter might not approve of that.' Rex frowned. 'Nor might the police.'

'The *police*? What on earth for?'

'Richard told me he saw Tobias Rocke emerging from it yesterday morning, just as Mr Trotter came along. Cross words were exchanged, to say the least. Anyway, Helen has enough photographs of herself to fill the National Portrait Gallery single-handedly,' he ended on a lighter note.

'Then just hold her hand and tell her she's wonderful.'

He just looked at her. 'No,' he replied simply, 'it doesn't work. It never has. I'm part of the scenery. That's all.'

'Not to me,' Sophy replied stoutly.

He planted a kiss on her cheek. 'Bless you, Sophy. If you weren't here, I'd give up my role of suitor-in-chief. It's a pantomime all by itself.'

'And woo another princess, Mr Beastly Rotter?'

'No princess would look twice at me,' he laughed.

Sophy considered this. Rex was – well, Rex. Reasonably tall, reasonably good-looking, reasonably good dancer – and very clever. Funny too. Besides, he was Rex, who took her impassioned outbursts on the benefits of communism seriously and pointed out the flaws in her arguments. Rex, who made her laugh and cheered her up when she was gloomy. That made Sophy wonder what on earth would she do if he stopped visiting Wychbourne. 'Do keep on coming, Rex,' she pleaded. 'If Helen's mucking you about, I'm always here – and you might find another princess or two at our parties,' she added, somewhat reluctantly, she realized to her surprise.

'No more parties like this one, I hope,' he said sombrely.

'No,' she said contritely. 'That poor little man, so funny, so kind. Why would he be killed? And by whom?' she managed to add, as all the terrible possibilities rushed through her mind.

'It was too cold for tramps to be passing through and too late for them to be out tramping anyway,' Rex said. 'That still leaves someone from the village, probably someone who was in the pub or in the audience last night.'

Sophy forced herself to put her fear into words. 'Or one of us here at Wychbourne Court.'

'I couldn't face attending church this morning, Nell,' Lady Ansley said. 'I'm sorry to have called you away from your work.'

'All in hand,' Nell cheerfully lied. In fact, it was nearly luncheon time and there was still much to do.

'You were with my husband and the police last night,' Lady Ansley said abruptly. 'He won't tell me much on the grounds that I would be upset. Nonsense. I'm *already* upset and that's hardly surprising. Who would want to kill Tobias? He was the peacemaker among us. He can't have been killed by anyone who knew him.'

Which Nell translated as Lady Ansley's fear that that might indeed have happened.

'Did he have a family?' she asked.

Lady Ansley thought for a moment. 'He told me he married early and his wife died at a young age, but I don't know whether he remarried or whether there are other relatives. The Sevenoaks police arrived early this morning asking the same question. My husband did his best, but I had to talk to them too. They already knew that his home was in a house in Earl's Court and that a housekeeper and her husband lived in. The police can find out things so marvellously quickly and the Metropolitan police are going to the house today. There's a funeral to arrange of course,' she added despairingly, 'so they need to know about relatives. Oh, Nell, I cannot believe it. Tobias of all people. He was so kind to me.'

'To all your friends as well?' It dawned on Nell that the reason she wanted to find out more was not mere curiosity. It was fear that it might affect Wychbourne.

Lady Ansley glanced at her. 'Perhaps not all of us. Is that what you are thinking, Nell?'

'The police will have to check that,' she said gently.

Lady Ansley's next words came out in a rush. 'Nell, I did not dare suggest this to my husband, but could all the secrets that Tobias kept have resurrected themselves here?'

'You mean about Mary Ann Darling?' Nell answered bluntly.

Lady Ansley blenched. 'Yes. What *have* I done, Nell?'

What she, Nell, had *not* done, she realized belatedly on her way back to the kitchens, was find that brooch for Lady Ansley. It was her treasured possession, her good luck charm. If she lost it, Nell knew Lady Ansley would see it as a dark omen of even more misfortune coming her way.

She would just have time if she went to look for it at the pub now, Nell thought, even if it did mean missing her own lunch. She knew from Lady Sophy that all the props and costumes were still at the Coach and Horses in view of what had happened, and no one was likely to collect them today.

How, Nell wondered as she hurried through the Great Hall, could everything look just the same when something so dreadful had taken place? And yet was it normal? There was no one to be seen here, although the Great Hall was the commanding centre of Wychbourne Court. Not even Mr Peters to be seen, although he usually worked from a room just off the hall, which was conveniently near Lord Ansley's office. Not today, though.

The Gaiety Girls postcards and posters looked almost forlorn as if they too felt the loss of one of their number. For Pete's sake, Nell, she muttered to herself, don't be so mushy. Nevertheless, she stopped for a few moments to look at them. There was a grinning Mr Rocke in *The Flower Shop Girl*, cast as Algernon Bly and wearing a baker's hat and apron. Here was Alice Maxwell playing a maid in a musical called *Kitty of Kensington* and another of her as Medea; and here was Neville Heydock as an obviously comic servant in *Lord Henry's Bride.* And there was another postcard from *The Flower Shop Girl* with a young Katie Barnes (now Kencroft) playing a fashionable young lady with the flower shop girl herself, Mary Ann Darling, leaning behind the chair on which Katie sat.

Nell picked up the photograph to study it closer. It struck her that there was something faintly familiar about this picture of Mary Ann Darling, perhaps just because of the way she was looking down towards that chair. She must have seen the postcard before, she presumed as she replaced it, but as she went on her way to the east wing she wasn't entirely convinced of that. Passing the darkroom on her way, she remembered where she'd seen a face at that angle before.

Yes! It was the spirit image on Mr Trotter's photograph of the former Gaiety Girls.

Triumph rapidly evaporated. *So what?* she thought dismissively. Perhaps his spirits always appeared in poses from their former lives. Or could it have happened because they had all been concentrating so hard on Mary Ann when the photographs were taken on Friday, and that their joint subconscious image of her was the one they had recently seen in the Great Hall photographs of Mary Ann? That was one explanation of spirit images, even if Mr Trotter wouldn't agree.

As she left for the village, once more elegantly shod in her wellington boots, she could see there had been even more snow since she'd returned to Wychbourne Court in the small hours. It wasn't snowing now, thankfully. Indeed, it felt a shade warmer. Nevertheless, as she ploughed her way along the drive, she realized that the footprints she had seen last night which had already become partially covered by the time the police arrived would now be completely obliterated.

She opened the rear door to the Coach and Horses, relieved to see there was no sign either of the police vans or of the police themselves or, thankfully, of the body. The door to the downstairs room they'd used for costumes and props was open, but there was no sign that the costumes had yet been brought down, so she ran upstairs to the stage. It was a desolate sight. Before her was a great yawning space filled only with empty chairs. The Pierrot costumes were still in the piles as she had left them last night, so she took up the search once more.

The empty hall was eerie and its silence was in stark contrast with the songs, dances and general uproar last night. Images of a living Tobias Rocke performing for the last time seemed to echo across the stage. Nell gritted her teeth and persevered with the job in hand, anxious to be done with it and back at Wychbourne Court.

There it was! She'd found it. The brooch was caught up on a snagged thread of a Pierrot sleeve and she rescued it with a sigh of relief. Time to go. *Now.*

'What are you doing please?' A commanding voice came from the hall behind her, and with a stab of shock she realized it was one she knew.

She scrambled to her feet – which of them had the greater shock? she wondered. She or the man now staring at her, his murder bag in his hand.

'Good morning, Inspector Melbray,' she said trying to sound perfectly normal. Alexander Melbray. When she had met him last year, he'd said she should call him Alex, but how could she with those impersonal steely eyes looking at her? Scotland Yard had arrived.

FIVE

'Blithering bloaters, what are *you* doing here?' Nell blurted out after a moment of shock.

Something that might have been a smile appeared on the inspector's face, but if so, it was quickly suppressed while he carefully placed the murder bag on one of the chairs. In there would be rubber gloves, tweezers, test tubes, a magnifying lens – all the paraphernalia he might need. All Nell could see now, however, was that impassive gaze with which she was all too familiar.

'My job, Miss Drury. I've checked the props and costumes downstairs and was about to check these. I had specifically requested this room should be left as it was last evening and closed.'

'You forgot to tell *me*,' Nell retorted, aware she sounded like a thwarted three-year-old. Even though she had guessed that the local police would have called in Scotland Yard, given that Mr Rocke had been a guest at Wychbourne Court, she had feared but not expected it to be Inspector Melbray. They must have more than one detective at the Yard. But here he was, and it was clear that he was at work. The human side of him – if that still existed – was firmly closed.

'I'm here because I came to find a brooch,' she added awkwardly.

He stared at her. 'There's been a *murder*. One of the Wychbourne Court guests, I understand. And you're looking for your brooch?'

Nell flushed. 'Here it is.' She opened her hand to show him. 'It's Lady Ansley's. A special one. I remembered it this morning. Lord Ansley and I were in the middle of our search last night when we heard Jethro James shouting outside.'

It seemed to her that the inspector relaxed a little. 'I had wondered why you were both here so late. I shall be coming to Wychbourne Court shortly. Perhaps you can save your version of events until then? You may take the brooch now, though.'

'There's something I want to show you—'

'Thank you. No,' he said dismissively. 'I prefer to look for myself.'

To her annoyance, he was already walking towards the main stairs down to the bar and she knew what she had to say shouldn't wait. 'The footprints,' she shouted at his retreating back. 'They might already have gone, but—'

He stopped instantly, albeit still stony-faced. 'Footprints?'

'You know where the body was lying?' she began carefully.

'I do.' The reply was almost curt.

'When Lord Ansley and I reached it there were clear footprints leading to and from the church, as well as the disturbed ones across the green in both directions as Jethro James had been there. There were two tracks coming from the direction of the church porch and one returning, which must mean—'

He cut her off, although not so abruptly. 'Thank you, Miss Drury. The meaning I can work out for myself. However, I would be grateful if you could show me where they are or were more precisely.'

He didn't seem inclined to talk further as she led the way down the back stairs and out into the cold morning air. Nell longed to know if anything did seem to be missing from Mr Rocke's possessions, despite Lord Ansley's searches last night, but even if the inspector knew he wouldn't tell her at this early stage. Even more importantly, she wanted to know how Mr Rocke had died and if he had been stabbed as well as hit with that stone – and if so had a weapon been found? She didn't want to think about that stone, though. It conjured up too many memories of what she had seen last night.

They walked in silence along the roadway, the chill of the icy snow reaching her feet and legs even through the wellington boots, socks and stockings. A service was still in progress. A brutal murder had taken place just outside, and yet inside St Edith's the lamps were lit, the organ was playing and voices were raised in harmony, Nell reflected. Everyday life, Sunday or weekday, had to continue, side by side with its horrors, but she struggled with the contrast.

Two policemen were guarding the spot where Tobias Rocke's body had lain; there were still a few signs of blood despite the further snowfall. Two more policemen were guarding the churchyard gate and the porch and by the side of the green groups of villagers were watching in silence. Another policeman, well-built and in plain clothes like the inspector, was walking towards the inspector. He might look a bluff, no-nonsense sort of man, Nell thought, but his eyes were as shrewd as his superior's.

'Miss Nell Drury is a witness, Sergeant Caring,' Inspector Melbray introduced her. 'She was early on the scene last night.'

The sergeant gave her a friendly nod. He was a tall man, in contrast with Inspector Melbray's medium height, and yet one's attention would always rest on the inspector, regardless of rank, Nell thought, then wondered why that was.

'It will look different now. There have been motor cars and horses passing along the road this morning,' Inspector Melbray told her briskly.

She could see that for herself. The snow was packed solid and discoloured with mud. That meant the footprints she had seen in the roadway wouldn't be visible even if the further snowfall hadn't obliterated them already. She stomped over to the church gate, which was still open, in the hope of seeing whether they were still visible on the path up to the church porch.

'Even though there's been more snow, there still seem to be some signs of indentations on the path,' she reported back to the inspector, trying her best to sound professional. Though why the walloping walnuts did she want to do that? she thought crossly. She was a professional chef, nothing more. She *had* on one occasion been a very amateur sleuth, but a fine mess she had made of that.

'Too far gone,' Inspector Melbray said. 'We have only your description of what you recall seeing.'

Only? She didn't like his use of that word. 'The two sets I told you about,' she continued, determined to make him regret it, 'coming in this direction towards the green weren't uniformly side by side. They were uneven and sometimes mixed together, perhaps one person following the other. And,' Nell continued steadily, despite the lack of reaction from either man, 'the set going back must have been returning to where the two sets came from.'

'Which was – in your opinion?'

'The church porch.' So much police work seemed to be stating the obvious.

'What do you deduce from that, Miss Drury?'

Was he being sarcastic? Laughing at her? Apparently not. Both men seemed to be waiting for her answer.

'As the door isn't locked at night, I thought Mr Rocke might have been talking to someone inside the church or in the porch,' she said bravely, 'and he or they might have come along the other path from the lychgate from Mill Lane.' She pointed to the west of the churchyard. 'That path then goes on to the gate on the east side of the churchyard which is at the end of the drive up to Wychbourne Court.'

Belatedly she remembered the splodges of blood. 'He might have been attacked in the porch,' she added impulsively. 'There were splashes of what I thought looked like blood from here to the road, and there might have been others in the porch itself if he was attacked there. There didn't seem to be any just inside the church gate, though.'

She saw Inspector Melbray glance at his sergeant, who shook his head. 'Nothing left now, Guv. Too much snow since and too many folk trampling it down.'

'Check again for bloodstains,' the inspector told him.

'If he was attacked in the porch,' Nell added unwisely, 'he could have tried to run to the green in an effort to escape.'

'Why would his attacker then return to the porch? If and could are words to consider, Miss Drury, but not to work with.'

That did it. She could take no more, but she wasn't going to lose face before either the inspector or his sergeant. 'Then I'll leave you to consider, Inspector. *If* you come to Wychbourne Court and *if* you wish to interview me, then I *could* tell you more.'

She marched away, feeling like a prize idiot. Was it the cold wind or something else that seemed to be making her eyes water? Of all the detectives in London, why did *he* have to come? They'd parted on friendly terms last summer, or so she had believed. 'Call me Alex,' he'd said, and there had even been a plan to meet again, for a picnic lunch.

Why the frost now?

Nell marched grimly back over the snow. Snow looked and felt so pretty drifting softly down, but as the days passed, it became increasingly hard and crunchy. Like love, it occurred to her. That at least made her laugh. So soft, so yielding, so sharable, but then came crunch, crunch, *crunch*, and however hard it snowed it was never quite the same again. That had been her experience in life, and so perhaps in Detective Inspector *Alex* Melbray's.

And then something else occurred to her. She still didn't know for sure that Tobias Rocke had been stabbed or whether a weapon had been found, let alone why he might have been attacked. Even for a failed amateur sleuth that was a poor showing. She'd have to do better if she was to stand by Wychbourne Court in this crisis. Especially, she thought with sudden horror, if it had anything to do with the disappearance of Mary Ann Darling – but surely that was too far-fetched?

Usually there was nothing like an early lunch to make the world seem a bright place. Not today, however. According to Mr Peters, the morning had passed with the family doing its best to pretend all was normal while the guests themselves were oddly subdued. That was natural enough, Nell thought, with one of their number murdered and a popular member at that. Yet that reasoning didn't entirely satisfy her.

'All longing to leave for the next train,' Mr Peters remarked. 'I know the signs. Running like rats, they are.'

'One of their friends being killed doesn't help,' Nell pointed out.

'That's nothing to do with Wychbourne Court,' Mrs Fielding said promptly.

'Pity,' Miss Smith put in pertly. 'It's certainly put some life into the old place, eh, Mr Briggs? You're very quiet.'

Nell stiffened. Although she had now been warned, Miss Smith had obviously forgotten about Mr Briggs' reason for silence, perhaps not surprisingly with all that was going on.

Mr Briggs rose to his feet, smiled at everyone at the table, and left. Nell knew better than to try to stop him.

'What's wrong with that man?' Miss Smith asked.

'The war,' Mrs Fielding replied tersely.

'Oh. I'm very sorry. You did tell me. I'll be more careful.' Miss Smith seemed genuinely contrite, and Nell liked her a little more. 'Can I do anything about it?' Miss Smith asked.

'No. He's happy enough with his birds,' Mrs Fielding answered.

'*Pardon?*' Miss Smith looked startled. 'Here or village floozies?'

Mrs Fielding looked blank but Nell intervened. 'The feathered kind, Miss Smith. Mr Briggs is very fond of them, particularly at night. He likes the owls and nightingales.'

'Thought the owl went off to sea in a boat?' Miss Smith observed brightly, but this poetic reference fell on deaf ears.

Time to call a halt to this, Nell thought. 'Luncheon,' she said briskly, rising to her feet. 'The kitchen calls.'

'Oh, Miss Drury, I forgot to tell you,' Miss Smith added, 'that old gent's coming to see you this afternoon at two o'clock.'

Old gent? No use pressing any further, Nell thought. Miss Smith might be a breath of fresh air in the stuck-in-the-mud servants' hall of Wychbourne Court, but fresh air can be chilly at times.

'That old gent' who arrived at two o'clock promptly was Arthur Fontenoy, as Nell had assumed. Even so, seeing his trim figure was a relief. For a moment she had feared it could be the gamekeeper, Jethro's father. He had a habit of turning up on a Sunday to thank her for the gift, which was actually the spoils of his son, of which Harry remained in blissful ignorance. He put the occasional appearance of game birds on his own table down to generosity on his lordship or Nell's part and she never had the heart to tell him his son was the poacher whom he sought so diligently and with so little result.

'Just in time for a cup of tea,' she greeted Arthur. 'I stole two Jersey Wonders from the still room to go with it.'

'An excellent fortification against the ills of this world. My dear Nell, tell me how Gerald and Gertrude are taking this terrible news? I have seen nothing of the family today. Even dear Clarice is mysteriously otherwise occupied – I suspect with Mr Trotter. Perhaps she is hoping that he will catch the image of Tobias's killer on his camera.'

'I hadn't realized he was still here.'

'Indeed he is. The police and the snow between them have contrived to keep him in our presence. He spends most of his time with Lady Clarice, either stalking the ghosts of marquesses past or sharing the delights of his previous successes with her.

Tell me, were you convinced by his delightful photograph of the Gaiety Girls with an unknown spirit lady? Lady Clarice is quite sure she is Violet, the dairymaid mistress of the fourth marquess, but everyone else was led to believe it is the spirit of Mary Ann Darling.'

'Was I convinced, Arthur? Only that it looked remarkably like the postcard displayed in the Great Hall of Mary Ann in *The Flower Shop Girl.* The poses are the same.' The more Nell thought about it the more she dismissed any notion of the collective subconscious bringing about such phenomena. 'You think Mr Trotter might have been up to jiggery pokery? Lady Sophy told me that Lord Richard had seen Mr Rocke coming out of the darkroom – could that have been connected? Perhaps he had his suspicions too.'

'Who can tell? Richard certainly distrusts Mr Trotter, and did indeed see Tobias emerging from that sacrosanct darkroom of Trotter's. Spirit photography has long been a matter of contention between its doubters and its defenders. However, with a murder on our hands, there are more urgent matters to discuss than Mr Timothy Trotter's photography. Tell me how Gerald and Gertrude are.' Arthur never took luncheon at the house, which he considered the dowager's right.

'Shocked, worried and on edge,' Nell said bluntly. Even the return of Lady Ansley's brooch, received with great relief, had not changed that.

Arthur sighed. 'I'm told that Scotland Yard is once again with us – in the form of Detective Chief Inspector Melbray, as he is now. He has been assigned this area, covering cases for which Sevenoaks police have appealed for the Yard's assistance. He is a most remarkable young man to gain such rapid promotion so early in his career.'

Chief inspector? 'Yes,' Nell managed to agree through clenched teeth. Was that why he had been so distant with her? Was she now beneath his notice as a mere top chef?

'I understand he has refused Gerald's offer of a room in Wychbourne Court from which to operate. Instead he prefers a working room at the Coach and Horses. Perhaps that is wise, in view of the fact that his fellow guests might, should the necessity arrive, have to suffer the indignity not only of being interviewed but also having their luggage searched. Mr Hardcastle is also far from delighted at the inspector's presence. He fears it might affect his trade and give his inn a bad reputation.'

That made Nell laugh, as no doubt Arthur had intended. The Coach and Horses was a highly respectable inn, but every village has its bad 'uns and Wychbourne was no exception. As it only possessed the one public house, the bad 'uns mixed with the good 'uns.

'To our muttons, Nell,' Arthur continued. 'I'm naturally greatly perturbed about Tobias Rocke's murder. Firstly, on his own account, as he was far too good a comedian and actor to lose, but more importantly on behalf of the family.'

Nell looked at him sharply. 'And especially if one of their guests was involved?'

'It is a possibility, given the circumstances that brought them here. I'm told by Lady Clarice that Chief Inspector Melbray is keeping Lord Ansley informed and nothing appears to have been stolen from the deceased. The police believe he was killed some little while after the Follies finished and judging by Jethro's evidence some while before he came along.'

'But *why* kill him and why there?'

'There is the possibility that an inebriated customer of the Coach and Horses decided to attack him or, that valuable gentleman, the passing vagrant, who so conveniently appears in detective stories, perhaps disliked the cut of his jib. The question is why, of course.'

'Why would they dislike the cut of his jib?' she enquired, tongue-in-cheek. 'If any passing vagrants had been trudging over the snow last night they'd have stood out like a lobster in a shrimping net and why would they bother to kill Mr Rocke and leave his money and watch behind?'

'I do agree and jibs are henceforth dismissed from consideration. However, my question was *why*, meaning why was Tobias Rocke there by the church when most of the party had departed for Wychbourne Court either by foot or by such transport as was available on such a night?'

Another black mark against her as an amateur sleuth, Nell thought crossly. That hadn't occurred to her.

'The Follies – a quite delightful performance – finished at ten o'clock,' Arthur continued, 'and the audience dispersed quickly, as did the family. Richard's governess cart, I noted, also bore Miss Smith back in style. I had been squeezed in on the downward journey but was now stranded. Fortunately, Sophy, Helen and Mr Beringer took pity on myself and the delightful Muriel and brought us back with them. I was thus at Wychbourne Court for a speedy supper at ten thirty, and we must have been one of the last to arrive. Whether in the transport home or in the supper room I noted no absentees among Gertrude and Gerald's guests. When did stalwarts such as yourself return? I know you and Robert valiantly agreed to help clear the scene.'

Nell thought back. 'Robert left before me. I was back at the Court shortly before eleven o'clock and Lord Ansley and I set off back again about twenty to twelve. We hadn't long started our hunt for Lady Ansley's brooch when we heard Jethro shouting outside – so Mr Rocke must have been dead by about eleven thirty as we saw no signs of anybody or anything amiss when we reached the Coach and Horses. And Jethro claims he saw no signs of anyone around when he found the body. The blood was still fresh,' she forced herself to add.

'You're sure Lord Ansley, Mr Hardcastle and yourself reached poor Tobias shortly after midnight?'

'Yes, I remember hearing the church clock strike as Lord Ansley and I were in the pub.' Much as she liked Arthur, she longed to be done with this and back to what she understood best: kitchens and the excitement of her menus. But it seemed there was no stopping him and she was fearful of what this might be leading up to.

'You and I know this village, Nell. Rumour travels so speedily that the Red Baron streaking along in his Albatros would have been impressed. Is it at all possible that a villager, perhaps someone in the audience, knew Tobias was a guest here and murder was the result?'

She was hoping she could say yes – but could she? She lived here, she liked the village and its residents. 'Perhaps,' she answered Arthur reluctantly. 'Mr Rocke might have been seen by somebody he knew in the audience and stayed behind to talk to him.'

'It is indeed possible.' Arthur paused. 'Alas, there is that other possibility. That Wychbourne Court is involved.'

As she had feared, but it had to be faced.

'I mean the guests of course,' Arthur added. 'It is highly unlikely that the family or anyone else who lives here would have wanted to kill him.'

Nell fervently agreed with that. 'Why kill him on the village green though, when so many people might still have been around? Doesn't that look like a spur of the moment act?'

'Yes, but the field of suspects must still therefore include Wychbourne Court and its guests.'

Concerns had to be put into words. 'You told me that Tobias Rocke was known as the keeper of secrets,' Nell said.

'I did. That is what Gertrude and her guests called him.'

'So we could be back to Mary Ann Darling?'

'Not necessarily. Don't forget our Mr Trotter.'

Gertrude Ansley summoned up her courage. Gerald had never seemed so distant. She was mystified as to the reason and it added to her bewilderment over what was happening to her innocent reunion. She tracked her husband down to his office next to the steward's room just off the great hall. Goodness knows where our guests are, she thought despairingly. The library? The billiard room?

She thought she should begin with the practical question. 'Now that the inspector has requested none of our guests leave, Gerald, and the police are searching Tobias's room, they are very discontented. It's very hard on them – Hubert is currently appearing in a play and Neville rehearsing for his new one at the Albion; Lynette too is busy, and Mr Trotter also has other engagements to fulfil – and they must feel they might be under suspicion themselves. That puts us in an awkward position. Is there anything we can do?'

Thankfully, Gerald did at last pay some attention to this. 'I doubt it. I'm hoping this sorry business can be wound up by tomorrow, at least to the point when they are free to leave.'

'That seems unlikely to me,' Gertrude replied firmly. 'Even if Tobias's murderer is found and arrested, there are other issues to deal with. Inquests, funerals, and so forth. We have to do something, but what?'

'We shall wait, Gertrude.'

When Gerald spoke in that tone of voice, she knew there was nothing to be done.

'The police have his address and are in contact with his housekeeper, who will know about any surviving family,' he continued. 'We should know the position shortly, and I hope our guests can then leave.'

She was silent, then decided to speak out. 'This reunion was a mistake, wasn't it?'

'You could not have known a killer was to strike. And the Follies were a success.' He spoke with such detachment that it brought her no comfort.

'But it has resulted in bringing old issues to the fore.' There, she had said it. Even if Gerald was annoyed at her worries, they did exist and she had to continue. 'Suppose it was because Tobias was the keeper of our secrets that he was killed?'

Gerald did not reply, and that terrified her. Gerald *always* knew how to handle difficult situations.

She'd spoken though, and she couldn't hold back now, whether he was upset or not. 'The police will have to look into his past as well as his present. Suppose Tobias knew who killed Mary Ann?'

And still Gerald did not reply.

Katie Kencroft grew more and more doubtful as she studied her fellow guests. How well did she know them after all this time? They *were* all as shocked as she was, weren't they? Tobias had been a friend to all of them, but it did seem to her that one or two of them, while appearing to be shocked, seemed almost relieved at his death. That was possible, she accepted. Even though Tobias had been trustworthy, knowing someone is in possession of your secrets could make one uneasy, and there was no doubt there was tension in the room. Lynette was prowling around like a caged tigress, fussing because she hadn't brought a black dress with her and had to make do with a grey silk dress more suitable for evening attire.

'It's snowing again,' Lynette said crossly, as though it were time someone had a word with Mother Nature for disrupting her plans.

'It seems much lighter now,' Constance ventured.

Horrible Hubert, as Katie privately termed him, glared at his wife as though this displayed sheer incompetence on her part. 'We leave tomorrow morning, with or without Scotland Yard's approval.'

'How very brave of you, dear Hubert,' Neville observed.

'I agree with Hubert,' Alice said. 'I shall follow suit.'

That must be the first time in her life she'd ever agreed with Hubert, Katie thought. Even at the Gaiety they'd fought like cat and dog.

'How brave,' Lynette drawled. 'Personally, I don't care if I have to miss all my engagements for a week or more. I simply must find out what happens in the next instalment of this thrilling yarn. Poor Tobias,' she added belatedly.

'I imagine it'll soon be sorted out,' Neville said. 'It's that poacher fellow. Has to be.'

'Sorted out might be a somewhat double-edged expression,' Charles Kencroft observed drily, 'in view of the fact the chief inspector clearly thinks he might have plenty of other suspects close at hand.'

'You mean us?' Alice looked shocked. 'Why should any of us have wanted to kill Tobias?'

There was an awkward pause, which amazed Katie. Could any of them have wanted him dead, she wondered, unlikely though that was? And that raised the question once again of whether Tobias knew who killed Mary Ann. Could one of them have killed her? The idea was ludicrous. And yet Mary Ann had carefully guarded her privacy; none of them had known where she lived, and she came and left the theatre in a cab. That surely confirmed she was fearful of something or someone.

'Who knows which of us might have harboured naughty thoughts about Tobias?' Lynette asked lightly. 'Perhaps our hosts are under suspicion too.'

'Gertrude and Gerald?' asked Alice, horrified.

'Why not?' Neville said languidly. 'They invited him after all.'

Katie frowned. She had always had her suspicions about Neville. He was *too* good looking, *too* suave, to convince her of his genuine warm-heartedness. Nevertheless, he'd been jolly decent over the divorce, Lynnette had told her; he hadn't made a murmur about setting off on the usual trip to Brighton for the ritual photograph of being caught in bed with another woman.

'Steady on, Neville,' said Charles sharply.

'I'm never steady when I'm under suspicion of murder.' He laughed.

'We don't know you are or indeed that any of us are,' Constance said firmly. 'The chief inspector's only coming to question us, not arrest us.'

'He had the impertinence to say the interviews will be with each of us individually,' her husband retorted instantly. 'Even our host is to be grilled, I gather.'

Katie had had enough of this. 'If for the sake of argument Gerald or any of the Ansleys had wanted to kill Tobias, they wouldn't have invited us all along.'

'Bravo, Katie.' Constance clapped her hands. 'Of course they wouldn't.'

'My dear Constance,' her husband said instantly, 'you have missed the point. We would be required here as a shield. Remember that Gerald was an avid visitor to the Gaiety.'

Katie was appalled. Even for Hubert this was going too far. She glanced at her husband and realized what was coming. Charles was always one for putting cards on the table.

'And so was I,' Charles said levelly. 'All in all, it's a pity indeed that Gertrude should have mentioned Mary Ann. Nevertheless, I shall tell the chief inspector about her. He might consider it relevant to his investigation.'

At last. Trust *Chief* Inspector Melbray to ask for her company, just as she was about to put the finishing touches to the stuffed leg of mutton for Sunday evening dinner. Thankfully it was a day in which Mrs Squires would be working late.

Nell strode through the Great Hall to the morning room where Mr Peters was serving coffee to the inspector and to Sergeant Caring. This meant business then. The 'Alex' she'd known seemed to have vanished for good, and one look at his face made it clear that he didn't want any mention of their earlier encounter today. She was glad she had taken time to change into her red jumper suit. If you looked better, you felt better, and she certainly needed to do that.

As always, though, Chief Inspector Melbray surprised her. 'I apologize for any discourtesy this morning, Miss Drury. A journey beginning at three in the morning, in the snow and by train, motor car and foot, does not improve one's outlook on life – or on death.'

'At least I had more sleep last night than you,' she replied inanely, relaxing slightly.

'Thank you. Now to return to—'

'The footprints?' She had relaxed too soon.

'No. Would you take me first through the events during and after the play?'

'The Follies,' she muttered.

He let that pass, wrong-footing her again. 'Did you see Mr Rocke after the Follies ended?'

'Only in passing, when I went to help clear up after the performance. He had changed out of his Pierrot costume and was about to leave.'

'Did you speak to him? Do you have any idea as to why he might have remained there and not returned to Wychbourne Court straightaway?'

'None. I didn't see him when I went back to the Court, or on the way. Perhaps he went somewhere else.' She was making a real Eton mess of this, she thought savagely. All the fruit and meringue of the facts mashed into creamy nothingness.

'Take me through your own movements,' he asked again.

She did so, then seized the bull by the horns. 'I know he must have died because of that stone, but was he stabbed in the back too?'

He shot a look at her. 'Yes. He didn't die prettily, Miss Drury. He was, we believe, first stabbed in the back and then killed by the stone. I remember your mention of blood splashes and quite a bit of it was found by the porch. That suggests he made a run for it and was pursued to the green. We have not, however, found any weapon, only the stone. Now would you kindly tell me about Jethro James? Would he, in your opinion, have any reason to kill him, if theft is ruled out?'

'None that I can see. He wouldn't even have known him. If Mr Rocke caught – no, I won't make guesses.' If he'd caught

Jethro red-handed and threatened to summon Lord Ansley or the police . . . No, that just didn't seem likely.

'Don't worry, Miss Drury. Motives don't provide evidence against a killer, but they can give signposts, as in this case.'

'You mean Mary Ann Darling,' she said without thinking and instantly regretted it.

He looked at her thoughtfully. 'A name that has been mentioned to me. If you have any evidence or even any indications of her being relevant, then I should be grateful to know of them.'

SIX

There are some days when there seems to be a perpetual skin over the custard of life's trifle, and today's looked ominous. Nell laughed at herself. Moping macaroons, look on the bright side. Tonight's dinner would only be for the family and Lord and Lady Kencroft, who would be rattling around like two peas in the very large pod of the west wing. Even Mr Beringer had returned to London. Only Lord Kencroft's valet would still be in the east wing. Much of the snow had now melted and so she presumed had the police's requirement for the guests to remain must have done likewise. There were still rumblings about the police's 'request' to search their luggage early yesterday afternoon, but the halibut à la Welsh 'rabbit' (another thank-you to Mrs Leyel's recipes) had wooed good or moderately good humour back.

If only all life's troubles would follow suit and tiptoe quietly away. But there was no doubt that the shadow that had fallen over Wychbourne Court was to remain here for a while. Tobias Rocke had been a well-known comic actor and so not only would there be an inquest, but newspaper reporters would once more be present in force. A fact of which Lord Ansley was no doubt fully aware.

As an unwelcome hors d'oeuvres to Nell's Monday morning, Mrs Squires had not yet arrived, an unexpected problem. She lived in Burnt Ash Lane, near enough for the remains of the snow not to trouble her. Something must be amiss, Nell realized. If she was ill, the butcher or milkman would have brought a message. But there had been nothing, which meant the servants' lunch would have to be covered by Kitty, Michel and Nell herself. Miss Maxwell (and her formidable dresser Doris Paget, thankfully) would be leaving this morning, as would the Jarretts, and after luncheon Mrs Reynolds and Mr Heydock would be motoring off together – to everyone's amazement) – in his Lagonda with the gentleman's gentleman, Mr Winter, presumably tucked in behind them with the luggage. The indefatigable Mr Trotter would not be leaving, but was staying in the Coach and Horses, courtesy of Lady Clarice, so Arthur had told her (with some relief that he had not been asked to host Mr Trotter's stay).

Meanwhile, the family luncheon was catered for, but how about the servants' hall? Nell made a whirlwind tour of the larders to see what Mrs Squires had planned and found the already prepared mutton pies. By eleven o'clock the crisis was abating – in the kitchens at any rate. Her morning visit to Lady Ansley had hardly convinced her that the atmosphere in the main house was brightening up. The cloud there remained firmly in place and would do so, Nell suspected, as long as Chief Inspector Melbray remained at the Coach and Horses with an unsolved murder case.

That was puzzling. Wasn't it strange that Mr Rocke's fellow guests were being allowed to return home so promptly? If that meant they were cleared of involvement in the crime, then that must look ominous for Jethro, who had come across the body on such a wintry night. That was by chance, he'd maintained, which was odd. He hadn't been in the Follies' audience, nor had Frank Hardcastle served him in the bar and he wouldn't go poaching in the snow. So what was he doing out? Nevertheless, Nell found it hard to think of Jethro as a killer – save of other people's game, of course.

She made a determined effort to study the organization of the dinner menu laid out before her in the Cooking Pot – or cook's room, as Mrs Fielding scathingly called it. A knock on the door and a breathless Kitty announced, 'Mrs Squires is just coming. She's putting on her apron in the hall.'

'Any sign of what's wrong?' Nell asked, following Kitty quickly to the kitchen.

'No, but she doesn't look happy,' Kitty hissed.

Mrs Squires was already at her post. She looked more than just unhappy, Nell thought in alarm, but Mrs Fielding bore down on Mrs Squires in full housekeeping mode before Nell could prevent her.

'And just where have you been, Mrs Squires? It's gone eleven o'clock.'

'I'm sorry, Mrs Fielding. It's my friend, Mrs Palmer,' Mrs Squires replied.

'Ethel?' Nell intervened. 'What's wrong? She seemed well enough at the Follies.'

'She's very upset, Miss Drury.' Mrs Squires turned to her with relief.

'We're all *upset*,' Mrs Fielding snorted. 'Miss Drury has been put to inconvenience.'

'Thank you, Mrs Fielding,' Nell said quickly, her eyebrows mentally shooting up at such apparent concern for her welfare. 'Upset about what, Mrs Squires? Is her husband ill?'

'No. He's been arrested. For the murder of Mr Rocke,' Mrs Squires burst out crying and Kitty flew to comfort her.

Gentle John? *Arrested?* 'Why?' Nell asked, completely at sea. This was incomprehensible. Not Jethro, but John? That huge giant of a man couldn't kill an aphid on a tree let alone a human being. And what possible reason would he have for killing Tobias Rocke? 'Can I help?' she added impulsively.

'Would you go and see Ethel, Miss Drury? She's in a right lather. You could find out who really killed that man, couldn't you?'

'But I didn't—' Nell broke off helplessly in the face of Mrs Squire's trusting expression. 'I'll visit her and then ask the inspector what's going on.' The thought of that appalled her, though.

There was still an expectant silence and Nell braced herself.

'I'll do what I can, Mrs Squires.'

Nell ploughed through what remained of the snow on her way to the village. It was turning into patches of ice and mud, rather like her mission, she thought wryly. With straight snowfall, one knew how to deal with the situation, but ice and mud had to be taken with care. She'd lost her footing badly over the murder of Mr Rocke. She hadn't known that John Palmer – Gentle John's formal name – was a suspect, let alone that he must presumably have had some motive for murder. What could it be? As far as Nell knew, he was one of Lord Ansley's handymen, able to fell trees on the estate or paint a cottage or whatever was needed. She'd seen him at the Follies with his wife but not afterwards, but what the spluttering sausages could have happened then?

Miss Smith, who seemed to have acquired her own means of obtaining information, probably through Lord Richard, had informed the upper servants that the guests had been delighted to hear after breakfast that Mr Rocke's murderer had been arrested.

'And perhaps relieved?' Nell had suggested.

'No signs of that,' Miss Smith had retorted with glee. 'Mr Jarrett insisted on an apology from the inspector, who refused to give one, even though Mr Jarrett said he wasn't feeling well and his performance this evening would undoubtedly suffer from his ordeal this weekend. His lordship and her ladyship were very grumpy to hear about that terrible man who murdered Mr Rocke, because he does work for them, and everyone else was complaining about the clumsy and stupid way Scotland Yard had behaved over the luggage being searched.'

Mr Peters had stepped in at that point with the full majesty of his position as butler. 'What takes place with the family is not for discussion here,' he said reprovingly.

Miss Smith had not felt reproved. 'A pity,' she had observed cheerfully. 'Takes all the fun away.'

Fun was not how Nell would have described a murder. Once upon a time, the butler's word would have been law, even for the upper servants. Not now, it seemed. Mrs Fielding had been shocked and even Nell thought it was out of order. Much as she liked Miss Smith's bounciness in most circumstances, this was not one of them. Miss Smith, Nell thought, might not be long for Wychbourne Court, whether Lord Richard wished it so or not. His singling her out to drive her to the Follies had been noted with disapproval in the servants' hall.

Nell doubted whether grumpy accurately described Lord and Lady Ansley's mood this morning, although no doubt Mr Jarrett had been as querulous as Miss Smith stated. If only Mr Trotter would disappear off the scene together with the Gaiety guests. He might be staying at the Coach and Horses but he seemed constantly to be at Wychbourne Court. She was beginning to see him in her dreams popping up everywhere, saying, 'I don't wish to be of any trouble . . .' That reminded her of the Mary Ann photograph and whether Mary Ann's spirit had chosen to appear exactly as she'd been photographed in her lifetime or whether the very human Mr Trotter had played a part in it.

What part had Mr Rocke played in the story? she wondered.

Had he been curious about the authenticity of Mr Trotter's work in view of the recent doubts over the work of spiritualist William Hope and prowled around the darkroom for proof? Could that have led to his death? Suppose Mr Rocke saw himself as another Harry Price and was set on exposing Mr Trotter as a fake? No, from what she'd heard, Tobias Rocke was a placid, likeable man, who went out of his way to calm difficult situations down, not stir them up.

Reaching the end of the drive, she decided to brave taking the footpath from the Wychbourne Court gates past the church porch where Mr Rocke had probably been attacked. There was nothing to show what had happened now, save for a pile of dirt-trodden snow on one side. No sign of the bloodstains though, and for that she was glad. Even in what was left of the daylight, the churchyard was a gloomy place in winter. The thick bushes along both sides of the fencing and the gravestones weathered by age made her feel trapped, and it didn't help that on a weekday afternoon the churchyard was deserted. She quickened her steps to the lychgate to Mill Lane and made her way up the lane to Birch Cottage where Ethel and John Palmer lived. Their daughter had worked as a chambermaid at the Court before she left to get married, so Mrs Squires had said. That had been before Nell arrived a year ago, so she had not met her or Ethel, but Gentle John was known to her as a familiar estate worker.

Am I here as comforter or investigator? Nell wondered, as she knocked on the cottage door. Both, she decided, as she followed Ethel into their parlour. This was clearly seldom used, as a fire had obviously been hastily lit, and the antimacassars on the armchairs looked immaculate. Ethel must be about fifty-five, Nell thought, though the worry and grief that had etched themselves into her face made her look older. She was tiny compared with Nell's five foot six, and in the displayed photographs a six-foot Gentle John towered over his wife. No wedding photographs that Nell could see, but plenty with their three children, none of whom now lived in Wychbourne, so Mrs Squires had said. The ornaments suggested a happy life of work and excursions, judging by the 'Present from Margate' shepherdess china figure and the photographs of the couple and their children at fairs and circuses.

'It isn't right, Miss Drury,' Ethel wailed, even before Nell had sat down.

'Then your husband will be released when the facts are known,' Nell said more confidently than she felt. 'It's some misunderstanding. Why would your husband have wanted to kill Mr Rocke? It seems very unlikely.'

'He'd no reason,' Ethel shot back at her as though this were an accusation. 'We come home that night from the Follies and didn't go out again. Police say he was out murdering Mr Rocke. But he wouldn't, he couldn't.'

Nell disentangled this. 'So why do the police believe he was out?'

'I don't *know.*'

'They must have witnesses,' Nell tried to explain patiently. Could they have got John confused with Jethro the poacher? she wondered. Very unlikely, and that still wouldn't fit Ethel's story since Jethro was out at about midnight. Could Ethel be lying? She seemed too genuinely distraught for that.

'Did you come straight home from the Follies?' she asked.

Ethel hesitated. 'Yes.'

Nell noted the hesitation. 'Did you stop to talk to anyone?'

Ethel seemed to clutch at this. 'Well, I had to, me remembering everyone from the Gaiety. But only for a minute or two and then we come straight home.'

The Gaiety again. Of course. Ethel had worked there. Surely, oh surely, this murder couldn't be connected to Mr Rocke's role as the keeper of secrets there? 'You were there at the same time as Lady Ansley?'

'No, I never knew her. I knew his lordship – a real stage-door johnnie he was. Lord Kencroft too. That's how I came to be here. His lordship told me I could have one of his cottages. I knew the others too. Recognized them right away. Miss Katie, Miss Lynette, Miss Constance, and Mr Neville of course. *And* that Mr Jarrett.'

'Mr Rocke too?'

Another hesitation, or was she imagining it? Nell wondered. 'Him too. I was her dresser, see.'

Of course! Nell remembered now that not only had Ethel been at the Gaiety but that she had been Mary Ann Darling's dresser.

Tread carefully, she warned herself. 'Were you there the night Miss Darling disappeared?'

'Course I was. That was my last night, almost, that is. I went in next day, found out she was missing, stayed on a couple of days and then I couldn't take no more. I was so fond of her, that Miss Mary Ann.'

Everything always came back to Mary Ann, Nell thought. And now Mr Rocke had been murdered.

'It's been said that Mr Rocke knew everybody's secrets at the Gaiety. Do you think he knew what happened to her?'

'I wouldn't know,' Ethel said woodenly. 'Didn't have much to do with him. Sweet on Miss Darling, he was, though. And a waste of time, that was.'

'Why was that?'

Ethel shrugged. 'All the men had a yen for her. And she wouldn't have nothing to do with any of them. Not her. Anyway,' she said pitifully, 'that ain't got anything to do with this murder. And nor has my John. How could it? I left the old Gaiety when Miss Darling went and didn't meet John for another three years.'

That was a load of gammon at times, Nell thought as she left. Ethel Palmer might be right or wrong about her and John's movements last night, but she certainly wasn't telling the whole story about the Gaiety and Mary Ann. Nell walked back along the churchyard footpath, uncomfortably aware that Tobias Rocke's murderer could well have taken this route.

As she reached the Wychbourne Court gates, she hesitated. Presumably Gentle John had been taken to Sevenoaks Police Station for questioning, and only one motor car remained outside the Coach and Horses. Could the inspector still be there? And if so, should she take the opportunity to tackle him now on the question of Gentle John? She'd probably get a flea in the ear as a result, but she'd risk that. What had she got to lose – apart from her temper?

There was no sign of him in the bar, and Frank Hardcastle directed her to the snug which he said Chief Inspector Melbray had taken over as his operations room. The snug was slightly more comfortable than the other bars, as it was the domain of those few ladies who dared to enter this male preserve with their husbands.

Come into my parlour, said the spider to the fly, and she'd have to be fly to get past this spider of a police inspector. Right. Nell mustered herself ready for the challenge. She was about to knock on the door when it was pulled open from the other side. Chief Inspector Melbray, clad in overcoat and hat and carrying his usual murder bag, was all too clearly taken aback at her unexpected appearance.

For once she had the upper hand because it was left to her to open proceedings. 'May I talk to you?' she asked politely.

A long hesitation, and then he held the door open for her. 'Come in, Miss Drury. I can delay my departure for a while.'

She walked into the spider's parlour, waited as he placed his murder bag on the floor and took off his coat and hat – reluctantly, as if hesitating to commit himself to a tête-à-tête. He didn't suggest that she sit, but at least he helped her off with her coat. She chose one of the upright chairs at a small table to sit down and he sat on the bench some way away. Nevertheless, she felt in command for once, despite the inelegant wellington boots.

'You've finished your work here?' she asked.

The question was redundant, as there was no sign of anything left other than the pub furniture, adorned by a tired aspidistra, a pile of old magazines and a huge old picture book on the life of the late King Edward VII, which she remembered once leafing through.

'I was just closing down here.' Another unnecessary statement. Good. He was still leaving it to her to make the running – unusual for Chief Inspector Melbray.

'I heard that you've arrested John Palmer.'

'That's correct.' Perhaps that steadied him, for he seemed back to his usual crisp self. 'In view of your interest, might I enquire whether you intend to take up your role of private investigator again?'

How could she answer that? Only by evading it. 'It seems so unlikely that Gentle John—'

'Do you have evidence of his innocence, Miss Drury?'

This pointless fencing match could go on all day and she

wasn't going to let him escape that way. It was time it ended, it was time for the head-on shock, and the time was *now.*

'I want to know why you keep calling me Miss Drury. It was Nell last year.'

He flushed. She expected that he would reply with some trite comment, such as that he was at work now, but he didn't.

Instead, he moved to sit down opposite her at the small table. 'I owe you an apology, Nell.'

'A second one? You apologized to me on Sunday.'

'It's the same one extended. I didn't expect to come to Wychbourne or to see you again.'

'Not relevant,' she whipped back. 'What happened to that picnic lunch I was promised?'

'If I said the offer was still open, would you accept?' he countered.

Neat, she thought. He was putting the carving knife back in her hand. 'Not unless you explain your icebox behaviour.'

He managed a smile which promptly then disappeared. 'I decided the lunch would get us nowhere, Nell. You're working here in a place you love at a job you love. I work in London at a job to which I'm dedicated twenty-four hours a day and though I don't exactly love it, I'm part of it. Is that still the case as far as you're concerned?'

'Well, strike me down with a coconut,' she answered slowly. Where might this be leading? 'Yes.'

'Suppose a picnic lunch led to another and then another,' he continued levelly. 'Would you be ready to give up Wychbourne Court?'

She was silenced. Give it up? How could she? She was needed at Wychbourne; it gave her all she needed to fulfil her dreams and, equally important, she was a part of it, just as he was of Scotland Yard.

'No,' she answered. The ramifications rushed through her head like peas bursting out of their pod. 'Not yet anyway,' she quickly amended.

'And nor could I give up my job for Kent. Not yet anyway.'

'Could we be friends and see what happens?' she said uncertainly. What on earth was she saying? Acknowledging that there could be something more?

'Friends? What happens if you deliberately leave a saucepan of milk on a lit gas stove?'

'It boils over,' she said crossly.

'I'm not good at boiling over, Nell. I can't risk it.' A long pause. 'There is, I grant you, such a plan as simmering.'

'Until it gradually boils away,' she countered. That didn't appeal.

'That is the danger,' he replied gravely. 'It could burn the pan too. Could you risk that?'

'That's unfair,' she shot back at him.

'Nothing's fair in love and crime, Nell. Shall we simmer for a while?'

'We can try.' Why the buttered parsnips did she feel like crying? After all, he could easily find another blinking saucepan and boil the beastly milk with someone else – and so could she. If she wanted to do so! But what *did* she want? Then Alex made her feel even worse by kissing her hand lightly.

'Let's declare a truce then.' A pause. 'Is that what you really came here for?'

'Perhaps,' she admitted. 'But I would like to know why you've arrested Gentle John.'

'Usual terms? Confidentiality?'

'Yes.'

'Because his boots had mud on them, he lied about his movements and we found one of those light mackintoshes with blood on it screwed up in a bush near the lychgate. There was also a glove in the lychgate half buried in snow, the pair of which we found when we searched his home. No blood on that, but there wouldn't necessarily have been any. We've also searched the guests' luggage, which revealed nothing helpful to the case.'

'Did you find the knife?'

'Only the stone you saw.'

'And that's all?' she asked bravely.

'No. Last Thursday night at the Coach and Horses and in a state of inebriation, John Palmer remarked to the world in general that he would like to wring the bastard's neck. The bastard under discussion was Tobias Rocke.'

That was still a long way from murdering him, she thought, after recovering from her dismay. What on earth could have roused Gentle John to such a state of ungentleness?

'How did you first pick on him as a suspect?' she asked.

'Going too far, Nell.'

'Accepted,' she said ungraciously, 'but why would he want to kill Tobias Rocke?'

'Ah. Slipping up on our detective skills, are we, Nell? You've interviewed poor Ethel Palmer, I take it?'

She nodded.

'Did she mention that Tobias Rocke was her first husband?'

'*What?*'

'Or that as far as we can check, they never bothered to get divorced?'

Holy mackerel, she thought dizzily, as she walked back to the Court. Some days just turn you upside down and shake you inside out. She apparently now had a new 'friend', Chief Inspector Alex Melbray, who had revealed a whole new side to himself. No, she was wrong. It wasn't new, it had just unexpectedly returned, a possibility she hadn't faced. After all, she hardly knew him and had moved on from their first meeting. On reflection, was that true? What she could not deny was that his image had an annoying way of popping up time and time again – but nothing more surely, despite the way she'd quickly changed that 'no' to a 'not yet'? Anyway, there was no drama about it. After all, the case as far as he was concerned was over.

Alex – no, she must think of him as the chief inspector, or she'd become confused between the two roles – thought the murderer of Tobias Rocke had been found, and now she realized that Gentle John had a strong motive for killing him, what more was there for her to do? It seemed as though Ethel might have been bigamously married to him with or without his knowledge, and so he could have killed Tobias Rocke in a sudden rage or if Mr Rocke had threatened to expose them. Ethel must have lied about his movements to her; either they had not returned home with each other or Gentle John had left again after their return.

Where did this leave her, Nell, though? She had more or less promised Mrs Squires that she would help prove Gentle John innocent. Did that mean she should take it at least a little further? (It might even lead to that picnic lunch with Chief Inspector Melbray.)

Stop this, Nell Drury, she told herself. Concentrate on Gentle John. Never mind the motive, did the facts fit?

If he had planned to kill Tobias Rocke, then he would have waited until Mr Rocke was about to walk or drive home and instead persuaded him to walk with him along that footpath past the porch as the quickest way to his home. Then he would have killed him. The problem with that theory was that the body would have been found well before Jethro saw it, as so many people must have been leaving the Coach and Horses at about that time. Perhaps Mr Rocke went back to Birch Cottage with Ethel and Gentle John. That was a thought. When they'd finished talking, John Palmer could have made some excuse to escort him back towards the gates to Wychbourne Court and killed him on the way.

But why would they have stopped in the porch? It wasn't snowing at that point. Did John Palmer come to the Follies equipped with a knife or did he pick one up at his home? Why use a knife at all? Gentle John was a tall and very strong man, Tobias Rocke was short and hadn't looked a man of much physical strength.

She was quite sure that Alex – no, Chief Inspector Melbray – had been thinking along the same lines. He had given one parting shot, as she'd left.

'Nell, we had to arrest John Palmer, because of the evidence. But there might be more to the story of Tobias Rocke than has emerged so far.'

Perhaps he wasn't overlooking Mary Ann Darling after all.

SEVEN

'Pray enter, Nell.'

She obeyed with pleasure. Tuesday morning, and Arthur Fontenoy was just the person to talk to about the arrest of John Palmer. If anyone could make sense of this, it was Arthur. In a sense, he was an outsider. He wasn't part of the Ansley family and yet he was close to its interests, and on good terms with them all (save the dowager, of course). Nor was he part of the village, although he was generally trusted.

'I am honoured to see you, Nell,' Arthur continued. He ushered her into Wychbourne Court Cottage. The word cottage was a misnomer, in Nell's view, as it had three storeys and was built in elegant Georgian-style red brick. Arthur led her to her favourite room in his home, which was his den; this was full of memorabilia of the Ansleys, his own family and of his great passion, the London theatre. 'Although Chief Inspector Melbray has vanished along with the snow, the Follies are over and that poor man has been arrested, do I deduce correctly that you consider this terrible business of Tobias Rocke's death is far from over and that is what brings you here?'

'It is, Arthur.'

'Nevertheless, it does seem a coincidence that Tobias's murder is attributed to the husband of a lady who was Mary Ann Darling's dresser. I do recall there was a rumour going around the Gaiety when the dresser first arrived that perhaps Tobias was secretly married to her; that was made all the more fascinating because of his apparent infatuation with Miss Darling. He was known to the cast as the keeper of secrets and his marriage seems to have been one of them. Dear Ethel. Of course I remember her in the past, but we don't talk of old times when we meet in the village.'

That was a relief. She could talk to Arthur without betraying police confidentiality. Nell remembered Ethel Palmer's hesitation when asked if she and Gentle John had talked to anyone after the Follies ended. Her answer had been yes, but only briefly. Tobias Rocke's name – unsurprisingly – had not been mentioned.

'This is going to be sticky,' she began. 'If he was known as a keeper of secrets, isn't it also a coincidence that he was murdered just as people who might have confided in him gathered together. On the other hand, if he had kept the secrets so long, why bother to kill him now?'

'Reminders of the past can be uncomfortable.' Arthur frowned. 'Look at all these smiling photographs of mine. Ellen Terry, Henry Irving, Ellaline Terriss, and with them Alice Maxwell, Hubert Jarrett, dear Neville Heydock – none of them would want the past raked up, no matter how insignificant or innocent their secrets might have been or, indeed, still are. None of us would like that. It's possible therefore that John Palmer took advantage of Tobias being on his own to eliminate the threat to his respectability and his children's legitimacy. I doubt if there was ever a divorce, with the laws as they were both then and now. Nevertheless, I take your point, Nell. Do you still think Mary Ann might be relevant?'

'I don't know,' Nell said in frustration. 'As murder was suspected, Mr Rocke might have known who killed her, but how do I find that out now?'

There must be *something* she could do to prove or disprove Gentle John's innocence or guilt, but what? Inspector Melbray – yes, thinking of him that way came quite easily to her – couldn't take Mary Ann's case any further, but perhaps she could. The key had to be Tobias Rocke himself and if Mary Ann's death had been the touchstone for his murder, then his relationship with her could have been the reason for his death.

'But I'll do my best to do so,' she added.

'My dear Nell,' Arthur commented, 'there will be no stopping you once you have set foot on the trail. A caveat, though. Impediments may block your path.'

She saw his point immediately. 'The Ansleys' involvement. But Lady Ansley wasn't at the Gaiety when Mary Ann disappeared.'

'Gerald *was*, however. I was not. I do agree with you that the gathering here for the Wychbourne Follies might have provided a perfect opportunity to ensure secrets of any sorts remained secret for ever. Nell, to use Mr Horace Walpole's excellent word, serendipity has provided another perfect opportunity in that Lady Kencroft, whom I find it impossible to consider a murderess, is shortly to arrive here for a chat. I suggest you delay your departure and join us. Shall we adjourn to the morning room?'

To Nell's pleasure, Lady Kencroft looked delighted to see her when Arthur ushered her into the morning room twenty minutes later. Slender and tall, her pleated day dress and cloche hat were the epitome of fashion and yet her sparkling eyes and lively manner made that seem of little importance. Take care, though, Nell warned herself. I'll be stepping back into her past here, and Lady Kencroft's view of it, like those of the others at this reunion, could have been coloured by time.

'I know from Lady Ansley that you are a force for good, Miss Drury,' Lady Kencroft greeted her, 'and also how much she relies on you – much needed at the moment. Arthur tells me you've been chatting and I'm very willing to help if I can, especially as Lord Ansley does have doubts about John Palmer's arrest.'

'As we have, Katie,' Arthur replied. 'Do you mind talking about Tobias?'

'Not if it unravels any of the truth. It was all terribly hush-hush at the time but the story going around was that Tobias was a married man. I can't believe that is true, though, because Tobias was so very fond of Mary Ann Darling. Oh dear.' Lady Kencroft pulled a face. 'I'm afraid it was Gertrude's remark that put a pigeon among the cats – my own reversal of the usual order. She was the pigeon and positively devoured as a result; she is still suffering from it. Mary Ann's disappearance has always been such a closed book. I don't even talk to my husband about it, although there's no reason at all that I shouldn't. Do you really think that it's relevant to Tobias's death?' she asked anxiously.

'One can't help but think that his death at this reunion is intriguing,' Arthur murmured.

'Be careful where you tread,' Lady Kencroft said lightly. 'My husband was very fond of Mary Ann too, and so were we all.'

'Did *you* think she was murdered?' Nell asked. Was this one of the impediments Arthur had feared? That guests' affection for Mr Rocke would stand in the way of the journey to the truth?

'Oh, Miss Drury,' Lady Kencroft replied, 'as she vanished so completely, we suspected it, especially when her body was found later. She did arouse passions in people. And yet she was the sweetest girl. She never actively stirred them up.'

'Did you see her after the performance that night?'

'Briefly, yes. I was dining at Romano's and so was Charles, although we were not married then and were sitting at separate tables with our respective escorts. In the nineties, Romano's was in its heyday. I gather it's declined since the war, but then it was such a lovely place. So unexciting outside, but inside! My dear, it was a stage all of its own. More diamonds to be seen than in Barney Barnato's mines. More champagne than the cellars of Cliquot-Ponsardin. The waiters were straight from *The Merry Widow* – Romano's was a Lehár operetta of its own, such frolics. And Signor Romano himself was such a character. The Guv'nor, Mr Edwardes, had an arrangement with Signor Romano that all we Gaiety girls could dine there half price so that's where we took our escorts. We were the attraction, part of the entertainment in the most respectable way, of course.'

'Were you dining near Miss Darling?' Nell asked.

'No. Charles and I were both at tables in the ground-floor restaurant, where one came to be seen, whereas Mary Ann was dining in one of the private rooms upstairs. I did see her briefly in the ladies' cloakroom.'

'Did she seem worried or upset?' Golly, Nell thought, I'm beginning to sound like the great Chief Inspector Melbray himself.

'Not worried. Excited, I think. Something might have been on her mind, because although she chatted to me she wasn't really *there.*'

'Who was she dining with?' Nell asked hopefully. 'Could it have been Mr Rocke?'

'I doubt it. He seldom came to Romano's. I didn't see Mary Ann arrive that evening, and although I caught a glimpse of her as she left with her escort the rear of one tail-coated gentleman looks much like another.'

'Did she have a regular escort?'

'Not as far as I recall. She liked dining at Romano's and went there often with different escorts. She was always very reticent about her life outside the theatre and she did have a problem with stage-door johnnies pursuing her – my apologies, Arthur. I remember your attending the Gaiety after some performances.'

'But hardly, my dear Katie, with designs upon the virtue of Gaiety Girls,' he laughed.

Lady Kencroft smiled. 'Mary Ann's problem with admirers was serious,' she added. 'She must have been scared, because I remember she asked me on one occasion if she could leave the theatre with Charles and me before taking a cab home. She always arrived at the stage door in a cab.'

'If she was being threatened, then that could have led to her murder,' Nell said.

'I suppose so.' Lady Kencroft looked worried. 'It may seem strange now, but her disappearance was never much discussed after the police visits stopped. Long before her body was found, we had all privately decided she had been murdered, and that just confirmed it. The strange thing was that Mary Ann wouldn't have dined at Romano's with someone who scared her.'

'Could that have been Mr Rocke?' Nell asked. 'You said he was very fond of her.'

'Good heavens, no. Far from it. He was a refuge not a threat. One longed to throw oneself into his arms and sob one's heart out.'

Nell laughed. 'Did you do that?'

'Back then in the nineties, yes. I was very fond of Charles, but he was so attractive and we Gaiety Girls were all eager to marry into the peerage that he and Gerald were much sought after. But Charles chose me, and now I wonder why I was so jealous. Tobias was our linchpin, holding us together. Alice isn't the sobbing sort, but even she confided in Tobias. We all did. Lynette used to alternately weep and rail about Neville and they married not long after Mary Ann disappeared. Constance too sought Tobias's help. She was so much in love with Hubert, who took not the slightest notice of her in that respect, although he was forever telling her what a great career on the stage lay before him. Tobias advised her to stick with it, but I'm not sure that was the right advice. They too married shortly after that terrible evening. Neville was pally with Tobias too – I presume because he saw him as someone who could open career doors for him, even though he opened them very efficiently by himself.'

'Did you know Mary Ann's family?'

'No, she never talked of it. I had the impression she lived on her own, though where I have no idea.'

Tobias Rocke, friend to everyone, very fond of Mary Ann. Did he see himself as her protector? Nell wondered. If so, wouldn't he have gone to great lengths to find out if she had enemies – and perhaps found one?

'I don't believe Gentle John killed Mr Rocke,' Sophy said firmly. It was impossible to get on with her work for the local Labour party with this new cloud hanging over Wychbourne Court, but it was hard to get either Helen or Richard stirred up over it, Helen because she spent her time mooning over the latest London club gossip and Richard because his new passion, Miss Smith, had taken over whatever brain power he had.

'Leave it to the police.' Helen yawned. 'They seem satisfied.'

'But what if they're wrong?' Sophy said. 'There were a lot of odd people here at the time.'

'Jenny Smith says—' Richard began.

'And she's one of them,' Sophy snapped.

'Don't say that,' Helen reproved her. 'Richard's got a pash for her. How do you fancy her for a sister-in-law?'

'Rotten.'

Richard flushed. 'She's a good sport.'

'More importantly, she's a good hairdresser,' Helen drawled.

Sophy tried again. 'This Gentle John business is serious, Richard. Ma and Pa are both involved in it.' If only Rex Beringer hadn't had to return to London. He was the most sensible one among them.

Richard frowned. 'It's over. They've arrested John Palmer. One good reason we should go on fussing, Soph?'

'Don't call me Soph,' she said crossly. 'Good reason? Yes. I saw Tobias Rocke talking to Gentle John and his wife after the Follies and heard a bit of what he was saying. It was something like "Let's have a little chat, Ethel, darling. Now. I've been having such a good time chatting with my old friends, but only one or two seemed really pleased to see me again, and I doubt if you are. What a sense of power that gives one." Then they all walked off together.'

'Did you tell the oh-so-polite inspector about this?' Helen asked, for once concerned.

'No. He didn't ask to interview me and I'd forgotten it anyway.

And when they arrested Gentle John I thought I might make it worse if I told them. Now I've had second thoughts because everyone seems to think Mr Rocke couldn't have been killed for quite a while after that.'

'And what, dear sister, will you do about these second thoughts?'

'Tell Nell,' Sophy said firmly.

Nell eyed Mrs Fielding warily. She had that look on her face that meant she was longing to impart information, and probably bad news. Lunch in Mr Peters' Pug's Parlour provided an excellent time for her doing so.

'They're coming back,' Mrs Fielding announced in tones of doom. 'All of them.'

'Staying here?' Nell asked, as Mrs Fielding was obviously referring to the Gaiety guests.

'They are, Miss Drury. The inquest's Wednesday, tomorrow. And no doubt the guests will be expecting the best of everything again.'

Nell immediately began planning in her mind. The fishman hadn't yet called. With any luck he'd be carrying crab in his van – and maybe some halibut and turbot. That would be good. The peach house was closed for forcing purposes, but there'd be pineapple and with her existing stock she could serve oranges with ratafia cream. That would be a start anyway.

The menus had to wait, though. When she returned to her Cooking Pot retreat, she found Lady Sophy patiently waiting for her.

'Why do you need all these cookery books?' she asked, leafing through Nell's precious hundred-year-old copy of Mrs Rundell's *Domestic Cookery*. 'You must know quite enough recipes already.'

'We build on the shoulders of giants,' Nell quoted pompously.

Lady Sophy giggled. 'I don't think Mrs Beeton is much of a giant except in the size of her book.'

'Which is why I don't build on her,' Nell shot back. 'What can I do for you?'

Lady Sophy hesitated. 'Something I haven't told the inspector.'

'Then tell me,' Nell said, heart sinking, and she listened with horror as Lady Sophy recounted her story. This was not going to help Gentle John but she couldn't be the judge of that.

'What shall I do?' Lady Sophy asked.

'He'll have to be told,' Nell said, rapidly thinking it through, 'but I'll do what I can.'

Lady Sophy was grateful, but that was premature, Nell thought. It would be a risk, but she would try tackling Ethel Palmer before breaking the news to Chief Inspector Melbray.

On her way out, however, she ran straight into Lady Clarice who beamed at her with pleasure.

'My dear Miss Drury, the most extraordinary event has taken place in the west wing. It was Tobias Rocke. I have no doubt of it.'

'His ghost?' Nell interpreted this. 'Is that possible? He didn't live or die at Wychbourne Court.'

'That is true. But Mr Trotter suggested Mr Rocke's sad spirit might have fled up here. It is my belief he is anxious to tell us something about his death. Could it be that he has come with a message about one of the guests who were here last week? Mr Trotter considers that is possible and has kindly offered to return to the Court after the inquest tomorrow. My brother tells me that their guests will be staying overnight. I would be so grateful if you could accompany us while we seek to find out if Mr Rocke will honour us again. The spirits trust you.'

Once again Nell had to accept graciously. It seemed a small thing to do, doubtful though she was about this new reputation she had acquired. It brought back her mistrust of Mr Trotter, unfortunately. A word about the darkroom with Lord Richard might be in order, she thought as she made her way down to Mill Lane and Ethel Palmer.

'Your friend Mrs Squires wants me to help,' she explained after Ethel Palmer had somewhat reluctantly invited her into Birch Cottage. 'But it's now emerged that your husband did have a motive for killing Mr Rocke, which is not what you told me earlier.'

'Maybe, but he still didn't kill him,' Ethel said defiantly.

Nell noted her crossed arms – a bad sign, from someone from whom she was hoping to extract truth. 'I've also heard that you were talking to Mr Rocke after the Follies ended.'

'Talking's not against the law. We may have said a word or two to him.'

Nell had had enough. Time for plain speaking. 'If you get caught out on the witness stand, you'll condemn your husband, Mrs Palmer. So better to tell the truth, no matter how bad it might look.'

Gradually the arms were uncrossed, to Nell's relief. 'He came back home with us,' she said sullenly. 'Said he wanted to talk to me about the old days. Then he went off and we didn't see him no more. And my John didn't know about me being wed before anyway.'

From the refolded arms and grim expression, Nell knew she'd get no further, so she tried a different tack. 'Were you already married to Mr Rocke when you went to work for the Gaiety?'

'Yes. He got me the job. No one knew we was wed. He said it was better that way. He had a twitchy nose where Miss Mary Ann was concerned and wanted me to keep him informed of every blessed thing she did. And he wasn't Tobias St John Rocke when he and I got wed. He was plain Billy Wagstaff. He said that wouldn't do for the London stage, so he went posh.'

An interesting side to the keeper of secrets, Nell thought. 'Were you still together with Billy after you left the Gaiety?'

She shrugged. 'No. While we was there he told me he wanted to split. Too dangerous for women in London, he said, and he'd a career ahead of him; he'd see I was all right for money, but I was on my own. I didn't mind leaving, not after Miss Mary Ann had gone. Billy and I had only a couple of rented rooms and he forgot all about the dosh he promised me. When his lordship heard I was being turned out of my rooms, he said I could have one of his cottages, so I comes here and meets my John, and we got wed in a year or two. I didn't see anything wrong in that, and no one was going to know about Billy and me here, not even his lordship. Billy had changed his name when he came to the theatre but I just stayed plain Ethel Wagstaff.'

'Didn't anyone at the Gaiety know?'

'There may have been rumours but no one really knew. We kept it dead quiet. You could have knocked me down with a feather when his lordship told me last week Billy was coming here with some of the old Gaiety folk. John wanted to go and gawp at them, so I thought why not? No one knew except us that Billy and me had been wed.'

'Did you know what happened to Mary Ann? Your Billy must

have been as upset as you were over her disappearance as I've heard he was fond of her.'

'And didn't I know it. Always pushing me for every little detail.'

One more try. 'Are you sure you didn't see who Mary Ann dined with that night? Wouldn't her escort have come to the dressing room door to meet her?'

'Never saw him if he did.' Then she reconsidered. 'Could it help my John if I tell you?'

'It might.' Nell held her breath.

'I've kept my mouth shut all these years. It were him, weren't it. Lord Ansley.'

'You wanted to see me, Miss Drury?' Lord Richard poked his head round the door of the chef's room. He came in, clutching his brow mockingly. 'Please tell me you're not going to scold me over my attentions to Miss Smith?'

'Not today, your lordship,' Nell replied demurely. She was glad of his arrival; it was a distraction from Ethel's revelation about Lord Ansley. She was still reeling from its implications.

'You're not a servant and you're not humble, Nell Drury. What's up?'

'Timothy Trotter is up.'

'Ah. Our spook-chaser. Pity he never quite catches one. I take it you have doubts?'

'Let's say there are interesting coincidences between published photographs of the spirit subjects before their death and those taken after by Mr Trotter.'

Lord Richard laughed. 'Really? What ho, as Bertie Wooster would say. Spirit photographers have been debunked before now.'

'How would our Mr Trotter be falsifying the photos?'

'Double exposures, perhaps. I've heard of that. Images of the subject cut out, photographed and the plates doctored. There were some scraps of paper and cardboard in the darkroom with pictures of people and all sorts of other things on them. He was certainly busy there all day. The pater doesn't trust him an inch.'

'You saw Mr Rocke coming out of that darkroom. Do you think he could have discovered Mr Trotter's little secrets?'

He looked at her in admiration. 'I say, Nell, that *is* a thought.'

* * *

Hanging over her like a dark cloud was the thought of having to relay all her new information to Alex Melbray before tomorrow's inquest. Late in the afternoon, Nell plucked up her courage to put through a trunk call to Scotland Yard to see if she could meet him before the inquest began.

To her relief, he sounded amused. 'A picnic lunch already, Nell? In the snow and ice?' He told her that he would be visiting Wychbourne Court after the inquest, but nevertheless he would be arriving early and could manage a brief meeting.

With that fixed, there was just one more annoying job to do before the day was over – checking the outside game larder for tomorrow's venison. The poor lighting in the kitchen yard made the covered path eerie at this time of night. Her pocket torch was helpful but hardly enough, and the rain was driving through the open side of the covered way. Nell picked her way carefully to the far end and over the gravelled yard and was much relieved when she reached the larder door. Immediately she opened it, though, she realized she was not alone. Sprawled on the floor, clasping a bottle in one hand, was a man whom she recognized, thanks to her torch. It was Jethro. What had he been helping himself to?

'What the cackling cobnuts are you doing here?' she exploded.

'Having a quiet moment, Miss Drury,' he sneered. 'And yourself?'

'Working,' she said briskly.

'Cooking ain't work.'

'Whereas poaching and pinching food are?' she retorted. What now? Ignore him and continue with her task? She was uneasy, aware that he too was deciding his next move. She had the door behind her fortunately, but she'd be blowed if she was going to retreat without what she'd come for just because of his leering attitude.

'Heard you were turning into a proper Sherlock Holmes,' he said, watching her as she checked the venison.

'Wrong. Get moving, Jethro,' she said when she finished.

'Who's going to make me?'

'Not me,' she snapped. 'But it will be a question of who comes to arrest you tomorrow if you don't leave. Especially if that's one of our pheasants I see in your bag.'

'You mind your own business.'

'Which you just informed me was detecting crimes.' Nell was on guard now. He was on his feet and moving closer. She could even smell his breath.

'Pheasants ain't crimes. Not like murder. Not like the bloke as was killed. Surprised the rozzers don't think I did it. I gets the blame for most stuff round here. But they arrested old Palmer and I'm told they charged him too. Did he do it? I ask. I could tell a story, I could. Shall I tell it you, Miss Drury?' He stepped even closer and this time she did retreat.

'Tell the police,' she countered. She'd have to risk turning her back on him if she was going to reach that door.

'Maybe I will,' he shouted after her, as she successfully reached the night air again.

At least she had discovered why Jethro was out on snowy nights. He probably had other customers than his father for the contents of the Wychbourne Court larders, *paying* customers. It put a new twist on the medieval custom of feeding the poor from the rich man's table.

When she arrived at the Coach and Horses on Wednesday morning, arrangements for the inquest were already under way, with motor cars and vans outside the pub and officials very evident inside it. This, she suspected, was going to be no friendly chat, and definitely not an 'Alex' day. This was business and she was facing an awkward conversation. She steeled herself as she entered the downstairs room to which she was directed. The chief inspector was already there when she arrived, rising to greet her. Oh yes, she could see immediately that talk of picnics was off the menu. He came straight to the point.

'Does this have to do with John Palmer or Mary Ann Darling?'

Take the bold path, she thought. 'Both.'

'John Palmer has been charged, as I expect you know. And I have read the files on Miss Darling. An interesting case. She was last seen on Thursday 8 June 1893. Her body was identified two years later by Mrs Elsie Humbold, her landlady, who had originally reported her missing shortly after her disappearance. There was a note that this was in agreement with Mr George Edwardes, as there was no known family. The investigation at the time of her disappearance into whether foul play or suicide might be involved was then closed.'

'What was the cause of death?' Nell instantly asked. 'Was she murdered? And if so who were the suspects? Was there another investigation?'

'One of the things I like about you, Nell, is that you leap straight into the boiling cauldron. It must be all those potatoes you cook.'

'This cauldron isn't boiling,' she said indignantly. 'It's had over thirty years to cool down.'

He laughed. 'Then why the eagerness to speak to me this morning? I'm delighted of course. Very much so. However, to answer your question: the coroner's court verdict was cause of death unknown owing to decomposition. She had been identified through her jewellery, and with the passing of time the inquest failed to catch the attention of the newspapers, save for a few brief notices. In those days, cases of unfortunate women found drowned in the Thames were not uncommon. The Yard closed the file, having concluded that the investigations it carried out in 'ninety-three were satisfactory and a further one could not be repeated with any hope of their shedding more light on the verdict given by the coroner's court.'

That meant murder was a possibility – even a probability given that Mary Ann disappeared late at night and accident was as unlikely as suicide. Now, Nell braced herself, she had to tell him about Ethel Palmer and Lady Sophy. The latter first.

He listed grimly while she told him, and then said: 'That's not good news for John Palmer, Nell. I'll have to follow it up. From what you and Jethro James tell us about the state of the blood when he was found, we don't think Tobias Rocke had been dead for more than, say, three-quarters of an hour. Which I'm afraid fits in with his accompanying the Palmers back to their home. Which means he must have been killed on his way back to the Court.'

The question of whether she should or should not tell him about Lord Ansley still bothered Nell. After all, the investigation of Mary Ann Darling had been closed. Nevertheless, given her own conviction that Tobias Rocke's past played a role in his murder, she had no choice.

'My visit to Ethel Palmer produced something else too,' she forced herself to say. 'She claims that Mary Ann Darling's dining partner that night was Lord Ansley.'

He stared at her. 'I understand why that cauldron's boiling now. Did you believe her?'

'Yes,' she said reluctantly. 'But I can't believe Lord Ansley is a murderer or involved in any plot that ended in a woman's death.'

'We have to take this information into account, however unlikely.' A long pause now. 'I would have arranged a picnic lunch shortly, you know.' Then another pause, while she waited, taken aback. Then he remarked. 'Your trust in Lord Ansley is a natural one, but he would have been a young man at the time of Miss Darling's disappearance. Passions sometimes decrease with age.'

'Not always,' she said obstinately. 'People don't change.'

'Fortunately, Mary Ann Darling is not my case, and I'm glad of that.' He reached out and took her hand. 'Don't worry, Nell. This goes no further.'

EIGHT

'Oyez, oyez, oyez . . .' The formal opening of the coroner's court. Only four days earlier this room had been alive with the singing and dancing of the Follies. There were no Pierrots on the stage now. Instead, the coroner and his officers were assembled, one or two of whom Nell recognized as policemen she'd seen in the village. The coroner was new, though. Lord Ansley had told her he was a Sevenoaks lawyer and very stiff and stern he looked, especially with the Royal Coat of Arms displayed behind him.

The inquest's legal purpose was to establish how Tobias Rocke had died, not who had killed him, and that perhaps explained why not many of the national press were here, although the local press was. Nell recognized a journalist from the *Sevenoaks Gazette*. She reasoned that from the national point of view, the story was temporarily over because of Gentle John's arrest.

From where she was sitting in the row of witnesses, she could see the Wychbourne Court guests, including Mr Beringer, sitting with the Ansley family and behind them the Wychbourne Court and the guests' servants – and the indefatigable Mr Trotter. Among those sitting near her were Jethro James, together with a defiant-looking Ethel Palmer, Lord Ansley, and of course Alex Melbray, together with the Sevenoaks police. Altogether an odd mixture, she decided.

She tried in vain to shut her ears to the gruesome details of Mr Rocke's injuries given by a pathologist from St Mary's Hospital in London, although her conscience told her she should listen. Obediently she concentrated on new facts. The blood on the mackintosh found in the churchyard bushes matched that of Tobias Rocke and the solitary glove found by the lychgate had been identified as John Palmer's. Both men were Group O, the most common group, so surely that did not lead anywhere, she reasoned. However, a lightweight mackintosh would hardly have been warm enough to wear on a cold January night, so that would suggest that the murder had been planned, as it could more easily be worn and disposed of after the murder had been carried out.

Once on the witness stand Jethro also produced something new. For once he was, amazingly, looking quite smart but otherwise he was his usual truculent self.

'And there he was,' he announced jauntily, 'lying there with his head bashed in. Midnight, it was.' He was clearly enjoying his big moment.

'Were you on your own, Mr James?' the coroner asked.

'I was, your lordship.'

'Why were you there so late at night? It was midnight.'

'My dad's the gamekeeper for his lordship, Lord Ansley,' Jethro said virtuously. 'I help him by checking his lordship's estate to see there aren't no poachers around.'

'And were there?' the coroner asked drily, clearly not believing a word of this.

'Not that I could see, sir. What happened was this. I did my usual tour in two halves. Poachers don't like folk being around, 'cos birds and game keep mum then, see, so I starts my tour before all those people come storming out of the pub and up the driveway which frightens the birds. Not seeing any poachers, I goes to check the outside larders to see whether they're being raided by poachers while the cat's away – beg your pardon, your lordship.'

'I take it there were none there either?' enquired the coroner.

'No, sir. Having done my checking, I decides to leave it awhile and go back to my home. That would be about quarter past eleven when I reached the churchyard making for Mill Lane. The bushes there were shaking a bit, a bit of nooky-nooky, if you ask me.'

'A cold night for it,' the coroner observed.

'True enough, sir.' Jethro laughed heartily, then must have seen the coroner's stony expression because he added hastily, 'It can't have been poachers, sir, there being no game around by the church. You need to be further into the estate for that.'

'Thank you, Mr James. I will bear that in mind.'

The coroner spoke with a straight face but Jethro looked at him doubtfully. 'Then I saw that beyond the bushes there was two gentlemen talking by the lychgate. 'Ello, I says to myself, poachers.'

The coroner regarded him grimly. 'You said there were none about.'

'That was earlier,' he said hastily. 'Anyways, these gents weren't poachers when I got closer. It was Gentle John and the tubby gentleman. Him that was murdered.'

The coroner frowned at this invasion of his court's prerogative in deciding how Mr Rocke had died. 'What did you do then, Mr James?'

'Not wanting to interrupt them, I climbed over—'

'*Climbed over?*'

'It's a quick way in and out of the grounds from Mill Lane, sir,' Jethro quickly recovered. 'I use it just because the poachers do, so it's a good way of catching them. Then I went the long way home so as not to disturb the gentlemen. The long way back being through the mill yard and round down Shepherd's Lane to the green where I live. I had a nip of something at home and then went out to do the second part of my tour half an hour or so later. It was when I was passing the green that I spots the lump on it and goes over to investigate. Gave me the fright of my life, it did, seeing him there like that, with the blood and all. So I hollers for help.'

Usually, Nell thought savagely, Jethro couldn't be trusted further than she could toss a pancake, but if his story *was* basically true, barring all this tommy-rot of looking for poachers, it was clear why Gentle John had been arrested. Ethel had made no mention to her of going out again. He had motive, opportunity and means. At least, Nell amended, he had the means as regards the stone. No knife had been found, according to Chief Inspector Melbray's evidence, only the pair to the glove. John Palmer could have disposed of the knife, Nell reasoned uneasily, snowy weather or not.

As for Jethro, he must have set out for his usual trip to scrounge what he could in the way of game either from the grounds or more likely, given the snow, the Wychbourne Court outhouses, and then had to make for the outhouses speedily to avoid people returning from the Follies. He must have waited there until the coast was clear and then made off across the grounds with his booty to his unorthodox exit to Mill Lane (or perhaps only part of his spoils which would explain his later planned return journey).

Her own interrogation on the witness stand and Lord Ansley's were mercifully brief, confirming Jethro's time of 'hollering', and that, she imagined, would be that, especially as Gentle John had already been charged with murder. She was wrong. Ethel Palmer was put through it next. This coroner was thorough, Nell thought; nothing was going to slip by him, and he could well get further with Ethel than she had.

'Mr Rocke wanted to talk to us,' Ethel stated reluctantly, 'so instead of standing in the cold when the pub closed, we said, "Come back home with us and we'll talk it over." That was just gone ten thirty. And so we did go home. He said he'd sort it all out somehow and we wasn't to worry about this marriage thing. He was ever so sorry that he'd given me the impression we was no longer wed when apparently we was.'

Nell pricked up her ears. That was new. Just an embellishment, or the truth?

'What then?' the coroner asked gently, as she came to a halt.

Or so Nell had thought, but she was wrong.

'Nothing,' Ethel said defiantly. She wasn't doing herself any favours, Nell feared. 'Well, John did go down as far as the church gate with him for a minute or two just to show there was no hard feelings. They had a chat and John came straight back here. He couldn't have been away more than five minutes and there was no blood on him or nothing like that.'

'What was he wearing when he went out?'

'His old jacket.'

'Under a mackintosh?'

'Yes.' Then Ethel must have realized what she'd said, because she added quickly, 'Not one of those light ones, though.' But the damage had been done.

By the time a procession of witnesses had given their evidence, the flurry of excitement had died down. The emphasis being on how Mr Rocke had died, most of the questions were devoted to that angle, although there was seemingly endless probing as to how the guests had left the Coach and Horses that evening: Nell made mental notes that Mr Peters had been first to leave, before the Pierrot finale, Mr Jarrett, having refused to take part in that, was the next, walking back to Wychbourne Court; Lord Richard had left with Miss Smith about five minutes past ten in the governess cart; Lady Sophy, Lady Helen, Mr Beringer, Mr Fontenoy and Muriel had returned by wagon; Mrs Reynolds, Mrs Jarrett and Lord and Lady Kencroft had walked; Mr Heydock and his 'Jeeves' had taken another wagon; Miss Maxwell and Doris Paget had walked back to the Court just before ten thirty; Lord and Lady Ansley, accompanied by the dowager, had left promptly at ten o'clock; and Lady Clarice had commandeered another wagon for herself and Mr Trotter.

Nell therefore deduced from their evidence that they had all left by ten thirty and it had also been established that all of them had appeared for supper, at least briefly, and then retired to their rooms or to the drawing or billiard rooms. But suppose, she thought, one of them had slipped out again? No, that wouldn't work. Tobias Rocke had not returned to the Court and how would any would-be killer there know where he was?

The jury, unsurprisingly, having retired to the bar parlour, didn't take much time in reaching a decision of unlawful killing.

Here's a load of bubble and squeak, as her father used to say, Nell thought ruefully. How was Mrs Squires going to take this? Convinced as Nell still was that Gentle John was no killer, she had as much hope of proving it as a snowman surviving a heat-wave. She was about to leave the Coach and Horses when Arthur Fontenoy beckoned to her.

'Nell, a word in your ear, if you please. I did with some difficulty,' he explained, 'persuade Lady Clarice not to insist on giving evidence at the inquest, but only at the cost of suggesting she talked to your Chief Inspector Melbray. I also suggested you might accompany her.'

'Thank you, Arthur,' Nell said grimly. She had a shrewd suspicion what this 'evidence' might turn out to be. This was no time to point out she was needed back at Wychbourne Court, as Lady Clarice was already advancing towards Chief Inspector Melbray, who was engaged with the Sevenoaks police. By the time Nell caught up with her, it was too late to stop her.

'One moment of your time, Chief Inspector,' Lady Clarice said, as the inspector turned to her politely. 'I have some good news for you.'

'Relevant to this case?' he asked, glancing at Nell as though this were her idea.

'The fifth marquess is eager to help,' Lady Clarice said triumphantly.

'The fifth? But he must have lived some time ago,' Inspector Melbray observed, as Nell inwardly groaned.

'Certainly he did. Simon Ansley, like Mr Rocke, was cut off in his prime. He came into his inheritance in 1856 and died, one suspects courtesy of his twin brother, in 1857. He is entitled to his say *now,* however. Unfortunately, he can be a fibber on occasion but I'm sure you are used to that in witnesses, Inspector.'

The inspector did not comment. 'Did the marquess communicate directly?'

'Ghosts rarely do,' Lady Clarice pointed out. 'One requires a medium to be sure of the message. If you wish, Mr Trotter might oblige in this respect, although his speciality is spirit photography, rather than Ouija boards and such devices. He appeared quite unexpectedly last night. His message was quite clear. There is a murderer among us who walks free and who must not be allowed to do so.'

'We believe we have him in our charge, Lady Clarice,' Inspector Melbray said.

'Nonsense. You may have Mr Rocke's murderer in charge,' Lady Clarice replied earnestly. 'I refer to quite another murderer. The fifth marquess referred to the murder of Miss Mary Ann Darling.'

Nell squirmed. Chief Inspector Alex Melbray must think that everyone at Wychbourne Court was cuckoo, but privately he proved amazingly understanding. 'After all, Nell,' he pointed out, after Lady Clarice had left with his full assurance that he would give this matter his full consideration, 'the fifth marquess is working on the same lines as you.'

'I'm flattered,' she retorted.

He laughed. 'It's true. You both believe the real answer to why Tobias Rocke was killed lies in his past life.'

Nell was only partially mollified. 'And you don't?'

'Officially, no. I'm coming up to Wychbourne Court again, remember?'

'You're right,' she grudgingly agreed.

'Always words I like to hear. Let's hope the fifth marquess hears them too.'

He returned to the pub and once again she set out for Wychbourne Court, only to run straight into Jethro James.

'You spoke splendidly, Jethro,' she said, stretching the truth as far as she could in the interests of diplomacy. After all, he had given a splendid statement from his point of view.

He smirked. 'Thanks, Miss Drury. I like to do my bit for his lordship.'

'His lordship could do without some of your help in reducing his game supplies.'

He shrugged. 'Cottagers' rights. He ought to be grateful to me for checking his game larders.'

'Why?'

'Justice, that's why. I see his posh guests come back after the Follies, and I see them go out again.'

Nell stiffened. Had she been misjudging him? Could Jethro really have seen something to shed some light on what had happened that night? 'That's Mr Peters' job,' she said cautiously.

'The butler don't always see everything. He's at the front door. He can't see those who come out the side door by the toffs' breakfast room, now does he? There was someone.'

'Who was it?'

'How could I know that? Dark, wasn't it? You don't light that yard too well at nights, Miss Drury.'

Another setback for Nell the Great Detective, she fumed, as she stomped back to the Court. Mrs Rundell or Elizabeth Raffald or Mrs Acton didn't take time off from their dedicated work on their cookery books in order to investigate murders, and here was she, Nell Drury, being out-manoeuvred by Jethro James. Stick to the jobs you understand, Nell told herself. Luncheon called, and it would have to be a speedy one, as Chief Inspector Melbray wanted to speak to them all in the drawing room while coffee was being served and then he had to return to London.

A distressed Mrs Squires was in full flow when Nell reached the kitchen. 'They don't understand, these judges,' she said as soon as she laid eyes on Nell. 'Why didn't that coroner fellow set him free? Gentle John couldn't kill a chicken – Ethel has to do it. As if he'd kill a gentleman like Mr Rocke.'

'It's ever so exciting, though,' enthused Miss Smith, blundering in once again. 'I thought it was going to be dull down here in the country but this is as good as having Jack the Ripper around.'

'Or that Patrick Mahon,' Kitty said with a shudder. 'Fancy cutting up your lady-friend into little pieces and boiling her.'

'Not here, Kitty,' Nell said firmly. There were limits to what she permitted in the way of idle kitchen chit-chat. 'We've enough on our hands.'

Although he had not expressly said so, Chief Inspector Melbray's request to speak to everyone at the Court did seem a sign that he was beginning to have doubts about Gentle John's guilt, despite Ethel Palmer's revelation. He couldn't ignore the coincidences of this reunion, Mr Rocke's death and the presence of so many people who knew Mary Ann Darling. Even the fifth marquess had his views on her murder.

Luncheon over (not entirely satisfactorily owing to the rush), it proved to be a larger gathering in the drawing room than Nell had bargained for. It wasn't just the family and their guests whom Chief Inspector Melbray wished to see. Mr Trotter was here and the upper servants too – save for Mr Briggs, who was already upset by the commotion in the house and would not understand what was going on, and Mrs Fielding who was nobly coping with coffee together with her still-room maid. With trepidation as to what was going to happen, Nell took her place beside Mr Peters and an excited Miss Smith.

'I cannot think why you wish to talk to us, Chief Inspector,' Mr Jarrett began querulously. 'You yourselves have charged Tobias's killer with murder. What more is there to say?'

'A great deal, I hope,' Inspector Melbray replied. 'The Department of Public Prosecutions would be knocking on my door if I neglected to present available evidence to the defence as well as the prosecution. Especially in this case. The motive for the killing stems back to the days when Mrs Palmer was married to Mr Rocke and was also dresser to a lady whose disappearance was subject to a Scotland Yard investigation that involved him. I refer of course to Miss Mary Ann Darling.'

Nell was torn between relief that the inspector was indicating that Mary Ann was a definite factor in the case and pity for

Lady Ansley who looked distraught. Lord Ansley had a face like thunder.

'Really, Melbray,' he barked. 'I fail to see how this can possibly be relevant to Mr Rocke's death. As you said, you consider that the motive for that is clear enough – Ethel Palmer was bigamously married to John.'

'Even so, it's my duty to examine all avenues.'

'Including Miss Darling's murder?' Mr Trotter piped up excitedly.

'If relevant to Mr Rocke's death,' Inspector Melbray replied.

'Surely,' drawled Mrs Reynolds, 'we all suspect that Tobias Rocke killed her?'

Nell felt like a batter pudding being vigorously beaten. So did everyone else judging by the uproar that took place.

'No, Lynette, we did not,' Lady Kencroft declared loudly.

'On the contrary,' Miss Maxwell shouted, red in the face with anger, 'you are quite right, Lynette. Mary Ann was terrified of him. She came to me for help.'

'And I agree with Lynette too,' snapped Mr Jarrett, pink with emotion. 'He was pushing himself on her constantly, the poor girl.'

Their polite society masks are falling off, Nell thought, her head still whirling. Just as the inspector had hoped perhaps?

'It's entirely possible he killed her,' Neville Heydock agreed. 'It's what we were all privately thinking. Tobias hung around the stage door in Wellington Street to see her arrive or leave.'

'You're all wrong,' cried Constance. 'I did not like Tobias but he adored Mary Ann and I do believe he might have known who did kill her. He was the keeper of secrets and—'

'Let me speak, Constance,' her husband thundered. 'Mary Ann was indeed fearful for her life, and certainly it was Tobias of whom she was scared. She made a practice of never walking alone through the stage door and then she regularly took a cab home to Cheyne Gardens as well as taking one to the theatre. Oh yes, Tobias was her killer. She rejected his advances – who would not? – and that was his revenge.'

'No, no, *no*,' Lady Kencroft cried. 'I agree with Constance. Tobias was our friend and Mary Ann's friend.'

'Muddied waters indeed,' Inspector Melbray broke in dispassionately. 'Mr Rocke couldn't have been murdered for knowing who killed Mary Ann *and* because he killed her himself.'

'He did,' Miss Maxwell shouted angrily. 'She hated him.'

'I cannot believe this is Tobias you are talking about,' Lady Ansley faltered, but the quarrelling continued.

Jumping jellies. Nell was appalled. Had Alex Melbray planned this? Those masks were well and truly down now.

'Perhaps you should ask yourselves what kind of person Tobias Rocke was,' the chief inspector said, as the noise began to die down. 'He was the keeper of secrets so what might that tell us? Perhaps that he might also have been a murderer, but what else?'

What did that mean? Was anyone going to answer? Nell wondered. *Could* anyone answer?

It was Mrs Reynolds who broke the silence with a burst of laughter. 'It might be of interest, Chief Inspector, to enquire how dear Tobias *used* those secrets. Surely no one here will deny that Tobias, our darling friend, was the gentlest, nicest, most implacable blackmailer one could ever dread to meet?'

Blackmailer? Just now he was a murderer. Who was this man? Nell took a deep breath. She'd seen him only a few days earlier, chubby cheeked, cheerful, pleasant – and now this. She was an outsider of course, so was it even true? Judging by their faces some at least thought so. There was a stillness in the room caused by more than bewilderment.

'Blackmailing the killer of Miss Darling?' Chief Inspector Melbray asked briskly.

'Perhaps,' Lynette Reynolds replied, not smiling now. 'Or perhaps his net caught other fish too. All sorts of fish swarmed around the Gaiety, and there might have been some swimming here. What do you think, Mr Trotter?'

NINE

Even Chief Inspector Melbray looked startled. All eyes had turned on the unfortunate Mr Trotter, and it seemed to Nell there was a general air of relief. Imagination, she told herself firmly, and yet her own doubts about Mr Trotter's activities reared up again.

'How dare you, madam!' Mr Trotter stood up, trembling. 'How could I possibly be connected with Mary Ann Darling's murder? I had the privilege of communing with her spirit last Friday, as you all know, but I had no previous contact with the lady.'

Lynette Reynolds lifted one eyebrow. 'I said Tobias had many other fish, Mr Trotter,' she replied coolly. 'Perhaps he fried you. He delighted in winkling out secrets from the most reticent of people and then tormenting them with his knowledge thereafter.'

'I still cannot believe it of Tobias.' Lady Ansley looked outraged.

'I can, Gertrude,' Neville Heydock said briskly. 'Several people – none here today of course – have suffered greatly.'

'I confided no such secrets to him,' snapped Mr Trotter.

'I did see Mr Rocke coming out of your darkroom, Trotter,' Lord Richard commented. 'Perhaps he'd been checking out your credentials, old chap. Studying your glass plates, for instance.'

Before Nell could add her pennyworth, Lady Clarice entered the fray.

'Richard,' she cried, 'you speak ill of a guest. Mr Trotter has the highest credentials. You have seen for yourself the splendid results of his work.'

'I have indeed,' Lord Richard replied in amusement. 'And Miss Drury noticed that your spirit photograph, Trotter, is identical with the postcard of Mary Ann displayed in the Great Hall. Isn't that so, Miss Drury?'

'It is,' Nell confirmed.

'I popped inside the darkroom to see what was what,' continued Lord Richard. '*Most* interesting.'

Mr Trotter was spluttering with rage. 'Are you impugning my integrity, your lordship? If the photograph looks the same as other pictures of Mary Ann, it merely means she liked that pose, that's all. You imply I am some kind of trickster, but I, sir, am a spirit medium.'

'There was that William Hope business last year,' Lord Richard pointed out. 'He faked pictures with double exposures, combining the originals with existing images. He had enough tricks to rival Houdini.'

'Mr Houdini is a friend of Sir Arthur Conan Doyle, who is of the opinion that Hope is a first-class spirit medium, as am I,' Mr Trotter shot back.

Richard laughed. '*You* a first-class spirit—'

'Enough, Richard,' Lord Ansley intervened. 'This is no place for such exchanges. We have guests, you are upsetting your aunt and we have a chief inspector of police with us investigating a murder.'

'Quite,' his son instantly shot back. 'That's why we need to know more about what Rocke was up to. But my apologies, Father.'

'If I may speak,' Chief Inspector Melbray said quietly. 'If anyone in this room was being blackmailed by Tobias Rocke, I wish to know. I should stress that at this point details are not required.'

'It's hard to see how anyone here could have suffered,' Lord Ansley said. 'This reunion was held because we rarely if ever meet each other, and although many of you are still active on the stage, meeting Tobias during the thirty years that have passed must have been an equally infrequent occurrence. It is unlikely therefore that any systematic blackmailing could have been in progress, as Lynette has suggested.'

'Blackmail is *such* an ugly word,' Mrs Reynolds pointed out, 'and an elastic one. Very elastic as far as Tobias was concerned. One doesn't have to meet people in order to blackmail them. Does one?'

'Lynette is right,' Mr Heydock said abruptly. 'But Tobias wasn't a blackmailer in the sense you would presume, Chief Inspector. Money was not always involved, not in cash payments anyway. He liked power. Power over people. The more people who confided in him, as I suppose many of us did in the old days, the more powerful he felt.'

'Oh, darling, how true,' Mrs Reynolds drawled. 'He gleaned information from his victims and then ensured they were always aware that he might spill the beans at any moment. He'd give a knowing wink or there'd be talk of a chat, or let's take luncheon together.'

'This conversation is making me feel quite ill,' Mr Jarrett complained. 'However, I should speak. As Tobias was a character actor, his career rarely coincided with mine, but nevertheless I believe what you say to be correct, Lynette. Wouldn't you agree, Alice?'

Miss Maxwell turned an icy stare on her *bête noire*. 'As it happens, I would. I've already mentioned Miss Darling's terror of him. I believe he blackmailed her and then killed her. I have never had the respect for Tobias that others seem to have held.'

'Once again, I really can't agree with this,' Lady Kencroft exploded in anger. 'He was always so kind to us, wasn't he, Gertie?'

'Yes,' Lady Ansley said stoutly. 'He supported us. He was our friend. It's true I had nothing to hide though, and nor did you, Katie.'

'Except an undying passion for Charles,' Lady Kencroft managed to laugh – obviously in an effort to diffuse the situation, Nell thought.

What was Chief Inspector Melbray making of all this? Nell wondered, glancing over at him. Everyone was talking as though he wasn't in the room and regardless of who else was. He had certainly listened very carefully and now drew the discussion to a close.

'Miss Drury,' Inspector Melbray called, as she was leaving, her mind whirling between the needs of her dinner schedule and the notion of Tobias Rocke as a blackmailer. 'May I have a word?' he asked politely, coming over to her.

'By all means,' she said formally. She could hardly commandeer the drawing room. It would have to be the Cooking Pot for their meeting. With its recipe books, files, photographs and pads of paper, she was proud of her room, but it was small and so perhaps she'd made a mistake in bringing him here. He was too close for her to think clearly about what she had to tell him – and vice versa. He leaned towards her, their knees almost touching where she sat in her chair at the table.

This isn't a personal discussion, she told herself. It's business.

'That meeting opened up rather more than I had bargained for,' he said.

'It didn't help John Palmer much,' she said ruefully.

'In a roundabout way, it did. I always try to look at the character of the victim, his or her upbringing, circle of acquaintances, etc. In this case, if one rules out a random attack – and with the weather conditions here last weekend we can do so – then the character of Tobias Rocke and his life do become important. No doubt Mr Heydock was right about the blackmail being in the form of power, but what matters is how much he threatened to use it.'

'As with Mr Trotter perhaps?'

'Quite.' He paused. 'Rocke could have seen John Palmer as another opportunity, I'm afraid. There's strong evidence—'

'From a poacher,' she snorted before she could stop herself.

'A poacher with a lot to lose if he lies in a case in which Lord Ansley is involved.'

'You're right – Alex.' Shouldn't it be 'inspector' if this was business? No, don't fuss, Nell, she told herself. Instead she told him about Jethro's claim that someone had left by the side entrance about eleven o'clock. And she had a feeling there was something else interesting that had been said recently, something she could no longer identify.

'Assuming that's true,' Alex Melbray said, 'it could have been a perfectly harmless mission by anyone in the Court.'

'Not anyone. It is officially only for the family and guests. Are you looking at them more closely now that the blackmail issue had arisen?'

'Same old story, Nell. I can't discuss that officially. I'd be a fool to ignore it, though.'

'Even though Tobias Rocke hadn't asked for money?'

'We don't *know* he didn't. And regarding the power issue, there are some things that are highly sensitive to talk about in company. Sex, for instance. Naturally enough your Wychbourne guests weren't going to announce their peccadilloes and preferences to all and sundry this afternoon.'

'Speaking as another all and sundry,' Nell said, 'do these peccadilloes also tie in with Mary Ann Darling's death?'

'I've no idea. I'll follow it up though *and* Mr Trotter. What's this about Mary Ann's spirit photograph?'

'I'll fetch that and the postcard from the Great Hall.' On her return, she found the inspector studying her childhood copy of *Alice in Wonderland,* and he hurriedly put it down.

'Look,' she said, laying both photographs on the table.

He stared at them for a while. 'You're right,' he said at last. 'It's the same image. It has to be.'

'Similar doubts over William Hope's photographs don't seem to have affected his career, though, so perhaps this doesn't mean that Mr Trotter is a complete fake.'

'You're too kind-hearted, Nell. It's time we took a closer look at Mr Trotter.'

'We?'

He smiled. 'The CID, Scotland Yard, on that one. About Mary Ann Darling, though. Her family were apparently non-existent, which suggests that might have been a stage name. You could enquire.'

'How?' she asked, taken aback.

'Ask Signor Antonio Murano.'

She blinked. 'Who the sizzling sausages is he?'

'He works at the formerly highly fashionable and romantic Romano's in the Strand. He looks after the grill-room bar on the lower floor, where Romano's kitchens used to be once upon a time. Before that he worked under the great Romano himself and then with his successor Luigi. But it's Mr Murano you want. He was there in the 1890s when our folk were at the Gaiety. I took the liberty, Nell – with Lord Ansley's permission – of saying you'd visit him tomorrow. He would, I think, respond more easily to your interest in the Romano story than to a Scotland Yard interview. About three is the best time, after the lunch rush is over. Unfortunately, it's not so much of a rush these days so far as Romano's is concerned. It's a relic of a former age and so are most of its customers.'

Nell laughed, highly pleased at this suggestion. 'Tell me what I want to find out, please.'

'As much as you can about the Gaiety actors and actresses who were here today and on the night of Mary Ann's disappearance.'

She whistled. 'One night more than thirty years ago?'

'A night that would be stamped on Murano's memory. He won't have forgotten even if the story has become twisted a little over the years.'

'But can't Lord Ansley tell you all that?'

He looked at her. 'Not necessarily in view of the fact that he was a frequent visitor to the Gaiety before he met Lady Ansley and that he was with Mary Ann Darling on the night she disappeared.'

'Yes, but—' She longed to ask him if he had spoken to Lord Ansley about that evening but did not dare. A step too far at the moment.

'Did you hear about his visits from him or from his father's friend, Mr Fontenoy?' he asked.

Nell grinned. They had crossed swords before over him. 'Arthur Fontenoy,' she replied. Then she realized what Alex was implying. 'Do you mean Lord Ansley might have been one of Mr Rocke's blackmailing victims because he was with Mary Ann at Romano's the evening she disappeared?' she asked incredulously.

'Obviously that question arises. Particularly as he is, I gather, reticent on the subject.'

'Have *you* asked him about it?'

'I have. He was reticent on the subject.'

Dismayed, Nell pulled herself together. 'But I can't see Lord Ansley either submitting to blackmail or murdering Tobias Rocke.'

'I can't see it either, but why not?'

'Because . . .' she cast around wildly for an explanation, '. . . Mr Rocke was a guest in the house.'

She caught his eye, bit her lip and then burst into laughter, as did he.

'Oh, Miss Drury,' he said, still shaking with laughter, 'I fear the rules of etiquette are sometimes ignored in such circumstances.'

'Never,' she said solemnly, '*never* in Wychbourne Court.'

London. Once this city had been her home. She'd been born in its East End, worked in the Carlton, then on Monsieur Escoffier's retirement taken a job in Hampstead and finally moved to Kent and Wychbourne Court. Did she miss London? Sometimes, Nell remembered those early years with her costermonger father at Spitalfields market in the early dawn and her later visits to Covent Garden market for the Carlton. Oh, the smells of all those fresh vegetables and fruit, brought in from far and wide. They were surely what had first kindled her love of good food, the spark that began her determination to use them as the basis of her own recipes.

The sheer sense of being part of London had overwhelmed her as she stepped off the train at Charing Cross. Would she exchange Wychbourne for it, though? Never. She'd been at Wychbourne for over a year and loved it. She loved the kitchen garden, the pigs of Home Farm, the smell of sawdust in the carpenter's shop, the sails of the mill flying majestically around, the smell of mown grass on the cricket pitch, the pit-pat of tennis balls. She loved it all – even at such terrible times as this when murder clouded its skies.

'*Star*, *News* and *Standard*,' yelled the paperboy she passed and, ignoring the rain pattering on her umbrella, she stopped to buy the *Evening Standard* hoping that it would no longer be carrying the Tobias Rocke story. She loved the Strand in particular. This *was* London to her. It didn't have the splendour of the wealthy West End, or the commercial appeal of Oxford and Regent Street, or the fun of Soho, but the Strand was the street that linked east and west London. This was the street that had housed the rich and famous of the past with their magnificent mansions and gardens leading down to the River Thames. Now the river had been pushed farther back, the horses and carriages had given way to motor cars and vans and the huge mansions were now hotels, shops and theatres. The Gaiety theatre building that Lady Ansley had known was no more, having been lost when the Aldwych was built. The theatre had resurrected itself further along the Strand but for many it lacked the razzle-dazzle of the earlier years.

Nell had passed Romano's many times in her career, and here it was, still proudly presenting its name over the doorway. She had visited its kitchen too on errands from the Carlton. Even Monsieur Escoffier had spoken in awe of its magnificent cellars.

'The Still White Champagne Cramant, Nell, *c'est magnifique*.'

She could hear Monsieur's voice now, as he had nodded with pleasure. Even then the bohemian atmosphere of Romano's was fast changing, so Monsieur had said. Signor Romano himself had died and excellent though his successor Luigi was, it was never quite the same as with the eccentric Romano. Physically it had changed too. The bar and grill room had replaced the kitchen on the lower floor, and it was there she was to meet Signor Murano today.

Here we go, Nell thought, shaking the rain from her umbrella. There were no diners remaining as she walked down to the grill room, but she was clearly expected as an elderly short man with a moustache and welcoming beam advanced to meet her with an old-fashioned bow.

'Signora Drury,' he greeted her. 'What honour, Signora.'

'The honour is mine, Signor,' Nell returned graciously.

'A glass of the Château Yquem perhaps?'

'*Grazie*.' Monsieur Escoffier would certainly approve of that.

'The pleasure is mine, Signora.'

The formalities over, Nell was able to take in her surroundings. She immediately felt at home here, since the walls were plentifully adorned with familiar-looking photographs of clients past and present, and even one or two Gaiety posters. If the current Romano's needed evidence of its glory days, here it was. Lynette Allison, as she then was, the bubbly Katie Barnes, Neville Heydock of course and a wonderful one of Lady Ansley. Nell lifted her glass of Château Yquem to them in tribute and Signor Murano followed suit.

He sighed. 'The signor from Scotland Yard say you wish to know about an evening from long ago, which the signora is too young to remember.'

'I've heard enough about it to believe I was there,' she replied. It was true. Here in Romano's itself, glory days past or not, it was all too easy to think of them as yesterday. 'Were you here on that day, the day Signorina Darling disappeared?'

'Not all the usual staff were working that evening, but I was, although I did not see the lady. I was at the main restaurant bar, and the police interviewed us all. When you have finished your wine I will show you Romano's, as the inspector asked me to.

Your Gaiety girls and boys would not have known this grill room but they did know the great Romano. The Roman as everyone call him. He *was* Romano's; he was the greatest showman of them all. Everyone come here then, not just the theatre people; everyone come to meet everyone else. The Prince of Wales, he loved the place – the *old* Prince of Wales, not the Bright Young Man we know today. Now we are more respectable, Signora, but we are not *fun.*'

She followed as he led her upstairs to the ground floor to show her the entrance hall. 'Signorina Darling would have come in here, perhaps her gentleman friend would buy flowers at the stand here. Now I will show you our restaurant, Signora.'

'Is that where most of the Gaiety Girls would dine?' Nell asked, remembering Lady Kencroft's account.

'Some were in private rooms, but that night many were in the restaurant. I will show you. When Romano's first open, everyone met in the bar and then walked through to the restaurant, but by the nineties, when Miss Darling come, the door open straight to the restaurant. More à la mode.'

He paused before the doors and then flung them dramatically open.

'*Ecco*, Signora.'

And there it was. The glory of Romano's. And an odder restaurant Nell had never seen. She felt she was walking straight into the *Arabian Nights*, with two long side walls composed of Moorish arches with brightly coloured Oriental scenes on them. And yet, unusual though it was, the décor worked, and it was possible to see how exciting a place this had been thirty years ago. The tables were in two long rows, against the side walls, and the floor space in between was used for dancing, Signor Murano told her.

'Your lady, she was not here,' he said, 'but other ladies from the Gaiety were here that evening. She dine upstairs.'

'Up there?' Nell pointed to where a trellised balcony stretched across the far wall.

'No, no. That not there in the nineties. Miss Mary Ann was in a more private room, much more private.'

'And you're sure that was the night she disappeared?'

'I am. Many people swear to that when the police came the

next day after she had not appeared at the theatre. Mr Edwardes, the boss at the Gaiety theatre, took a cab to her home but no one there.'

'Was Darling her real name or a stage name?' she asked, remembering Alex's instructions.

'That I do not know. I knew her only as the beautiful Signorina Darling.'

That line had petered out then. Nell stared at the restaurant, imagining it full of exotically clad ladies sparkling with jewels and dancing the night away. 'Can you show me the private rooms too, please?'

'Yes, Signora, but they will tell you little about Miss Mary Ann.'

He led her upstairs and Nell saw his point immediately. All were still furnished with heavy dark tables and dark plush-covered chairs. Mary Ann's was the first in a row of four but the room spoke only of the past, not of the people who had dined there.

'Were all these rooms occupied that night?' she asked.

'The room next to this one was booked. I do not know about the others.'

'The diners wouldn't have seen her leave, would they?'

'No. The doorman would have seen them.'

'Does he still work here?' she asked hopefully.

He smiled. 'No, Signora. He left us many years ago.'

No luck there then. 'Who was in the other private room?' she asked, trying to see some sense in this story.

'Signor Jarrett. He has become very famous since. He was with a signorina from the Gaiety, Miss Constance Wilson.'

Did that get her any further? Nell wondered. She pushed on. 'Did Mr Rocke dine here that night?'

'I do not think so. Only rarely did he come, and then he liked to be near Miss Darling, whoever she was with. If she discovered he was coming, she would try not to come herself that night. Perhaps he not like it if she dining with other gentlemen.'

That sounded creepy, she thought. Tobias Rocke had seemed to her such a pleasant man, but now he sounded like Svengali in the Du Maurier play.

'There were others from the Gaiety here, in the restaurant,' he continued. 'Miss Lynette Allison, Miss Katie Barnes, Miss Maxwell, and I believe Miss Wilson joined them later. She had arrived with Mr Jarrett, who had to leave early. All so very long ago. We tell the police all this, and that is how I remember it. Very long ago. Imagine our restaurant, Signora, as it was then. It is changed and now no more are we as grand as the Savoy.'

'I used to work at the Carlton.'

He beamed. 'Then you know the hotel world. It has many nations working there. You are a great chef, Miss Drury. Our chef in the nineties was from the Hapsburg family, one of the young waiters, Louis, was the son of a nobleman in southern France, another was Mario, from a poor village in the south of Italy – the south is not so good as the north of course, where I was born. None of them work here now, nor were they present that evening, but I was, and still I work here, as does the man who look after the cellars, Bendi. He and I, we are maturing like our wine of which we are so proud.'

'You age perfectly, signor.'

He bowed. 'I thank you, but there is a story in the Bible of a woman who named her child Ichabod. The glory is departed, she said, after all she loved in life save for him had been taken from her. I am Ichabod, Signora Drury. The glory of Romano's is departed and soon it will take me with it.'

Alex Melbray had said nothing about her reporting to him on her visit to Romano's and an enquiry at the reception desk of Scotland Yard proved fruitless, as he was out that afternoon.

Time was passing and Nell needed to be back at Wychbourne Court for dinner preparations. She had only just arrived there when Mrs Fielding thumped on her door.

'Gallivanting in London, Miss Drury? I suppose you realize that I had to order more apples for your fancy puddings and Kitty has been trying to get your jellies and junkets ready for dinner. She needed that as much as a toad wants a side pocket. She'll be glad you're back.'

No point in defending herself. Instead, Nell smiled at the Kentish saying. 'I'll make up for it. Luckily it's only the family dining.'

Mistake. 'Only the family?' Mrs Fielding retorted. 'Mr Beringer has stayed on and Mr Fontenoy's dining here with Lady Clarice as the dowager is staying home. It all has to be catered for.'

'And Mr Trotter too?' Nell asked with a straight face. Mrs

Fielding had taken exception to Mr Trotter, who had unwisely observed in her hearing that the scones were overcooked.

Mrs Fielding stiffened. 'Her ladyship wouldn't invite the likes of him, but Lady Clarice insisted.'

'Thank goodness you're here to see all goes well, Mrs Fielding,' Nell said diplomatically, dumping her bag and turning to leave.

'And his lordship wants to see you now you've returned,' Mrs Fielding added offhandedly, blocking the door. 'If you've the time to spare, of course.'

'Plenty of it,' Nell tried to say sweetly, squeezing past her to pick up the house telephone. She could make a good guess at what this was about. Crackling crumpets, though, was she going to be cross-examined before she had even disentangled the afternoon in her own mind? Apparently yes. Lord Ansley would like to see her before dinner if at all possible.

If Lord Ansley asked, anything had to be possible. Why so quickly though? There could only be one answer to that. He would want to know about her visit to Romano's. Chief Inspector Melbray had told Lord Ansley his plan for Nell's visit in full awareness that his lordship had been with Mary Ann Darling on the night she disappeared. Did that mean that Lord Ansley really was a suspect either for Mary Ann's death or Tobias Rocke's?

Tread carefully, she thought, then reprimanded herself. Hadn't she said that there was no way that she could believe Lord Ansley guilty of anything evil, let alone murder?

She whipped off her apron, hurried up to her bedroom on the first floor to organize her hair and change, then rushed straight to his study, as he had asked. He used the steward's room for his estate work, but this summons did not fall under that category. The study was on the first floor, and it was here that he wrote private letters and, yes, studied. He kept a formidable array of books there, chiefly on his main interests. Kentish history, farming and archaeology together with a few political memoirs.

'Thank you for coming so quickly, Miss Drury,' he greeted her formally. He was already dressed for dinner, with dinner jacket and white waistcoat, which made him look far more formidable than his usual Norfolk jacket and trousers. 'I hope you enjoyed Romano's. Not what it used to be, but then we can't turn the clock back.'

'Would you want to?' she asked boldly.

He smiled. 'When you yourself are older, Nell, you will find that giddy youth is not always a joy to look back on.'

Giddy youth at the Gaiety stage door? she wondered.

'I asked you to come,' he continued, 'because the ramifications of this murder case are spreading at such a pace that it's time I spoke both to you and to Chief Inspector Melbray as he is formally engaged in uprooting the past. I have been under an obligation not to speak of this affair, but as Mary Ann Darling has become an issue in another death, I bow to the necessity of breaking my word.'

So that was it. Nell breathed a little easier, but still plunged right in. 'I was told it was you who dined with her that night.'

'It was. At Miss Darling's request.'

'In a private room, so Signor Murano said.' This sounded accusatory to her ears and she regretted it.

'And you will understand why, when I explain,' he said quietly. 'Mary Ann – I think of her that way and not as Miss Darling because I was very fond of her. Not so fond, I hasten to add, that I suffered the pangs of unrequited love when she told me her heart belonged to another. I was young, but even then knew that I would recover. As indeed I did, since I met Gertrude almost immediately afterwards when she came to take Mary Ann's role in *The Flower Shop Girl*. Mary Ann's understudy had been taken ill and Gertrude had made a name for herself at the Albion in a play that had just closed.

'But I digress,' he continued. 'That evening Mary Ann was a very scared young lady. She told me she had had a miserable time, pursued and pestered wherever she went, and she felt in great danger. She did not go into details, but she was sufficiently alarmed to believe that her life might be in danger because she had rejected this man's advances. She told me therefore that she had a plan to disappear without trace in the company of a gentleman who loved her greatly and whom she wanted to marry.'

The truth at last. Thank heavens. 'Did she name him?'

'No. All she said was that she had planned for him to draw up outside Romano's one evening. She would join him there and he would look after her. She would leave her home for his. She was upset at the thought of letting Mr Edwardes down without notice, but she had confidence in her understudy, who, as I said, was unfortunately then taken ill just as she was needed. I asked Mary Ann if she trusted this man, as I was most concerned, but she was quite sure she could. I had the impression it was not someone with whom she worked at the Gaiety, and that perhaps was an advantage. All she asked of me was that I would escort her through the Gaiety's *front* doors on the Strand and not through the stage door in Wellington Street, which was the usual exit for the cast. I would then take her to Romano's for dinner. She hoped that whoever was dogging her footsteps would assume that she was spending a normal evening with me, as she did from time to time. She asked me then to escort her after dinner out of Romano's and into a cab that would be waiting for her with her lover.

'This seemed to me a plan full of holes and I told her so,' Lord Ansley continued. 'Even if I did as she requested and she was driven away in the cab with her beloved, she ran the risk of being followed and attacked either then or at a later date, whether she was married or not. We therefore concocted a plan to make it seem that she had disappeared for good. It did require the help of another male friend at the Gaiety however. She suggested Neville Heydock.'

'She trusted him?' Nell was amazed. To her he seemed flippant and unreliable, but perhaps that was just outward show.

'Yes, just as she trusted me. The plan was that Neville would wait until the cab – a growler so that the cabbie could not see what was happening – drew up with her gentleman friend in it towards the middle of the road. Neville would come into Romano's to alert Mary Ann and myself, then immediately return to summon a second growler, which would wait at the kerbside directly outside Romano's while Mary Ann and I were coming downstairs. Neville would get into that cab himself, ostensibly to await Mary Ann's and my arrival. The first cab would be parallel to the second – which would not draw any attention as the Strand then was even more crowded than it is today with carriages higgledy-piggledy everywhere as they waited for theatres and restaurants to empty.

'The moment I came out of Romano's with Mary Ann,' he continued, 'I would go up to the cabbie to give him directions and pay him, while Neville slipped away on the far side of the growler unnoticed. I could then usher Mary Ann into the growler on the near side, go to the cabbie again to change the directions or some such pretext, then return and bang the door as though I had entered, giving him the shout to leave. Then I'd step smartly back into the milling crowd. Meanwhile, of course, Mary Ann had also left the growler on the far side and jumped straight into the cab with her sweetheart.'

Nell gulped. Quite a story! 'Did it work?'

'Amazingly, looking back, it did. I returned to Romano's. The cabbie duly drove on only to find no passengers when he arrived at the false address. He'd been paid so he had nothing to worry about. Quite a lot might have gone wrong, but we were lucky and nothing did. Except in one particular.'

'Which was?'

'Mary Ann really did disappear,' he said soberly, 'and I fear met a terrible death. We had realized that investigations would follow because of her fame and role at the Gaiety, but I had no reason to doubt that she was safe, despite being somewhat baffled by this mysterious lover. Revealing our plan to the police could well have brought more trouble for her, and in any case I had promised to keep silent. Only as the years passed did I wonder whether I was right to do so, especially when I learned that a body had been identified.' He paused. 'I concluded that Mary Ann's love affair had gone seriously awry and that either her lover had killed her or she was so distraught that she ended her own life.'

'That must have been truly dreadful for you,' Nell sympathized. 'Did your Gaiety friends who'd been at Romano's think you were to blame for her disappearance?'

'Mary Ann and I had a private room and as far as I know no one saw us come or leave. Certainly not those in the restaurant. Fortunately for my reputation, I did meet Signor Romano himself who could verify that I had returned after Mary Ann's departure. He was surprised to see me alone as he knew I'd arrived with Mary Ann, but as Romano was used to such surprises he showed the utmost discretion and I wasn't questioned by the police. I had chatted to Signor Romano for ten minutes or so before returning upstairs to have a reviving brandy. The usual waiters weren't on duty that evening, so the Roman, as we called him, brought it up himself and we talked of the lovely Mary Ann. I couldn't know of course that that would be her last appearance. I suspected that she would not return, although not for such a terrible reason.'

'Mr and Mrs Jarrett were in the room next you,' Nell remembered. 'Did they not see you?'

'Luckily, I think not. Hubert was greatly attached to Mary Ann and it hadn't been the first time that Mary Ann was dining there and he managed to be seated in the adjoining room. His attachment was not reciprocated. I always – I know you are the soul of discretion, Nell – thought that Constance was second best for him; he married her very shortly after Mary Ann's disappearance.'

Another persistent suitor then, Nell thought. 'Mr Murano told me today that Mrs Jarrett joined Lady Kencroft, Miss Maxwell and Mrs Reynolds in the restaurant later on that evening, because Mr Jarrett had left early.'

'I didn't know that.' Lord Ansley frowned. 'I suspect that Hubert merely walked off in a huff having realized that Mary Ann had slipped away. I can't believe he was the mysterious lover in the cab. He's an odd fish though.'

Nell hesitated. 'Mr Rocke was a great admirer of Mary Ann too.'

Lord Ansley looked at her. 'And where does that take us, Miss Drury?'

She grimaced. 'I don't know. It's hard to see how he could have been too persistent an admirer because he was married to Ethel then.'

'I don't believe that would have greatly inhibited Tobias's life,' Lord Ansley said drily. 'But then who knows with Tobias? He remains the best kept secret of all.'

TEN

Nell felt like a yo-yo, whirled between the story of Mary Ann Darling and raspberry dumplings – that being the particular recipe her eye had fallen on. True, raspberries were out of season, but would it work with raspberry preserve? Back to Mary Ann: did Lady Ansley know the story? She could always fall back on whip syllabubs. Good standby. And what about that other favourite of Dr Johnson's, veal pie with plums and fish sauce, for an entrée? What could have happened to Mary Ann after she set off in the cab with her lover? Had she met her death at his hands? Fruit – she must find some fruit. How would that have affected the Gaiety? Stop this, she ordered herself. Daily life deserved her full attention – even if Mrs Squires was late again.

It was because of Ethel once more that Mrs Squires bustled in breathlessly at ten thirty on Sunday morning. 'I'm sorry, Miss Drury. Ethel's in a real lather.'

'What's happened?' Nell asked, alarmed. Ethel's situation had been bad enough already without more trouble.

'I can't think what's come over her,' Mrs Squires lamented. 'Mr Rocke's funeral is tomorrow and she's running around like a dog with two tails. I don't know how we're going to manage either.'

'How *we're* going to manage?' Nell frowned. 'It won't affect us much here if the family has to go to London to attend.'

'No, they'll be here, won't they? The funeral's at St Edith's. It's all arranged.'

'*Here* in Wychbourne?' This didn't make sense. Gentle John was in prison awaiting trial for the murder of a man from whom Ethel appeared to have parted with little regret and must have even less regard for him now.

'Ethel thought it best, there being no one else to make arrangements at Earl's Court. That's where Mr Rocke lived, and the housekeeper there wasn't going to lift a finger, so Ethel said. Mr Rocke's to be buried in the new cemetery.'

'New' was a misnomer, but everyone called it that, although it had been opened thirty years ago when St Edith's churchyard had been closed for new burials, and a separate cemetery consecrated further up Mill Lane.

'I don't understand,' Nell said. 'Why can't his heirs arrange the funeral?'

'Ethel is the heir, Miss Drury. He never made no will and had no children so it all goes to her, so the solicitor says. She was still married to him by law, but as he'd changed his name and she'd had no word from him since he told her to hop it, she's been told she was entitled to think him a goner. Ethel says it's her due to get his money as he treated her so rotten.'

His heir? Another shockwave hit her. Assimilating this information was making her mind feel like an unset jelly. To Nell's dismay her immediate thought was to wonder how much Ethel might be inheriting.

Mrs Squires must be reading her mind. 'Don't know how much she's going to get, but a tidy sum, Ethel thinks.'

What, Nell wondered, would Chief Inspector Melbray think of this, because with this revelation the noose around Gentle John's neck would surely tighten? The inspector might well suspect Ethel of complicity in the murder, remembering the notorious Thompson and Bywaters case in which Mrs Thompson was hanged for inciting her lover to murder her husband.

Mrs Squires was still talking. 'Ethel's going to do him proud, she told me. Tomorrow afternoon it is.'

'We're not holding the funeral gathering here, are we?' Nell was even more alarmed. The thought of Jethro striding through the Great Hall as if he owned it was not appealing.

'No, Miss Drury. Ethel's fixed it with the Coach and Horses to serve a nice sandwich tea.'

Thank goodness for that, Nell thought, although Mr Hardcastle was hard put to it coping with the Follies, a murder, an inquest and now a funeral all in ten days or so.

'Everyone will be eating here in the evening, though,' Mrs Squires blithely continued.

'*What?*'

'That's what Lady Ansley said while you were out Friday.'

Lady Ansley hadn't mentioned it yesterday morning, Nell

thought. Who exactly was 'everyone'? Lady Ansley's silence was one more instance of how far from normal 'normal' life was at present. She took a quick look at the menu she was about to present to Lady Ansley. The fishman had promised oysters for Monday and she'd planned on using the cold lamb from today's roasts for Mrs Leyel's lamb à la Marie recipe, which involved a curry sauce. That wouldn't do for the threatened 'everyone'. Oh well, curly kippers, she would cope somehow. But would Lady Ansley?

Lady Ansley was contrite. 'I'm sorry for not telling you yesterday about the funeral, Nell. It all happened in such a flurry on Friday, and since then so many people have been telephoning and causing problems.' She pulled a face. 'However Constance came to marry Hubert Jarrett, I'll never know.'

'Mrs Squires told me Ethel has booked the Coach and Horses for tea, but what about the evening?' Nell asked with foreboding. 'She said that everyone would be coming here.'

Lady Ansley sighed. 'Not quite everyone, just those who were staying here for the Follies, but that's quite enough. Mrs Palmer seems to be quite determined to hold the funeral in the village, firstly as she's inheriting the estate she feels she should do so, even though he behaved like a bastard – I'm afraid that was the word she used – to her during the time they were married. No, they were still married of course. I mean while they lived together as man and wife. The second reason is that not only is she naturally convinced that Gentle John is innocent, but that "one of them", as she put it, meaning my guests, is guilty.

'Oh, Nell,' she continued, 'what else could I do, but ask our friends to dine here and stay overnight? I fully expected them to refuse, but because they're all coming to the funeral, they all accepted. Isn't that surprising?' Lady Ansley asked.

Nell agreed, privately wondering which of them thought they *should* be there, and which of them thought it would look strange if they weren't – especially if one of them were a murderer.

'Mrs Squires informs me that the sandwiches will be made at the Coach and Horses and she's been rallying helpers,' Lady Ansley continued. 'Muriel offered too, and so did all three of our guests' servants. Your Kitty suggested that she'll be there as well, as I do hope you will be, Nell – although you won't be making sandwiches of course. Chief Inspector Melbray will be joining us for dinner tomorrow evening, although not staying overnight. Perhaps he sees so much hobnobbing with the suspects as a step too far.'

Lady Ansley could well be right, Nell thought. 'And Mr Trotter?' she enquired in the hope of bringing a smile to Lady Ansley's face.

It succeeded. 'That I don't know and I'm not going to ask. He's staying at the Coach and Horses. Lady Clarice can invite him to dinner if she wishes, but I imagine the prospect of having to face my son's onslaught again will deter him. Richard talks of getting his activities investigated for fraud. Oh dear, I'm getting to the point where I just want to hold my wrists out and say, cuff me now, Inspector, just don't ask me any more questions.'

Nell laughed. That was more like her ladyship. It cheered Nell up too – as did the prospect of seeing Alex again. Just in the interests of proving Gentle John's innocence of course.

Lady Ansley hesitated. 'I know my husband talked to you yesterday. He has told me the whole story too. Thank goodness, Nell, thank goodness.' She flushed, as she must have realized this sounded as though she had suspected her husband of involvement in abduction or even murder.

Nell echoed the thank goodness. Lord Ansley was the rock of Wychbourne and at present Wychbourne needed all the rocks it could muster.

St Edith's was a large church for a small village such as Wychbourne but its ancient stained glass and the pews dating from centuries past gave it a comfortable feeling. For centuries it had looked like this, Nell thought, and we're just temporary visitors. There had been plenty even more temporary visitors here today. The service over, the congregation was spilling out into the churchyard. The Reverend Higgins had seemed somewhat overwhelmed by the fashionable gathering that had poured in by motor car or taxi cab, the women clad all in black or the now acceptable dark violet, the men in their stately mourning coats. Not only were the actors and actresses she had seen at Wychbourne

Court here, but many more, together with journalists from national and local newspapers, plus, it seemed, most of Wychbourne village, chiefly men, as the old habit of men-only funerals was dying hard in Wychbourne.

Nell watched them paying their condolences to Ethel – surely only lip service in the circumstances? They moved slowly, like carved figures on the chiming clocks that emerge ritually on the hour, each playing their part. The only person who looked human, she decided, was Chief Inspector Melbray, sombre in black suit and tie. For the most part people were heading for the Coach and Horses rather than to the cemetery for the burial.

'Nell, are you going to the pub?' Alex caught up with her, walking alongside her towards the Coach and Horses. 'I've another mission for you.'

'Another Romano's?' she asked, intrigued. 'I enjoyed that.'

'This one may not be quite so enjoyable, but it could be interesting. There may be a chance to find one or two of those secrets Tobias Rocke held before they get thrown away. Ethel Palmer isn't wasting time. Tomorrow she's going to inspect Tobias Rocke's home in Earl's Court. It's an imposition, I know, but I'd like you to go with her – I'll explain to Lord Ansley. My men have finished there and so have I. We found the usual papers, some relating to his marriage, but nothing that suggested any line of enquiry other than the ones that lead to John Palmer. I can't help feeling that *if* there is more to this story you might possibly sense a clue there.'

'Relating to blackmailing activities?'

'Certainly including that.'

Nell wavered. 'I'm not trained.'

'You can spot a fly in the soup, can't you?'

She laughed. 'That I can do. Done then.' She was already looking forward to it, Ethel or no Ethel. Piecing together Tobias Rocke's life might be a fascinating task.

'I've checked the Darling investigation records, Nell. You'll be interested to know that Tobias Rocke couldn't have been responsible for her abduction or murder that night. He didn't return home until two in the morning, because he had dined at your old stomping ground, Nell. The Carlton Hotel, confirmed by several reliable witnesses at the time.'

'Mistake over the timing?' she asked hopefully.

'I think not. One of his fellow diners was Marie Lloyd of music hall fame and another a rising young officer, now a fellow chief inspector in the City of London police. I spoke to him and he assured me that Rocke was indeed at the Carlton with him. He only left the table for a while to see Marie Lloyd safely into a cab. I can't confirm that as Marie Lloyd is no longer with us, but my colleague remembers it clearly because it became such a talking point with Mary Ann's disappearance reported two days later. We have to assume that in all probability Tobias Rocke did not murder Mary Ann Darling at least on that night unless he had several accomplices. Marie Lloyd would not have been one of them.'

'And yet Mary Ann was scared of him.'

'Rocke could have been a rejected lover or the importunate lover who followed her everywhere, but that doesn't make him a murderer, unless after her disappearance he discovered her whereabouts and killed her. If so, why no outcry from the true lover?'

'But Tobias might have known who killed her.'

'Indeed he might. An excellent victim for his blackmail. Keep your eyes open at his house, Nell. You might find something we missed.'

'You're flattering me,' she said uncertainly.

'I never flatter anyone,' he said simply, and once again she felt wrong-footed.

Funeral gatherings were strange occasions, Nell thought, looking round the room, which was even more crowded than on the night of the Follies. Either conversation flowed as people relaxed, or they remained as formal as the service itself. This one had elements of both. Tables lining the walls held glasses and drinks, sandwiches and cakes. Mrs Squires, her team and the guests' servants, even the guests themselves, were busy taking small trays around the gathering and offering drinks. There was no sign of Lady Helen, but Lord Richard and Lady Sophy (and Miss Smith) were busy helping too.

'I'm hunting for clues, Nell,' Lady Sophy hissed at her as she floated by with a plate of what looked like salmon and cucumber sandwiches.

'You need a magnifying glass for clue-hunting,' Nell retorted amiably, 'not plates of food.'

She braced herself to walk over to murmur appropriate words to Ethel, who looked flushed and out of her depth.

'Thank you, Miss Drury,' she said stonily. 'Inspector Melbray said he'd asked you to accompany me tomorrow. I don't know why, I'm sure. They've finished their investigation, he said, but I'm to leave everything in the house until the solicitor says it's legally mine. I've no objection to you coming, though. The housekeeper will still be there and that husband of hers.'

'It must be hard for them as they lived in.'

'Not my fault if he didn't leave them nothing,' Ethel snapped. 'What will you be looking for there, Miss Drury?'

'Anything that might help show who killed Mr Rocke. I don't believe that was Gentle John.'

Ethel had the grace to soften a little. 'It wasn't. He's no murderer and nor was Billy.' She hesitated. 'Billy wasn't home that night Miss Darling disappeared, but he didn't kill her. Not his way of doing things.'

'What was his way then?' Nell asked, but there was no reply.

Nell was glad to reach the warmth of the Wychbourne Court kitchens. Here, she thought with relief, she knew exactly what she was doing. It was all very well for Alex Melbray to think of her as a makeshift detective, but detective work, like cooking, needed ideas to follow through, and she couldn't be as sure of the outcome. Talking of cooking, tonight's dinner required attention. She needed to check that Muriel had cleaned the mussels of their beards and hadn't let any open ones slip through before cooking. And, Nell remembered, she hadn't checked that there was enough parsley available. There was an old saying that parsley takes so long to germinate that it goes nine times to the devil before it springs up and Mr Fairweather was in full agreement with that.

'They're saying in the village, Miss Drury, that you're going to find out who really killed Mr Rocke,' Kitty observed trustingly.

'Are they indeed?' Nell replied shortly. 'Are they also saying who it was? And who's going to do my work when I set off in my deerstalker?'

Kitty took the point. 'No, Miss Drury.'

She looked crestfallen and Nell apologized. She shouldn't be adding to the tensions in the kitchen; she should calm them. As it was, Kitty was dreaming of her boyfriend, Michel was casting passionate eyes on Miss Smith, Miss Smith was sitting like a cuckoo in the midst of the servants' nest, Mr Peters seemed to think the end of civilization was near because Miss Smith was consorting with Lord Richard, Mrs Fielding was perpetually up in arms, and the family itself was not in much better shape. Lord Richard was spending too much time trying to please Miss Smith instead of taking care of his estate work, Lady Helen was floating around dreaming of the next London party and Lady Sophy was running around trying to save the Labour party and organize her sister's love life, ignoring the fact that she was far more suited to Mr Beringer than Lady Helen. To crown it all, even Mr Briggs seemed to have taken a fancy to Miss Smith and was pathetically trying to please her with apples acquired from the apple store.

Detective indeed, Nell scolded herself. Physician, heal thyself, she ordered. Just get moving. Her next step was dinner; the one after that was serving coffee in the drawing room.

'It was sex of course. It always boils down to that,' Lynette Reynolds remarked, once the party settled in the drawing room and Nell was inconspicuously (she hoped) superintending the coffee trolley. 'Take Noël Coward's plays. Sex of all sorts,' Mrs Reynolds continued. 'Tobias's death will boil down to that in the end.'

In Nell's experience, boiling down could be a long patient business. Perhaps that's what sex was like too, she thought, then quickly took her mind off that subject. What was past was past, and what was to come— No, she wouldn't think about that either. Not with Alex Melbray close at hand. 'Tobias was a lech,' Mrs Reynolds pronounced. 'That's what happened to Mary Ann. He was disappointed with his own sex life, so he muscled in on other people's.'

'He couldn't have done the night she left us,' Lady Kencroft said patiently. 'Now Gerald has told us what has happened, we know that Mary Ann was leaving with her lover, and that wouldn't have been Tobias.'

'We don't know that, Katie,' Alice Maxwell objected. 'Some wolf was continually and mercilessly harassing her. It could have been Tobias or someone else. One of the troubles we women have. Fortunately, I can stand up for myself.'

Nell saw her point. Miss Maxwell was a sturdy woman and Nell wouldn't want to cross her path.

'I have to tell you,' Lord Ansley intervened, 'that I've been told by Chief Inspector Melbray that Tobias had an impeccable alibi for that night. He can't have murdered her, but as you say, Alice, he could have been the man who was pressing his attentions on her and scaring her so much.'

'That could equally well have been any of the Gaiety backstage staff or any of the cast,' Lady Kencroft pointed out, clearly annoyed.

'I still maintain Tobias was in some way responsible for her death,' Miss Maxwell declared.

'You seem very sure of that, Alice,' Lord Kencroft observed.

'Aren't you?' she retorted.

'No, although I agree the situation suggests it. She told me on several occasions about this menace.'

'Did she name him?' Mrs Jarrett asked.

'I fear not, and perhaps that was because he was one of us,' Lord Kencroft calmly pointed out.

'By us, you must mean anyone at the theatre,' Mr Jarrett said impatiently. 'Constance, as I informed you earlier, I am not at all well. I shall retire to my room.'

Here we go again, Nell thought, as Mrs Jarrett rose to her feet to accompany him. What a guest! Any difficult situation and he does not feel well. How does that nice woman stand him?

'That's Hubert's way of escaping the fire,' Mr Heydock observed, after they had departed.

'Darling, what do you mean by that?' Mrs Reynolds whipped back smartly. 'Can it be you agree that it all comes down to sex?'

Mr Heydock flushed. 'Think about it. Hubert married Constance very quickly after Mary Ann's departure. And didn't you tell me that Constance joined you in Romano's restaurant at some point that evening? She and Hubert had been in a private room upstairs and so he must have left early.'

'Not feeling well, perhaps,' Lynette said languidly.

'I suggest,' Lord Ansley said quietly, 'that we change the subject. It's all too easy to speculate without evidence.'

'Hear, hear,' Miss Maxwell agreed. 'Mary Ann loved the Gaiety and loved *all* of us. Let us remember that.'

Mr Heydock would not be deterred. 'Whoever he was, I still believe that the man who was persecuting her was behind her disappearance, and probably her death too, then or later.'

'We may never know,' Lady Kencroft said firmly. 'But Alice is right in saying that Mary Ann loved us. If she had escaped safely away from the Gaiety and its problems she would have sent some sign that all was well. We heard nothing. Let her rest in peace.'

ELEVEN

Tobias's home was in Radpath Gardens, which was only a short walk from Earl's Court station in west London. For that Nell was extremely grateful, as travelling with Ethel Palmer had been difficult, naturally enough, she supposed. Once the legal formalities had been ironed out, Ethel would have the task of disposing of his possessions. Would Ethel resent or welcome her presence while she was sizing up her inheritance? You'll be treading on eggshells, she warned herself.

The tall, white-painted terraced buildings looked attractive even in the harsh grip of winter and suggested that Tobias Rocke had had a comfortable life but not an ostentatious one. She could hazard a guess as to why he had decided to live here. These houses were in the hinterland of society, well positioned without being at the centre of the glittering world of theatreland or part of fashionable Chelsea. Here he could have watched without drawing attention to himself.

A ring at the bell in the stately porch brought the housekeeper to the door. Dickens would have approved of her, Nell thought. Beaming and substantially built, she looked the picture of welcome and reliability. Her husband, even more powerfully built, loomed behind her.

'You'll be Mr Rocke's widow,' the housekeeper addressed Ethel. 'You come in, dearie. I'm Mrs Jolly. Jolly by name and jolly by nature, that's what Cyril always says.'

Behind her, Cyril murmured agreement.

'I've a cup of tea waiting,' she reassured them. 'We'd have been at the funeral if it hadn't been for my rheumatics.'

The beaming continued while Nell was introduced, but she noticed it became somewhat forced, when it was mentioned she was here at the police's request.

'Thought they'd finished,' Cyril grunted, as Mrs Jolly led the way into an austere and obviously little used room off the hallway, where teacups were laid out on a table. The fact that she then had to disappear to the basement to bring up a large teapot herself underlined the decrease in servant numbers since these houses were built well before the war.

'We've been wondering,' Mrs Jolly said firmly, once settled, 'what you'll be planning to do with the house, Mrs Rocke. Once everything is settled, that is.'

For a moment, Nell thought Ethel was going to snap back, 'That's my business,' but to her credit she was diplomatic. 'I'll have to think about that, Mrs Jolly. If I sell it of course I'll make it clear you and your husband go with the house.'

Mrs Jolly's beam stopped being forced. Relief was evident on both their faces.

'You're from the police then,' Cyril grunted, still regarding Nell with great suspicion.

'Here at their request,' she amended.

'That Inspector Melbray wanted to know a sight too much if you ask me,' he muttered. 'Wanted to know who Mr Rocke's guests were, rummaged through all his belongings. Nose into everything. Nothing to be touched or removed, but for what? Nothing, because they've got the bloke who did it banged up, begging your pardon, missis.'

Ethel stiffened at such lack of tact. 'That'll be all, Mr Jolly, Mrs Jolly. We'll begin looking round now.'

'We'd best show you.' Mrs Jolly immediately rose to her feet.

For all the housekeeper's beams, Nell suspected some items might already have made their way into the Jollys' quarters. Enough, Nell, she reproved herself. Good sleuths don't make premature judgments. Anyway, whatever Alex Melbray thought she might find, it was hardly likely to be valued in gold and silver.

'We've given everything a nice tidy-up,' Mrs Jolly announced proudly.

So much for the inspector's order that nothing should be touched, Nell thought ruefully. 'Thank you.' She smiled as warmly as she could in the higher interests of the task ahead.

'Much appreciated, I'm sure,' Ethel said less warmly.

'Was Mr Rocke a tidy man in his habits?' Nell asked, looking round at the main room on the ground floor – an uninspiring dining room.

'He was, Miss Drury. Except for his study,' Mrs Jolly added.

'But you won't find anything of interest there,' she assured them. 'The inspector went through it. There's a basket where Mr Rocke kept his lucky tokens – daft, these actors are. Fancy taking a hare's foot to the theatre for good luck. "You ought to try some real work," I felt like telling him.'

Nell was beginning to tire of the Jollys. 'Nevertheless, I'd like to see the study.'

Reluctantly, the couple led them upstairs past a characterless drawing room at the rear of the first floor, and then to the far more interesting-sounding study at the front. 'In there.' Cyril Jolly pointed.

The study was indeed a contrast. Bookshelves with drawers beneath them and stuffed with papers, files and books of all sizes covered three walls of the room. A table with a typewriter stood by the window, and a large basket spilling over with what looked like cuddly toys was wedged between the table and the nearest bookshelves-cum-drawers.

'Just look at that pile of old rubbish,' Mrs Jolly sniffed.

Nell didn't see rubbish at all. She saw a pile of something interesting. For a middle-aged man a basketful of toys – and now, looking closer, she could see other knick-knacks – was an unusual choice. Is that the sort of thing Alex Melbray wanted her to consider? For instance, she recognized a Steiff teddy bear that was only designed a year or two ago so this couldn't be a collection of Tobias Rocke's childhood memorabilia.

'I remember that rabbit,' Ethel said suddenly, peering over Nell's shoulder. 'Picked it up at some theatre when we first came to London. To think he still had it. Silly old chump. And that's the vase from *The Flower Shop Girl.* I remember it because Miss Darling was so fond of it and, bless me, if that isn't Mr Heydock's toy lion. Called him Henry, don't know why. It went everywhere with him.'

Nell studied the collection for some time, wondering what stories might lie behind the items. Perhaps none, but perhaps some that might possibly tie in with something else. The more she learned about Tobias Rocke the greater her chances of finding the link to his murder. But frustratingly Ethel recognized no more of the now abandoned toys.

'I'll begin looking through the files now, Mrs Palmer,' Nell said firmly.

Ethel sniffed. 'Nothing much here that I can see. Only old papers.'

Only! Nell disagreed with that word. Here must surely lie some answers. The study was overlooking the street not the garden, although that might have been quieter. But Tobias Rocke wouldn't have been interested in peaceful places. He wanted to look out over the street where the world was passing by. He seemed to have been the sort of person with a nose into everything, a picker-up of unconsidered trifles. That to him would constitute power over people and their lives.

'If that'll be all, Miss Drury, I can show you the bedrooms,' Mrs Jolly announced edgily.

'Don't let me hinder you,' Nell said sweetly. 'As you can see, I haven't yet finished.'

Ethel was on Mrs Jolly's side. 'I haven't got all day either.'

Time to call a halt to this situation, Nell decided. Ethel was tactfully despatched to make an inventory of the rest of the house and the Jollys sent to accompany her, thus leaving Nell on her own. The Jollys had not been happy about that.

'I'll telephone to Scotland Yard for permission if you wish,' she had told them anxiously. That pleased them even less, and grudgingly they departed, leaving her to explore further. This room was her oyster, and she was going to make full use of it.

'Blithering bloaters, Tobias Rocke,' she muttered to herself, looking round at the giant task ahead. 'What on earth is this all about?' If he was indeed a blackmailer, then there had to be something in this chaotic study to indicate it. He had expected to return here and wouldn't have removed incriminating material before he left for Kent. Thankfully it was clear that the Jollys had no interest in papers and their 'tidying up' had not included this room.

She began with the easier tasks, on the grounds that if she tackled the files and papers first she might overlook the obvious by mistake. Good plan, but unrewarded. She could see nothing of interest on the table or in its drawer that contained only writing materials and spare typewriting ribbons. There was no paper conveniently left in the typewriter, and the only file on the table itself was a household budget book, which revealed merely an interest in fine wines.

Next she tackled the books on the shelves. They seemed just

what might be expected from a theatre lover and performer: *The Stage Year Book* going back to well before the war, John Hollingshead's book on the Gaiety theatre, Macready's diary, books by Sir Herbert Beerbohm Tree, Everyman pocket series play texts, and hundreds more. Nothing there for her, she decided.

The heavy loose-leaf files must surely be a different matter, she hoped, as she withdrew them one at a time. They didn't carry titles, but they all had the same content: page after page of newspaper clippings, with the dates and sources neatly noted above them and with photographs, either postcards or drawn from magazines, interspersed with them. The clippings appeared to be reviews of every play under the sun, from Euripides to Coward, together with articles on actors and actresses from *The Era*, *Play Pictorial* and other magazines dating from the 1880s until modern times.

She studied them for a few minute. Was there a link between the files? If so, it wasn't a record of all the plays in which Tobias Rocke had appeared because there was no mention of him in many of the cuttings she looked at. Then she spotted the name of Lynette Allison, Mrs Reynolds's maiden and stage name, in two clippings on one page and closer study revealed that every clipping in this file was of her. So that's all it was. Each file was centred on one of his friends.

Friends? She had been about to put the file down when it fell open at the last page. A large photograph of a young Lynette took up most of the page – and it had a huge black cross crayoned over the face.

What the devilled duck is this about? Nell shivered. Was this a glimpse of the real Tobias Rocke at last? Alex's men could well have passed over it, thinking it an insignificant detail, but yet it was just the sort of thing that he had asked her to look out for. Take it slowly, she thought as she began to check other files. Be sure of where I'm going with this. Only a few files had photographs similarly defaced at their end, despite the fact that all of them had photographs of differing sizes within the main content. Some of the files had more than one subject, so it was not always easy to pick up the name that had interested Tobias Rocke. And wasn't it odd that she hadn't found a file for Lady Ansley or for Lady Kencroft?

And Mary Ann Darling? Would there be one for her? Feverishly, she hunted through them, passing files with familiar names, including Hubert Jarrett, Alice Maxwell and Neville Heydock. Only one for Constance Wilson, now Mrs Jarrett, carried a black cross so heavy it almost obliterated her face. And then Nell found Mary Ann's. It was packed full of reviews and photographs, but not all of her. There were a few provincial newspaper reviews of an Elsie Hawkins, dating from the 1880s. There was only one photograph with these, a studio picture which was undoubtedly a young Mary Ann Darling but carrying the legend Miss Elsie Hawkins. That must have been her real name. Nell rejoiced. One mission accomplished at least.

Of Mary Ann herself, there were many photographs; she smiled out from every page, but in trepidation Nell turned to the end of the file. There was Mary Ann, a black cross so savagely drawn across her face that it had cut into the stiff card of the photograph. The hatred that had been behind it shouted out at her.

She had to force herself to go on with the search even though she felt like turning tail and running. This whole room now seemed poisoned with hate. What else might she find? There was a key in the lock of two of the drawers beneath the bookshelves, and she made herself open them. The first contained a number of paper bags, each with a date on them. One dated 1893 contained a pair of ladies' silk stockings; the next held a corset cover; the next, dated 1909, pink knickers. That's enough, she decided. Tobias Rocke was one very sick man.

Right, now for the other drawer. To her relief, this seemed merely a collection of loose photographs, which though interesting suggested nothing more. One, marked *Cannes* on the back, was of Alice Maxwell and Tobias himself with Doris Paget in the background, another was of Tobias in the Ivy restaurant with someone she didn't recognize, another showed him with Neville Heydock, marked on the back *Ascot*. All of them featured Tobias. Did they tell her anything other than that he was pathologically addicted to seeing himself in photographs as well as having a salacious interest in women's clothing? Was all this research for potential blackmail? Possibly, she thought, but it wasn't clear how except that the clippings might help if he had wanted to keep tabs on his victims' lives.

I'm flummoxed, she thought crossly. All I've got is a pocketful of dead hopes, or at least dying. There were no diary records, no notebooks, no tell-tale letters, nothing. And yet the black crosses and the locked drawer of clothing had to mean something. And so might the basket of cuddly toys that stood by his desk. Why should he have Mr Heydock's toy lion and Mary Ann's vase?

What must have gripped Tobias Rocke was knowledge of other people's lives that could be dangerous if aired abroad in public. Did he threaten them with exposure, or just give winks and nods and revel in the knowledge, or did he make demands? There must be, for instance, many men like Arthur Fontenoy who preferred men to women in their private lives, but in public this could not be mentioned, not least because it was illegal.

She was about to push the drawer in when one last photograph caught her eye. It appeared to be just a garden with bushes and someone standing at a front door. Even though the photograph had been taken from a distance away, she still managed to identify Mary Ann. It was a sepia photograph, perhaps taken around the time she vanished, judging by her dress. Nell studied it more closely, simply because it was so unlike the other photographs in the drawer, each of which had been taken at some luxurious location. The bushes were dark, but it looked as though they were obscuring someone standing there, hiding. Someone Mary Ann could not have seen from where she was. There was something familiar about that figure – the way he was standing and she'd seen it in the files she'd just been looking at.

It was Hubert Jarrett.

'This isn't the way I envisaged our first private meeting, Nell.' Alex Melbray pulled out the chair for her to sit down.

'Nor me,' Nell rejoined cheerfully. 'I thought Paris at the very least.'

'Only for lovers or kept women, and I don't have any of either right now. Someday we'll get there, Nell.'

'Yes.' A vision of strolling by the Seine or the Eiffel Tower with him floated through her mind. 'Nevertheless,' she added gravely, 'Lyons teashops are very charming in their way.'

He laughed, and she thought how different Alex looked then to when he was on duty. She supposed that applied to her too.

Nell the chef hauling Michel over the coals for curdling the mayonnaise was not the same woman sitting with Alex Melbray in a teashop in London's Northumberland Avenue.

'You're quite right,' he said. 'I myself have a particular fondness for their chocolate eclairs. Let's order some.'

'Speaking as a chef I can't approve of afternoon snacks,' she replied in her best pompous voice. 'But as I'm not a chef at the moment, I shall have no hesitation in enjoying such exotic fare with you. Oh, Alex,' she said abruptly, 'I have to tell you about today.' She couldn't wait any longer. At last she had a theory about the files and photographs.

'I assumed that was why you wanted to see me.'

She spilled it all out while he listened – attentively she thought, although she could not tell what he was making of it, especially as the teapot and eclairs arrived. She was too intent on her story to pour tea, and eventually Alex reached for the teapot to pour it himself. Disconcerted, she stopped mid-flow.

'I'm listening, go on,' he said.

'I can't—'

'You can. You were ferreting through the cuddly toy basket. Just reached Henry the lion.'

Mollified, but only half convinced she had his full attention, she continued. His eyebrows shot up when she told him about the underclothing and the black crosses through the photographs. And at last she was able to blurt out her theory that the loose photographs in the drawer represented those he was blackmailing and that the files and clippings were tied in with it, probably together with the cuddly toys and locked underwear drawer.

He took over immediately once she'd finished. 'I'm not sure I agree with this theory of yours.'

'Why not?' she demanded, deflated. She'd done her best not to sound obsessed with her own idea.

'If you're right, Tobias would have taken some kind of evidence with him to Wychbourne to wave in front of his victims' faces; he wouldn't have passed up an opportunity like that. In which case I or my men would have seen it when we searched his room at the Court.'

'Perhaps the blackmail victims searched for it and hid it,' she said lamely.

'We're into speculation as well as theories then. Theories require at least some evidence. May I please have my eclair now?'

'Yes,' she said crossly, taking her own – just as she remembered that last photograph she'd found. 'But you can't dismiss my theory altogether.'

'Give me one reason why not.'

'This.' She handed over the photograph of Hubert Jarrett.

He struggled to look at it, while coping with the eclair. 'What's this photo doing here, Nell?

'It slid into my pocket by mistake.'

He heaved a sigh. 'Removal of evidence is frowned upon.'

'Even though the Mary Ann case is closed?'

'I'm temporarily reopening it.' He frowned. 'Joking apart, you must see what this means.'

'Yes, that if Hubert Jarrett was the man harassing Mary Ann, he might have been blackmailed by Tobias Rocke. The great Mr Jarrett wouldn't want his wife to know about his former little weakness, nor would he want to risk his reputation in the theatre.'

'There's more, Nell. If this is Jarrett in the photo, Rocke could indeed have been blackmailing him for persecuting Mary Ann and even more so after Rocke had identified her body.'

'You think he was blackmailed because he *killed* Mary Ann?' Nell thought this through. 'Mr Jarrett left Romano's early that night so he could have managed to get rid of Mary Ann's lover and sit in the second cab himself.'

'If you insist on speculation, Nell, there are all sorts of possibilities, none of them pleasant. This isn't a pretty Gaiety world. Whether Rocke was blackmailing Mary Ann or not, he certainly seems to have had other people in his power and Hubert Jarrett is probably one of them. In the best Sherlock Holmes tradition, I'm a mere Lestrade, but looking at this photograph again, I'm bound to say that I'm halfway convinced. There's still a problem, though. I can't ask my men to squirrel into the Mary Ann Darling case.'

Nell's hopes sank. 'But—'

'But I can look into it myself. Dare I mention though that there is one point you appear to have overlooked or perhaps not thought through sufficiently?'

'What's that?'

'This blackmail theory is fast developing as far as the Gaiety veterans are concerned, but why would Rocke have confined his blackmailing career to them? Even if he carried the threat on when he saw them in various productions, he might well have had other people in his sights. Not only in the past but the present.'

She could answer that one promptly. 'There were lots of other photographs in the drawer and plenty of other files.'

'But there is one person vulnerable to blackmail whose photograph would not be in that drawer. Timothy Trotter.'

'Surely he wouldn't *kill* somebody?'

'You say that dismissively, as once my predecessors spoke of Dr Crippen. Never underestimate the apparent underdog. They too have passions. Mr Trotter, it seems to me, has very strong ones. However, I too don't see him as a murderer. Unlike, perhaps, others of the Wychbourne Court guests.'

'My dear Nell. Just the person I wished to see.'

Much as she liked Arthur, Nell's heart sank; it was just her luck that she ran into him as she parked her motor car on her return from London. She desperately needed to find Mr Fairweather, who would already have gone home for the day.

'Can I call in on my way back? I'm on my way to find out how the potatoes are.' That sounded ridiculous, but it was the truth. She needed to restock even though, thankfully, the guests had long departed, judging by the lack of motor cars here. The Jarretts had disappeared even before she left, leaving before breakfast in their chauffeured Bentley.

'Make it later, Nell. Do come to the cottage after dinner. A gathering is to take place which I'm sure will interest you.'

'What is it?' she asked cautiously.

'Now don't demur. Clarice is bringing a Ouija board with her. Quite harmless, I assure you. It's almost a game nowadays and compared with her usual ghost hunts it *is* a game. She is also bringing Mr Trotter. She has been most upset at the revelations concerning him but is still convinced he is a genuine medium, despite his clearly having helped one or two photographs along. Clarice is determined to help lift this cloud lying over Wychbourne Court and he is equally determined to clear his name.'

Mr Trotter didn't look determined about anything when Nell,

highly dubious as to what would take place, duly arrived at Wychbourne Cottage.

'Thank you for coming, Nell,' Arthur said. 'Incidentally Lady Clarice is convinced that those appalling fake photographs can be explained, as Mr Trotter explained to her that he merely wished to encourage the spirits into coming by such means.'

He conducted her to his drawing room and she could see why she had been invited. Arthur, Lady Clarice and Mr Trotter were the only prospective players and she, Nell, was presumably there to declare to the world that Mr Trotter was a bona fide spirit medium. Why on earth had she agreed to this? Nell wondered, looking round.

The Ouija board was set up on a small polished table near the window, with the planchette with its pointer in the middle and the alphabet printed out around it, together with Yes and No – in order to make it easy for the spirits to reply to questions, Nell deduced, her dismay growing. It might be no more than a popular game at the moment but here at Wychbourne in these circumstances Nell felt dubious about it. True, Lord Richard had bought and used one without dire results (indeed without any results that couldn't be attributed to his sisters' comic touches) but then Lord Richard didn't have Mr Trotter, spirit medium or otherwise, with him at the time.

'What, might I enquire,' Arthur said plaintively, as he turned down the lights to their dimmest point, 'should we be asking the spirits, Mr Trotter? Will they even travel from the Court as far as my humble cottage here? May we ask questions of them?'

'First we concentrate, sir,' Mr Trotter said. 'Kindly do not interrupt me. The more I can summon the spirits of the Court to assemble here the more likely we are to be privileged with their presence to guide us to the truth.'

Nell, sitting meekly at the table, was extremely glad that Alex Melbray was not here, even though she had to admit a certain interest now in what might happen, despite the butterflies in her stomach becoming more active by the minute.

'First try to reach Mr Rocke,' Lady Clarice commanded. 'We can then enquire who murdered him. Place your fingers on the planchette, everyone, pressing them down hard.'

As simple as that? Nell obediently did so. Mr Trotter, with

eyes closed, was clearly in deep meditation, but if he was pleading with Mr Rocke to appear his request was ignored. The pointer stayed where it was.

'Mr Trotter has kindly offered to ask the questions,' Lady Clarice whispered. 'And that of course is only sensible, given his great powers as a medium. Do begin, Mr Trotter.'

For a moment Nell thought he would not oblige, but he did. 'Great spirits of Wychbourne, has Tobias Rocke joined your number?' He sounded most impressive.

Silence, and no movement.

'Tobias Rocke, do you wish to tell us who murdered you?' Mr Trotter enquired.

No movement, no sound.

Nell took her courage in both hands. If this was all faked nonsense, she could do no harm in speaking up. If it wasn't, then she might do some good. Leaving the questioning to Mr Trotter alone might be a mistake. Suppose the spirits didn't like his questions?

Firmly pressing her fingers on the planchette, she asked, 'Did John Palmer kill Tobias Rocke?'

A hiss of disapproval from Mr Trotter, but then all she could hear was the heavy breathing of her companions as she pressed down her fingers. Too hard perhaps, because she felt a quiver from the board. And another – it must be pressure from Arthur or Lady Clarice. But slowly, just as Nell began to feel uneasy, conscious that it was certainly not her causing this movement, the pointer began to move. Slowly, very slowly, it moved on and then stopped, still quivering slightly.

'Who did that?' Arthur demanded, sounding distinctly jittery.

Mr Trotter did not look happy either. 'Who's out there?' he cried. 'What do you want?'

Nell could have sworn he was genuinely nervous – and yet if he were a genuine medium then he must surely be used to it. Even as these thoughts ran through her head, the pointer began to move again. Surely she was imagining it? But she wasn't. Someone must be pushing it, but all of them looked as shaken as she was. And then the pointer stopped.

'That's a D,' cried Lady Clarice. 'Pray try again, Nell. I knew you had an affinity with the spirits.'

But there was no need for Nell to try anything. The pointer was quite happy on its own, moving to the next letter.

'E,' Arthur said, as though he couldn't quite believe it. Nor could Nell. She felt trapped, hypnotized into watching that pointer.

'Onwards, Nell,' shrieked Lady Clarice. 'Look, an A!'

Now the pointer was swinging wildly. Nell could hardly bear to watch, her fingers shaking but pressed down on the board. It was a U – no, she thought in alarm: it was T. She couldn't bear it, she had to turn away.

'H,' Lady Clarice pronounced solemnly. 'Tobias Rocke is here. He wishes to tell us of his death.'

'Or another's,' Arthur murmured quietly.

'I must admit I was shaken, Nell,' Arthur said after the departure of a delighted Lady Clarice and very quiet Mr Trotter.

'So was I,' Nell confessed. 'But what did it tell us, after all? Merely that Tobias Rocke had met his death. It doesn't necessarily portend another one.'

'Some experts believe that movements of the planchette are just our thoughts or unconscious coursing through our nerves to the fingers,' Arthur observed.

'Not comforting,' Nell said. 'Especially if it *does* signal another death.'

'I agree. Mr Trotter looked far too shaken for me to be convinced by that. But I'm sorry I let you in for it. How about a glass of my excellent brandy? Not as good as Romano's, I daresay, but passable.'

She accepted gratefully and relaxed with the warmth of the drink. She was about to leave him when the telephone rang.

'Strange,' Arthur said. 'That's the house telephone and it's nearly eleven o'clock.'

Alarmed, she saw his face change as he listened. 'What is it, Arthur?' she asked, as soon as he hung up the receiver.

'Lord Ansley,' he said soberly. 'He wants us to know there's been another death. Whether murder or accident or suicide is not yet known, nor indeed whether it has anything to do with Wychbourne Court.'

'Who was it?' she asked fearfully.

'Hubert Jarrett.'

TWELVE

Hubert Jarrett *dead*? Nell let herself in to the darkened and silent east wing, still trying to take this in. Usually Wychbourne Court was a comforting womb, but tonight, creeping upstairs with a flickering candle (the generator disliked working through the night), it felt to her as though all Lady Clarice's ghosts were ready to pounce on her at any moment.

'Gibbering jam pots,' she muttered. 'Get a grip on yourself, Nell Drury. This is home not a house of horror.' There were no malevolent ghosts waiting around the corner, nor any Ouija board spirits nipping back from Wychbourne Cottage to have another word with her. Whatever happened to Mr Jarrett, Wychbourne Court wasn't involved, she reasoned. He died in London by a frightening coincidence, that's all. She hadn't liked Mr Jarrett and could easily have seen him as having been Mary Ann's stalker, perhaps even her murderer and therefore one of Tobias Rocke's blackmail victims. Now he himself had died, perhaps murdered, and all her theories were probably wrong.

She tried to put the events of the day aside, but her dreams kept her half sleeping half awake all night, dreams in which Alex Melbray was crazily whipping a bowlful of egg whites, then waving the whisk shouting that meringues were just the thing to trap killers. Goodness knows what Mr Freud would make of that. Why dream of Alex at all? Repressed sexual desires indeed. Nonsense, she told herself firmly. This was Wychbourne, not a romantic picture palace with Rudolph Valentino galloping all over the place. Alex Melbray was certainly *not* going to be a sheikh sweeping her off her feet into his tent.

Wednesday morning breakfast over, Nell awaited her regular summons to the Velvet Room, not least because she was hoping for information about Hubert Jarrett's death. When the call came, however, it was not only earlier than usual but from Lord and not Lady Ansley. Was that ominous? When she reached his study, he was not surprisingly looking very tired.

'My wife,' he told her without preamble, 'is joining Lady Kencroft at her London home to see what they can do for poor Constance. I'm sure you've heard the news by now and as yet I know no more about Hubert's death. There is another development that might affect today's schedules, Miss Drury. My wife will no doubt stay in London, but unexpectedly Chief Inspector Melbray will be returning here to stay at the Coach and Horses. He tells me you met him yesterday after the visit to Tobias's home. How did that go?' He looked at her curiously. 'Your sleuthing powers were at full strength?'

'They don't affect my work here,' she replied anxiously. This was bad news. Much as she would like to see Alex again, his presence here was a sure sign that he was not only investigating a probable case of murder, but that he thought there was some link to Wychbourne Court.

'I can bear witness to that.' He managed a smile. 'Nell – forgive my informality, but these are unusual times – there is a strong possibility from his symptoms that Mr Jarrett was poisoned with arsenic.'

'Like Herbert Armstrong and Mrs Maybrick?' She tried to remember the details of those cases. Wasn't that a poison that took its time to kill although its symptoms could appear almost immediately? Her brain did a double-take, as she recalled Mr Jarrett's querulous complaint that he didn't feel well on Monday evening and that he and his wife had left by motor car early the next morning. Mr Jarrett had declared himself ill on at least a couple of other occasions, though, and therefore his complaints on Monday could mean nothing. But had he cried wolf too often and he was suffering the effects of poison even then? If so . . .

'Yes, indeed,' Lord Ansley replied. 'Arsenic is the poisoner's poison of choice. It's hardly likely to have been self-administered in Hubert's case.'

'He'll never get his knighthood.' Nell felt genuinely saddened, remembering his magnificent rendering of 'To Be or Not to Be' at the Follies.

'No. He is a loss to the stage, as well as to Constance. Nell, you realize this will affect Wychbourne Court?'

Just as she had feared. Nell braced herself.

'Hubert had complained of feeling ill here, as you may remember,' Lord Ansley continued, 'and retired to his room with what he assumed was a bout of gastric fever. It worsened overnight which is why they returned home so early on Tuesday, and Constance then sent for a doctor. As he so often claimed of feeling unwell – although I gather that it seldom affected his stage appearances – she was not unduly alarmed and nor was the doctor at first. Then his suspicions grew as all the symptoms of arsenic poisoning made themselves apparent. As Hubert took no breakfast I fear the spotlight might once again fall on us as he dined here on Monday evening. Thankfully, my wife recalled that he ate very little dinner, as he was already feeling ill. Nevertheless, the finger of suspicion must point to that dinner.'

Her cooking? Nell instantly thought. That was ridiculous. How could arsenic have crept into any of her dishes, without poisoning other people too? Reason asserted itself. 'What about the sandwich tea at the Coach and Horses? And where did he eat luncheon?'

'An early one at his home, which is of course being checked, but I gather the prompt initial reaction time to arsenic makes that less likely than the tea at the pub or, unlikely though it is, dinner here. That means, I'm afraid, that we face another invasion by Scotland Yard. The chief inspector will be arriving shortly with his men, so I must ask you to take a few steps beforehand. Dishes from Monday evening will obviously long since have been washed – though should there be any with leftover food in the larders then they must be retained where they are. Any other food prepared for that night must be kept for examination, and the whole place searched for traces of poison. All ingredients used for Monday night's dinner will need to be checked and none of them used for current cooking.'

Nell was dizzy with shock. '*All* the ingredients?' Sugar, butter, flour . . . Her heart sank.

'The lot. A precaution only, I'm sure. How could any of the communal dishes have been tampered with here? We would all have suffered.'

Nevertheless, *her* food under suspicion? She mentally raced through the menus, then the china used, leftovers, food bins, larders and all the many dishes she had served. 'I'll take care of it,' she promised. 'What about the food bin for the animals?'

'I'll speak to Ramsay about that and everything else for which he's responsible.'

Mr Ramsay was in charge not only of the motor cars and garages but also the outhouses and the yards with their dustbins and waste bins.

'Obviously the main thing the police must establish,' Lord Ansley continued, 'if you'll forgive me, Nell, is whether the food could have been tampered with in our kitchens or at the table. If not, then we are ruled out and the Coach and Horses would seem to be the source.'

'It has to be.' Nell fervently hoped so. 'It *couldn't* have been here.'

'The other angle is whether the arsenic could have been obtained from our flypapers or rat poison.'

'But no one in our servants' hall would want to kill him,' Nell pointed out in anguish.

'I agree, but in theory it would be relatively easy for anyone here to gain access to such sources, unlikely though that is. I'm told it takes time to extract poison from flypapers, and not everyone would know where to find rat poison on the premises – if indeed we have any. It would certainly seem to rule out our guests, although again in theory they could surreptitiously have stirred poison into Hubert's food at the table. Highly unlikely, though. Nevertheless, plain arsenic is a white powder, so, once again in theory, it might blend into some of your dishes, Nell.'

'Or easily be popped into a sandwich at the Coach and Horses,' Nell added, remembering too late that some of her staff had been involved in the sandwich preparation. It was too late to haul her words back now, and in any case, she thought dismally, they were true.

'To me,' Lord Ansley said firmly, 'the Coach and Horses has to be the likely source. Let us hope the chief inspector agrees.'

Nell returned to the kitchens, trying to wrestle with the new situation. There was no time to lose. She had to organize her staff before a pack of invading police descended on the kitchen and scullery. Every cupboard, every larder, all the jars and storage pots had to be identified for the police, as had every scrap of waste or leftover food.

Full of concern, Mrs Squires assured her that she could see no way the sandwiches that she had helped make with her team at the Coach and Horse could have been tampered with. True, she added to Nell's alarm, a lot of the ingredients had come from Wychbourne Court. Still, Nell reasoned, none of them could have been poisoned in advance since the poison had reached one person only.

'Mrs Hardcastle was in charge,' Mrs Squires explained anxiously. 'We took some cakes from here but we made up the sandwiches down at the pub. We piled them on those large plates on the side tables and filled the small ones with them for taking round to people as they were chatting.'

That's how she remembered it. Nell recalled the occasional voice rising about the general hum of conversation and calling out 'eggs and anchovy' (one of Monsieur Escoffier's favourites) or 'cod's roe on toast', sounding like the old London street cries she had loved. She relaxed. What a relief. There had been plenty of opportunities for the poison to have been added then. Risky, but possible. Her hopes began to rise. *Her* food indeed.

'There wasn't no plan about it,' Mrs Squires continued anxiously. 'Some of the people from the funeral were just taking platefuls to offer round themselves.'

Servants' hall lunch was a hasty one. The impending visit of the police was producing a numbed silence in some and ill-concealed excitement in others. When the pack of invading policemen Lord Ansley had warned her about arrived, however, only Chief Inspector Melbray eventually came to the kitchens to find her. He was at his most professional and a long way from the Alex with whom she had shared eclairs the previous day.

'I gather, Miss Drury, that the servants here have been told not to touch any food served on Monday or anything relating to it,' he said to her formally. He stumbled over the 'Miss Drury' so perhaps he was finding this difficult too.

'They have,' she said proudly. 'Dustbins, food waste, leftovers and ingredients are all ready for your inspection.'

'Thank you. My men will be along shortly.'

'The sandwiches,' she told him, adjusting to his formality, 'are surely the most likely source and they were made at the Coach and Horses, albeit with some of our ingredients.' She confidently went on to tell him about the sandwich service and the smaller plates, but his only comment was: 'How about the icing on the cakes? I'm told your kitchens produced several cakes for the day.'

Nell inwardly groaned. Mrs Fielding wasn't going to like suspicion falling on them.

'Why would the housekeeper or her staff want to poison one of the guests?' she asked, trying her best to sound impartial.

'I don't know – yet. But as some of your staff were present at the Coach and Horses to help out, we have to consider it. Hubert Jarrett dined here that evening. That is also a factor.'

'And Mr Trotter was staying there,' she whipped back. Then she felt guilty for picking on him by name.

Impasse. Steely eyes met hers. 'We've already searched the outside larders and are about to do the same here. A tin of rat poison might be missing from one of the outhouses, although no one seems sure of that.'

He was surely implying that the Wychbourne Court staff were lax, to say the least. 'The servants have checked in here,' Nell told him firmly.

The steely eyes informed her that country house servants were not to be compared with the efficiency of Scotland Yard, and especially not female ones.

'I recall,' he said, 'that at that funeral gathering plates were being handed round frequently by people weaving their way through the crowd. It's unlikely therefore that anybody would remember what Hubert Jarrett took or who presented it to him. His wife does tell us, however, that he had a fondness for seafood.'

'There were creamed shrimp sandwiches,' Nell said quickly, 'and egg and anchovy ones.'

'They might be the answer. The post-mortem report will confirm whether arsenic was present or not.' A pause and what might have been a smile. 'As regards the icing of the cake, I'm inclined to dismiss that.'

Relief. 'Why?' she asked cautiously.

'It would have required prior planning to get poison into the icing, which doesn't sit easily with the haphazard method of handing round plates of sandwiches and hoping the target picks the right one.'

He seemed to relax because he added quietly, 'Your theory about Jarrett might still hold, Nell. But in that case why was he killed?'

'Perhaps he knew who killed Tobias Rocke,' she said impulsively. Too impulsively because she rushed on to say, 'Lady Clarice held a Ouija board session at Arthur Fontenoy's home last night.'

He looked at her in disbelief. 'You went?'

'Why not?' she asked defensively. 'I thought I might learn something.'

'And did you?'

'Yes, that there might be another death. And there has been.'

He made an instinctive move towards her, but checked himself, and said gently, 'You're letting this case overwhelm you, Nell. Don't.'

'I've spoken to my wife over the telephone, Miss Drury.' Lord Ansley stopped her as they passed in the Great Hall. 'She plans to return on Friday – and possibly with Mrs Jarrett.'

'Doesn't Mrs Jarrett need to be at home?' Nell was amazed, given everything she must be coping with.

'She's naturally distraught, but journalists have seized hold of the story, scenting that there might be even more to it than the sudden death of a great actor. To have Lord Northcliffe's troupe constantly on the doorstep and telephoning is not what Constance needs at present. She asked to come here, perhaps thinking it might help. So far, the newspapers haven't made the connection between Tobias's death and Hubert's and indeed there may be none to make. But if there is, it could be that he did indeed take his own life. I fear I did not find Hubert an easy guest, but we must support his wife as best we can.'

He looked hopefully at Nell. 'Suicide is just possible, if Hubert thought that the police had discovered he was responsible for the death of . . . He paused. 'I almost said Mary Ann Darling, for I fear her shadow lies over us still, but I meant to say Tobias's death.'

'Because he was being blackmailed by Mr Rocke?'

'That seems the most likely explanation, but everything looks possible at the moment. We seem to be floundering, Nell.'

She agreed. 'When will the inquest be?'

'Very shortly, I gather. It will be in London of course, once the post-mortem is done. But Wychbourne isn't going to escape the eagle eye of the law. The outhouses are under inspection now, in case the rat poison came from us. Many people have access to that particular outhouse, though.'

'Not many of them had reason to kill Mr Jarrett, though.' Nell could have kicked herself for speaking frankly. Now was not the time.

Lord Ansley blenched. 'That's something we have to face.'

Returning to the east wing seemed a daunting task. It seemed to Nell that a malaise had fallen over the servants' hall and main house alike and the police search, although concluded, had only worsened it. Perhaps it had begun with John Palmer's arrest, or was it stemming from herself? Had she picked it up from Lord and Lady Ansley? Their home had been overshadowed with doubt and darkness, despite John Palmer's arrest, and Mr Jarrett's death with all its question marks had been the final straw. For once, despite the good meals she produced, they had not brought a solution. Salt marsh mutton and tansies can only go so far in remedying malaise.

Her mind was a blank about how to put the pep back into Wychbourne Court. The Follies seemed to have resulted not in happy unity at the Court, but in the opposite and she was at her wits' end as to how to turn the tide. Only the solving of Tobias Rocke's murder, and now perhaps Hubert Jarrett's, might do that and Nell felt little further forward in her attempts to bring that about, despite her delving into Tobias Rocke's past.

She was greeted by a mutinous silence as she entered the kitchen. There they all were, Kitty and Michel among them, standing in a group doing nothing by the door into the scullery. Even Mrs Fielding was there, and for a change Miss Smith too. The police search had finished but there were no signs of preparations for dinner, or even tea come to that. Nell hazarded a guess that they had been questioned by the police none too politely and taken exception to it. Now they were glaring at her as though it were her fault.

For once words deserted her. This situation needed more than just a jollying along. Then help came from an unexpected source. Mr Briggs rose to his feet. He'd been sitting by himself on a chair by the window and as so often staring into space. In all the time she had been at Wychbourne Court he had spoken very little other than the now familiar 'G/26420, Corporal Briggs, *sir.*'

But today he began to sing, first a croon and then louder and louder. 'The bells of hell go ting-a-ling-a-ling,' he bawled out time after time.

Taken aback at first, Nell suddenly caught his message and joined in, singing lustily:

'*The bells of hell go ting-a-ling-a-ling*
'*For you but not for me.*'

Mrs Fielding was the next to join in, then Michel, then Muriel, Kitty, the kitchen maids, the scullery maids and Jimmy, the lampboy. Mr Briggs then struck up with another ditty:

'*When this blasted war is over*
'*O how happy I shall be.*
'*When I get my civvy clothes on,*
'*No more soldiering for me.*'

'G/26420, Corporal Briggs, *sir.*' And with that, Mr Briggs sat down.

If soldiers on their way to the trenches had sung that (or their own versions thereof) then so could Wychbourne Court, Nell vowed, as the rest of the staff continued singing or humming as they returned to their stations. Order re-established itself remarkably quickly, and the prospects for fillets of sole, mutton and tansies finding their way to the Ansley table rapidly improved.

The Ansleys could do with a dose of Mr Briggs's medicine, Nell thought as she made a flying visit to the serving room. It seemed gloomy in the dining room without Lady Ansley there, and without the dowager, even if that did mean Arthur could join them. Even so Lord Ansley did not wish to change the custom of years and indicated Helen should take her mother's place at the far end of the table.

Lady Helen refused. 'Too foolish, Pa,' she said languidly. 'I really can't shout at you all from this distance. Too utterly boring.'

That would bring even more gloom, Nell realized, as she hurried back to the kitchen. Lord Ansley had looked highly displeased. What next? she wondered in desperation. Should she organize a cancan? She had a fleeting image of Mrs Squires and Mrs Fielding throwing up their frilly skirts and flashing their legs for the entertainment of the family. Be serious, she told herself. A magic lantern show? Lord Richard had been good with that until the unfortunate occasion when he decided to go in for phantasmagoria and had persuaded his Aunt Clarice that the Wychbourne ghosts had been captured on moving magic lantern slides. It had ended in disaster when, thanks to Lord Richard, the second marquess appeared to be embracing the fourth marquess's murdered wife. Lady Clarice had taken strong objection to it, and Lord Richard had been forbidden to present any repetition.

Tonight, Nell found to her relief when later she returned to serve coffee in the drawing room, Lord Richard had a far more sensible idea. 'We've eaten, we've drunk, so let's now dance and be merry.' He strolled over to the gramophone and within moments 'Tea for Two' was playing at high volume. Lady Helen leapt up, so did Lady Sophy, even Lady Clarice and Arthur Fontenoy rose to their feet. Lord Ansley did not.

'This is not the time, Richard,' he said quietly.

'Wrong. It's just the time, Father. There's Miss Drury watching us, feet itching to have a go, I'm sure. Come along, Nell.'

She needed no urging, coming to join them as they all now danced madly, captured by Lord Richard's enthusiasm. Even, reluctantly, Lord Ansley took part as 'Tea for Two' blared out on the gramophone. Nell was only just aware of the main front door bell ringing far away. A few minutes later the drawing room door opened and Mr Peters stood there.

'Chief Inspector Melbray, your lordship.'

The dancing came to an abrupt halt, as Nell saw Alex gazing round in astonishment. Then he pulled himself together. 'I came to warn you, Lord Ansley, that the London journalists are gathering at the Coach and Horses.'

'I'm grateful for your telling us, Chief Inspector,' Lord Ansley replied grandly. 'We are, as you see, doing our best to fight off the blues. From what you tell us, battle will recommence tomorrow. Tonight is our own, however, and you are very welcome to join us.'

For a moment Nell thought he was going refuse, but then Alex Melbray smiled.

'Thank you, Lord Ansley. Shall we dance, Nell?'

Wychbourne Court was, however briefly, itself again.

THIRTEEN

Resolutions are easy to make but carrying them out is tricky. Nell knew that only too well. Yesterday evening she had rejoiced that Wychbourne Court was proving itself strong enough to withstand the nightmare it was suffering, but on Thursday morning that confidence was fast evaporating. Lady Clarice's ghosts had an easy time of it. They might have their personal tragedies to lament, but they didn't have to *do* anything, whereas it was crystal clear that she must. But what? The police had searched the house for evidence, and there was nothing she could do about Mr Jarrett's death. The second murder this month to haunt Wychbourne.

The first journalists had duly arrived at the Court's front entrance and been courteously but efficiently repelled by Mr Peters.

'I told them his lordship cannot be disturbed until later this morning,' he told Nell. '"Oh," says one of them, "we've already spoken to Chief Inspector Melbray, who's told us all about it." "Then you won't need to bother his lordship," says I and smartly closed the door.'

Nell doubted very much whether Alex had told them anything at all, but almost immediately he himself appeared in the kitchen to find her.

'A word, if you please, Miss Drury,' he asked, looking around him with interest at the overalled and aproned staff scuttling round the kitchen and scullery beyond.

Nell took this to mean a word in private and escorted him to the Cooking Pot. This didn't go unnoticed by Mrs Fielding, who just happened to be emerging from her nearby still room.

'I'll keep an eye on Kitty for you,' she said gloatingly, heavy with the implication that Nell was once again sneaking off and leaving all the work to her. She was clearly delighted with the opportunity to score.

Nell schooled herself to smile in gratitude. 'Thank you, Mrs Fielding.'

Alex looked amused. 'My apologies, Nell.'

'Nothing new. If it wasn't this, she'd take the next chance that came along.'

'The Yard has its Mrs Fieldings too.'

'I'll suggest ours takes a job there then.'

'Too kind. Nell, you'll be relieved to know we've finished our search here, though less relieved that we are now treating this as a murder case. A large dose of arsenic was indeed found in the post-mortem. All our search came up with here, however, is that there's a tin of rat poison possibly missing from one of the outhouses.'

'They're usually locked, but I did find Jethro James in the game larder late one night. Either the door was left unlocked, or he managed to get in anyway.'

'Part of his so-called job he professed at the inquest, if I remember correctly. The possibly missing rat poison though would have been taken from the barn with the farm equipment and stores in it. The only keys to it are kept by Mr Ramsay and Mr Peters, as I'm sure you know, but they have admitted that they are sometimes left unlocked for periods of time.'

Nell's heart sank. This was not going to be plain sailing for Wychbourne Court then. 'Oh,' was all she could find to say.

'That's not a sleuth-like comment,' Alex replied lightly.

'Most amusing.' She was determined not to be riled. 'How's this then? The poison could *possibly* have come from Wychbourne Court, but it's easy enough to buy arsenic in some form or other.'

'Not so easy. These aren't the days of yore for the would-be poisoner. Under the Arsenic Act you can't simply put on a false moustache, pull your hat over your eyes and rush into any old supplier to buy it over the counter. Registers have to be signed and the seller has to know the buyer. Flypapers aren't so handy either. The law was tightened after the Frederick Seddon case.'

'There must be thousands of tins of rat poison and flypapers already in people's houses, just as there are here,' she pointed out.

'That's true, Nell, but think it through. One doesn't get invited to a country house and go ferreting around in the hope of finding a half-used tin of poison; nor does one climb up to grab a flypaper in one's host's drawing room; and nor does one attend a funeral service clasping tins of rat poison in the hope of finding some way of murdering someone.'

'If Mr Jarrett's murder was planned in advance, one of the funeral congregation could have come prepared with the arsenic,' she contributed. 'It wouldn't take up much space in a pocket or handbag.'

'That, I concede, is possible.'

Well done, Nell, she thought savagely. She realized she'd neatly trapped the shadow over Wychbourne Court instead of lifting it. 'What you say could apply to anyone at the funeral gathering,' she made haste to add. 'Except John Palmer, of course.'

'Agreed. Nell, I managed a brief visit to Rocke's home yesterday to look at those files and drawers you mentioned. One very strange man, to say the least.'

'Tell me what I missed.'

'What both of us might have missed. Like you, I'm sure there's something there, but what? Signs of an inflated sense of self together with an unhealthy interest in other people, chiefly those on the stage. I did notice one thing: the reviews and photographs in the files mostly cover the whole of each subject's career. The dates written on the photographs in the drawer are of the day they were taken, but almost every one of them coincides with the point in their file at which there's a neat line drawn across the page. Couple with it the as yet unexplained black crosses, and we have some important unanswered questions. There are crosses on only a few of the file subjects, Lynette Allison, now Mrs Reynolds, is among them and of course Mary Ann Darling. My sergeant thinks they were Rocke's random choice of victims, perhaps those who didn't pay up or pay enough.'

'Why would black crosses and lines be random?'

'He frowned. 'Unlikely, I agree. Tobias Rocke doesn't seem to me a man who did anything at random. See what you think. I broke my own rules and brought some of the photographs in the drawer and several of the files.' He hauled out the contents of his holdall and spread them out on her table.

'Look at Hubert Jarrett's file,' he said. 'There's a huge number of clippings from 1893 onwards and several photographs. None with crosses, though. A line is drawn under the clipping from June 1893, the month Mary Ann Darling disappeared, and there were photographs of him in the drawer: one of him – we think – in the bushes possibly at her home, and two others. The Alice Maxwell clippings date from 1896, the line is drawn under 1909, and again no black crosses. But the Cannes photo of her with Tobias and Doris Paget is taken the same year. The file on Constance Jarrett presents the same puzzle. And here's Mary Ann Darling herself.' He opened the file. 'Clippings from 1891 with a few interesting early ones, as you noted. I agree that Elsie Hawkins must have been her birth name. Line drawn under 1893. No photograph of her with Tobias, but a black cross scarring her photograph at the end of the file. Do you make anything more of it, Nell?'

'Only a custard definitely curdled,' she admitted. It should have been a smooth mystery to solve, but it wasn't coming together.

'May I leave this with you then? I have to return to London.'

'Certainly, Chief Inspector Melbray,' she replied in her best sleuthing voice, hoping she sounded more confident than she was.

'I'm obliged to you, Miss Drury.' He bowed to her gravely.

Alex Melbray wasn't the only caller that morning. Arthur Fontenoy also popped in unannounced, as she was about to begin the chrysanthemum salad. It was another of Mrs Leyel's exciting recipes and Nell had begged a few of the flowers from Mr Fairweather. He had been depending on them for providing flowers for the house, a difficult task in January, but he'd graciously parted with just a few of the precious blooms.

'I'm told Lady Ansley and Mrs Jarrett aren't arriving until tomorrow, Nell. After luncheon, I gather,' Arthur said. 'However, I thought I should mention, in the interests of your detective work, that Mr Trotter is very anxious to make his departure before she arrives just in case Mrs Reynolds chooses to reappear with them. I understand that she and Mr Trotter are not on good terms. I'm also aware that because of his faking spirit photographs he has a motive for Tobias's murder and possibly therefore for Mr Jarrett's. Furthermore, since his so-called photographic embellishments have come to our attention, he is clearly anxious to leave Wychbourne behind him. It occurs to me therefore that I could offer to take him by motor car to Sevenoaks station after luncheon, and so—'

'It might be essential for me to have an errand or two there. How wise you are, Arthur.' True, she had been intending to grapple with Tobias's files and photographs, but she couldn't miss this offer.

'What an excellent opportunity to hold Mr Trotter captive for the motor journey,' she declared, when she duly appeared outside Wychbourne Cottage after luncheon in her role of eager shopper. She insisted diplomatically on taking the rear bucket seat of the Armstrong-Siddeley, yielding the front one to Mr Trotter. That way he would effectively be 'trapped', rather than let him sit isolated in the rear. He was clearly nervous, and she deliberately remained silent while Arthur was cranking the engine. As he climbed back into the motor car, Mr Trotter was forced to speak.

'So unfortunate, this business of Mr Jarrett's death,' he said miserably.

'It is indeed,' Nell piped up from behind him. 'And worrying too, as we were all in the Coach and Horses when the poison might well have been administered.'

'As were many other people,' Mr Trotter replied immediately.

'If only there hadn't been all this misunderstanding over your photographs,' Arthur said helpfully, gently manoeuvring the Armstrong-Siddeley around a hedgehog plodding across the driveway. 'The police have necessarily had to look at everyone who had reason to dislike Tobias Rocke and by extension Hubert Jarrett – after all, he might have known who killed Tobias.'

Mr Trotter clutched the lifebelt he'd been thrown. 'A misunderstanding, yes indeed. They were merely touches to embellish the photographs in order to reassure the spirits I summoned from the spirit world.'

'Mr Rocke,' Nell observed, 'might have gained a totally different impression when he visited your darkroom on the Saturday morning.'

Mr Trotter totally agreed. 'He must have seen the extra glass plates and old photographs I brought with me to persuade their spirits to join us; also a flash-lamp, and one or two small wigs for the same purpose. There is nothing fraudulent about that.'

'Yet they might have created a false impression,' Arthur murmured regretfully.

'Only to the untrained eye,' Mr Trotter said indignantly. 'Mr

Rocke spoke most rudely to me. Even though my darkroom was in proper professional order, he threatened to publicize his findings to the Society for Psychical Research and put a most unfortunate interpretation on them. It might have ruined me.'

'And no doubt Mr Rocke took full advantage of that,' Nell said sympathetically.

A silence, then: 'Yes,' Mr Trotter mumbled. 'He wanted me to introduce him to Sir Arthur Conan Doyle and made other impossible demands.'

'Much better,' Arthur commented gravely, 'to have the truth on the table. Or rather on the Ouija board. Did that have embellishments too?'

'Pray don't discuss that with Lady Clarice,' Mr Trotter gasped. 'I did so much want to please and the Ouija board often doesn't work without encouragement, so I . . .'

'Gave it a little help?' Nell suggested when he stumbled to a halt.

'I tried to, without success,' he agreed unhappily. Then he rallied. 'But it moved of its own accord at the end. It really did. I was most alarmed. Such a triumph, though! If you recall, it correctly foretold Death.'

'So there we are, Nell,' Arthur remarked, when a still gibbering Mr Trotter had been safely deposited at Sevenoaks railway station. 'Do you really wish to pursue your errands? If not, I hope luncheon at the White Hart might be acceptable to you. We do seem to need sustenance, with all these unseen spirits gathering around us.'

The Wychbourne Court library was Nell's first port of call once the dinner preparations were finished. She knew there was a row of bound editions of *The Stage Year Book* published from 1908 onwards, which would provide a rich harvest of information on prominent actors, character actors, leading ladies and the plays they performed in. Primed with knowledge and a book or two on the earlier period temporarily borrowed, she returned to the Cooking Pot and prepared to buckle down to her task.

She began with Hubert Jarrett, as Alex had done, and studied the two other photographs Alex had found of him with Tobias Rocke. The first had been taken outside the Garrick Club in 1900, which, checking the clippings file, was the year in which he had come to fame for his Richard II, and a line had been drawn under the relevant review. The other photograph was more recent. It was taken in 1920, the year he had won universal praise for his Othello. This time the two men were standing beside a saucy-looking portrait of Etty's *The Bath*. Chosen by Tobias Rocke, perhaps, given his private interests, Nell thought.

Neville Heydock, subject of the next photograph she looked at, had been the leading actor in a play by Jerome K. Jerome in 1902, but the line was not drawn under his reviews until 1908. No black cross. Lynette Reynolds, then Lynette Allison, had clippings from 1896, but interestingly Nell could not find a dividing line drawn in. But there was a black cross. The same was true of Constance Wilson, as Mrs Jarrett then was. Otherwise, as far as Nell could see, the clippings files and photographs followed the link that Alex Melbray had noticed, the date of the photograph tallying with the drawn lines in the files.

So what could she conclude from this?

Nothing.

Nonsense, she told herself briskly. You've got the ingredients, so now make the dish. All you don't yet know is the order those dratted ingredients should go in. She'd have to make guesses and see which worked.

First, the murders: two killers or one? Probably one, which meant that Tobias Rocke must be the key. Why these photographs? Why the lines underneath the files' entries? Why the black crosses? Why the Garrick Club, why Cannes? and so on. Did the locations have any significance? For instance, the Garrick was famed as being the club of choice for leading male actors. It was a most exclusive club, so had Hubert put Tobias up for membership because he was being blackmailed by him? That was possible. Personally, she would have blackballed him.

Why would Hubert Jarrett have been a blackmail victim though? Easy one that. He had probably been the man who harassed Mary Ann and perhaps her murderer. What about Alice Maxwell? The review nearest to the line drawn in the file was for her role in *Medea* in 1909, and the photograph taken in Cannes with Tobias was the same year. Was he on holiday with them there, or was it by chance that they met? No black cross either for Hubert or Alice Maxwell. Nell considered Lynette Reynolds again. No line drawn in her file but a very definite black cross positioned in the 1890s' reviews. There was a photograph though, marked Diamond Jubilee 1897 and featuring both her and her then husband Neville Heydock with Tobias at an unnamed grand reception. Lynette did not appear happy in it.

For Constance Jarrett, the reviews were sparse, and no line had been drawn in the file. But there was a very heavy black cross on the photograph.

Black crosses. People who had stood up to Tobias Rocke and his attempts at blackmail? She checked again: Lynette Reynolds, Mary Ann, Constance Jarrett. So far there were no black crosses for men, only women. Not every woman, though. Where did that take her?

Could it be her saucepan was beginning to bubble at last? It could be coincidence, but suppose the black crosses were allotted to women who had rejected him sexually? And did the lack of files on Lady Ansley and Lady Kencroft imply that he had decided not to approach either of them because of their powerful admirers? Nell decided she could give a cautious *yes* to this and to her solution of the crosses. Tobias Rocke had let his injured pride fester.

The lines drawn in the files still puzzled her, though. It was possible that they had to do with the people he was blackmailing, which would explain why the files on some people – again Lady Ansley and Lady Kencroft – did not have them. Could the lines therefore indicate the date Tobias Rocke began the subtle blackmail? Above the line was the general information he had gathered on potential victims before he made his bid for power. Why though would those drawn-line dates tie in with the photographs of himself with the file subjects? She could award herself another shaky *yes* for the drawn lines theory, so now she needed to pin down the significance of the photographs.

Start at the beginning, she told herself. What would Tobias Rocke have asked for in return if not money? Were nods and winks enough for him, just to remind his victims that he was in control, that he knew their secrets? Did he demand – ever so gently – that the victim handed over their prize mascots and in the case of the women – she shivered – their intimate clothing?

Surely even the knowledge that he knew their innermost secrets wouldn't be sufficient to make his victim tremble over a long period? That could be where the 'keepsakes' came in, for him to gloat over and his victims to silently rage. Could he also have made it clear to the victim that it was time he had another little reward? He'd demanded from Mr Trotter a social introduction, to Sir Arthur Conan Doyle, so perhaps he did from his other victims. A membership for the Garrick, for instance, or a holiday in Cannes, an entrée to the Diamond Jubilee celebrations, and so on. A photograph at least would be taken at each such event. It could be shown to others and duly noted in society. He would climb the ladder of social importance and cease merely to be a tolerable character actor and instead become a principal in the world he coveted – if not on stage then offstage. Nell sat back, well pleased with this theory – no, surely it was good enough to be termed a *deduction* that she could share with Chief Inspector Melbray.

The opportunity to do just that came quickly – it would be the very next day. Apologizing for the short notice, Lord Ansley asked her to accompany him to London to attend the inquest. 'As my wife is returning to Wychbourne tomorrow, I should welcome your company. It might also assist you in your work for Chief Inspector Melbray,' he added with a straight face.

Opportunity, yes, although Nell wasn't too sure that sitting through the inquest would be the privilege it sounded. It was all too soon after the previous one. Nonetheless, she accepted graciously, with the other half of her mind rapidly concocting Friday's list and estimates for the weekend for Mr Fairweather. He liked matters orderly, did Mr Fairweather. Vegetables, fruit and flowers had to be ordered in advance, based on his weekly report of what should be available – Subject to Weather. Nell always allotted capital letters to this in her mind, given Mr Fairweather's often dire warnings in this respect.

The inquest was being held at the Coroner's Court of West London in Fulham, and immediately they arrived in the hall (driven there in Lord Ansley's beloved Rolls-Royce, another treat) Nell spotted Chief Inspector Melbray on duty and sitting in the witness seats by the coroner. She steeled herself for the morning ahead, rightly as it turned out, as the medical details seemed to go on for ever. She was much relieved when the jury took only a brief time to give a verdict of unlawful killing. Even so she had a long wait before she could corner Alex Melbray, who was busy talking to *everyone* save her, or so it seemed.

At last he was free, though looking very weary. Anxious to convey her theory, she then blotted her copybook by rushing in where she should have feared to tread. Half of her was conscious that this wasn't the time to do so, but the other half wanted to seize the opportunity to speak to him right away.

He listened carefully – and patiently, she admitted – but then he said, 'That's good work, Miss Drury, but I'm not convinced. Why would any of them suddenly decide to do away with Rocke or Jarrett after all these years of being victims? And why at Wychbourne, in the company of people they knew and on a snowy night? It doesn't add up.'

Thwarted, she tried once again. 'Perhaps Tobias Rocke was getting obstreperous. If Mary Ann Darling had rejected his amorous overtures, perhaps others had too. I'm sure that's why the black crosses were on the photographs and possibly the reason for that locked drawer of underclothing too.'

'Or the opposite,' he pointed out. 'If he was blackmailing them but not interested in them sexually, demanding such things would make the indignity worse.' He paused. 'That was good work, Nell. Just one thing, though. How do *you* know that the guests at Wychbourne Court or some of them were victims of Rocke's blackmail?'

She had an answer for that. 'Servants – and I count as one officially – aren't considered to have ears. I serve coffee, I stand and wait.'

'I thought so. And what if they do realize you have ears? Suppose you then had to be silenced too?' he said grimly.

That startled her. 'That's not likely. Anyway, lots of us overhear, not just me. We all know about Mary Ann Darling and about the other guests.' She paused, wondering if she dared go on. Why not? It was a legitimate question. 'Couldn't you officially reopen the investigation into Mary Ann's death?'

'Nell, you know the limits,' he said in exasperation. 'I go as far as I can with you, but I can't step further. Why is this so important to you?'

'I'm sure she lies at the heart of these murders.'

'Nell, *stop*!'

'I don't see—'

'And I can't open your eyes, Nell. You know I can only talk about my work up to a certain point.' He hesitated. 'It would *always* be like that. Could you live with that?'

'No,' she blurted out.

He sighed. 'I have to go now, Nell. This case is moving on fast. And I can't share it with you yet.'

She watched him go, itching to run after him to take her words back, apologize, but she couldn't. Could she continue to bear with always knowing half the story until after it had ended? She had assumed yes, but now she doubted it. She waited until he had disappeared down the steps of the Underground station and then turned to go home with Lord Ansley. Home to Wychbourne Court.

FOURTEEN

'It feels as though the Keystone Cops have taken control of Wychbourne Court,' Lady Ansley said despairingly. 'You work wonders with the kitchens, Nell, Peters does his best, I do mine, but events do seem to be running away with us.'

Lady Ansley had returned home alone yesterday and as Nell had had an urgent summons to the Velvet Room and as Saturdays with no guests were usually quiet days, something, she deduced, was clearly amiss.

'Keystone Cops bring fun,' she said lightly. 'They just haven't brought it with them to Wychbourne.'

'Far from it. I've been speaking to Mrs Jarrett on the telephone. Poor Constance. What with the funeral and the inquest she is overwrought, and no wonder. It was a private funeral, she explained, and a memorial service at St Paul's in Covent Garden will be announced in due course. But now she is concentrating on discovering the truth behind Hubert's death.'

Seeing Lady Ansley hesitate, Nell waited for the bad news. Sure as eggs were eggs, it was coming.

'I'm afraid,' Lady Ansley continued, 'Constance has some notion that whoever poisoned her husband will confess to us all. This seems to me extremely unlikely, but she is not to be deterred. If I may speak frankly, Nell, I have to admit that Constance was always a puzzle to me. She was devoted to Hubert, even though she was – and is – fully conscious of his foibles, and she told me that makes her intention to rout out his murderer all the stronger. She changed her mind about travelling here yesterday, but still wishes to come down here because this is where he must have been given the poison. Worse, she wants all the friends who were here for the Follies to be present. She has even spoken to them all – and, oh, Nell, they are *coming.* Even poor Neville, who is kindness itself, but *We Dine at Nine*, his new play, is just about to open, and it really is not a good time for him to hurrying down to Kent for several days, nor is it for the others.'

'Several days?' Nell picked up in horror. Usually stays of several days presented no problems, but this sounded ominously urgent. 'When are they coming?' She could see from Lady Ansley's expression that she was right.

'Today.'

Today? Nell's first thought was that Mr Fairweather would have her guts for garters, as her father used to say so elegantly. She was cheered up by the thought of what Mrs Fielding would say with so many extra bedrooms to organize at short notice. Nell congratulated herself on her foresight in keeping emergency plans, but even so there would be problems. Ah well, look on the bright side. The game larder (if Jethro hadn't been too greedy in depleting it) could cope, and Mr Fairweather's carefully stored grapes and forced vegetables would be available once he had recovered from the shock and been persuaded to part with them. Bread would be a problem, as the baker had already delivered today's orders for the weekend, but there might be time to organize that with the bakery today.

'They will arrive for dinner this evening,' Lady Ansley added anxiously.

Once Nell had reassured her that her guests, welcome or not, would not starve, Lady Ansley returned to her main worry. 'Constance's insistence on such a gathering is most worrying. I believe she intends to address it. She is a very good actress of course. She was always so retiring, but on the stage she blossomed. Such a waste that Hubert would never allow her to perform again after their marriage. The same arrangement suited me well when I married Gerald but, unlike me, Constance seemed as dedicated to the stage as Alice.'

Goggling garlics, Nell thought, now truly concerned, as she raced back to the kitchens. The last thing Wychbourne Court needed at the moment was a repressed Sarah Siddons sweeping on stage. She quickly reproved herself. The poor woman had just lost her husband. Domineering he might have been, but that surely would make it harder for her to adjust to life without him. Nevertheless, let a mouse out of its cage and it might scuttle off anywhere.

'You haven't seen me for another fifteen minutes,' she informed Mr Peters, as she hurried past him. 'Have you heard what's happening today?'

'Mrs Fielding just told me. Tell you what, Miss Drury, Lady Clarice asked to see you, so I haven't seen you for half an hour. I'll convey the news to her ladyship that you're thought to be in the kitchen gardens.'

'Blessings be upon you,' she said fervently, and dashed on her way for a conference with Kitty and Michel. What emerged from that was a triumph of hope over practicality in the form of a list for Mr Fairweather divided into emergency (for today) and provisional for four days. (Surely they wouldn't want to stay longer than that?) After a somewhat fraught meeting with him, she managed to reach Lady Clarice only about ten minutes outside Mr Peters' period of grace.

'Ah, there you are, Miss Drury.'

Lady Clarice was poring over a pile of books from the Wychbourne Court library at the table by the window in her drawing room. Nell recognized at least one of them, Thiselton Dyer's *Ghost World.* Luckily Lady Clarice seemed not to notice her tardiness. She was looking too excited.

'You're just the person to help,' Lady Clarice continued. 'Pray do seat yourself.' A hand was waved at the chair opposite her, and Nell slid into it, hoping this did not portend a long stay. 'I'm concerned, Miss Drury, about Wychbourne Court and particularly about Lady Ansley and my brother. It seems to me that there is a definite cloud hanging over this house and over them. Would you agree?'

'Yes, Lady Clarice,' Nell replied cautiously. She did indeed agree, but with Lady Clarice it was never clear where such conversations might lead. Mr Briggs had cheered the kitchen staff up and Lord Richard had organized impromptu dances but the cloud still remained – naturally enough, since two unsolved murders had taken place, and both victims were Wychbourne Court guests.

'My nephew,' said Lady Clarice firmly, 'is neglecting his estate duties in favour of Gertrude's maid, Miss Smith; my niece Lady Helen is spending far too much time in London unsupervised; and Lady Sophy is forgetting her heritage and spending too much time admiring Bolshevik Russia and English socialist movements. I put all these factors down to the lack of progress in these murder investigations. John Palmer is still in prison, we have had no word from the police that they in any way consider this an injustice, and we are not giving the village the leadership they expect from us. In short, Miss Drury, Wychbourne Court is not itself. And nor, incidentally, are you, Miss Drury.'

That jerked Nell into attention. 'My work?'

'No. Yourself. I have noticed a certain amount of *tendresse* where Chief Inspector Melbray is concerned. That of course is your own business, but if it affects your endeavours to lift this cloud then I do plead with you to consider the importance of Wychbourne Court. We are all very fond of you, Nell,' Lady Clarice added anxiously, before Nell could burst out with a reply she might have regretted. 'Wychbourne does need you.'

'And I Wychbourne,' Nell managed to say. 'But I am doing all I can.' Lady Clarice must have something else in mind, though, she was sure of it.

'Good. I intend to play my own part in lifting the cloud. I have been consulting Mr Trotter.'

'Oh no.' The words were out before Nell could stop them, but fortunately Lady Clarice did not take this amiss.

'I'm aware that Mr Trotter is not popular with everyone, and he has perhaps behaved foolishly in encouraging spirits by unorthodox means, but nevertheless he has remarkable powers as a medium.'

'Does that help Wychbourne?' Nell couldn't help asking.

'We need to know who killed Tobias Rocke, Miss Drury, and by assumption Mr Jarrett too. We cannot have Wychbourne Court marked down as a place where actors meet unfortunate ends. Moreover, if we do not move quickly we shall find Gentle John at the Old Bailey convicted of Mr Rocke's murder.'

'Which would leave Mr Jarrett's murder still unsolved.'

Lady Clarice looked at her solemnly. 'Perhaps even with Mr Trotter himself as a suspect.'

Nell was instantly on the alert. Coming from Lady Clarice this was unexpected to say the least.

'No doubt that surprised you, Nell. But think of it this way. Tobias Rocke was most unpleasant to Mr Trotter, threatening to end his career, and Mr Jarrett too was very rude to him. Mr Trotter therefore might be considered to have a motive for killing both of them, and although I do not for one instant consider he might be guilty, he himself is concerned that the real murderer should be unmasked quickly. That is why he is willing to return to Wychbourne again to settle the matter once and for all.'

It was only two days since he had left, Nell thought, and that was because of his not wanting to face Mrs Reynolds. Lady Clarice, she suspected, had made her wishes for his return clear. But Nell could forgive Lady Clarice a lot. Her ladyship was ever hopeful that the ghost of her fiancé, Jasper, would return to her. He had been killed in the Boer War and taken with him all her hopes and love.

'He arrives today,' Lady Clarice continued, 'and will be staying at the Coach and Horses again.'

That was one relief. The idea of bumping into Mr Trotter at every turn would not have made life easier. 'How will he help the investigation though?' Nell asked, wondering what on earth Lady Clarice had in mind this time.

'I have asked my brother's permission for him to come to Wychbourne Court to do so. He was somewhat against the idea at first, as I can see you are, Nell, but then he saw reason.'

'In what way?' Stay calm, whatever it is.

'We shall be holding a tribunal in the Great Hall,' Lady Clarice explained triumphantly. Nell must have looked blank because Lady Clarice added impatiently, 'Mr Trotter will assist him.'

'Assist whom, Lady Clarice?' What new nightmare was this?

'Why, Sir William Ansley, of course. Sixteenth century, later became the first baron. I have persuaded him to attend.'

Nell was muddled. 'Mr Trotter?'

'No, no. Sir William, of course. He is the perfect spirit to preside over a tribunal when poor Mrs Jarrett arrives later today. He will lead us to the truth.'

Rapid thinking required, Nell realized. From Sir William's portrait in the Great Hall he looked a jolly man, and paternally interested in all that was going on around him, but as to how he could act as judge and jury over this, goodness only knows.

'How could he do so, Lady Clarice,' Nell ventured to ask. 'The police have not yet succeeded.'

'Because Sir William is a spirit. He sees more than we can,

and no doubt can communicate with Tobias and Hubert in the spirit world, where they are all located – well, not Hubert perhaps as he may prefer London, but his murderer will be here. Mr Trotter's presence will ensure that he attends and then Sir William will pronounce his decision.'

'But who will be present at this tribunal?' Nell asked, aghast at the thought of Mrs Jarrett and all the guests sitting through this ordeal. It was too much.

'Quite a small gathering,' Lady Clarice said reassuringly. 'You, Nell, myself, my brother and Gertrude. Lady Sophy is otherwise engaged this evening, I am not inviting my nephew as he has *doubts*, and Lady Helen is in London. Mr Fontenoy will also be present. We shall hold it in the Great Hall before the guests begin to arrive. Dusk is not a good time for Mr Trotter, but he gallantly informs me that darkness is not essential if the shutters are closed.'

She must have seen Nell's expression for she reassured her. 'Don't worry, Nell. Sir William will see that justice is done.'

Fresh air. That's what she needed if she were going to cope with both attending this tribunal to please Lady Clarice and deal with the unexpected rearrangements for dinner this evening. Whatever happened at the tribunal (or didn't happen) Nell had her own priorities. After dinner she would once more be at her post in the drawing room. Mrs Jarrett was clearly set on discovering who killed her husband, Nell intended to be listening.

Meanwhile, she was going to do her best to be prepared for this showdown. Two murders. Could Hubert Jarrett have murdered Tobias Rocke, or did he know who had? Fresh air would help her think, Nell decided, even though the light was beginning to fade. Perhaps walking around the churchyard would help her concentrate. Perhaps I'll bump into Tobias Rocke's ghost, she thought, then rapidly dismissed the idea.

As she approached the churchyard, she remembered the bushes stirring in what she had thought was the wind on the night of his murder. Was that linked to the rustling on the far side of the churchyard that Jethro heard about half an hour later?

Mr Fairweather and his wife who lived in the lodge had reported nothing suspicious taking place outside their home that night, which suggested Tobias Rocke was indeed coming from the direction of the lychgate towards the church porch where he was attacked. The rustling in the bushes could well have been Mr Rocke's murderer awaiting his return home.

Could a third party have been present – Ethel perhaps? Could she have dealt the first attack on Tobias Rocke? It was Ethel who had organized the gathering at the Coach and Horses where Hubert Jarrett had been poisoned. Nell recalled the medical evidence that he had eaten nothing after the brief amount at Wychbourne Court the evening before his death and at the Coach and Horses gathering. Don't speculate, she told herself, remembering Alex's warning, but surely the opportunity to kill and her strong motive were evidence in a way?

'What be you doing here, Miss Drury. You poaching again?'

Jethro had loomed up behind her, as she reached the lychgate where Gentle John and Tobias Rocke had been talking – perhaps arguing – on the night of the murder.

'Reconstructing the crime,' she said briefly.

'His lordship won't like it if old John gets off the hook, will he? Nice and handy having him locked up so the family secrets don't get an airing.'

'Suppose you talk sense once in a while, Jethro.' Keep your temper, Nell. 'Show me just where you heard that noise in the bushes, would you?'

He shrugged. 'Playing detective again, are we?'

'On occasion,' she said amicably. 'Do you have secrets you'd like to share?'

'You'd like that, wouldn't you?'

Nell lost patience. 'Show me, Jethro, or I'll split on you to your father.'

That worked. He grinned. 'About here it was. Them bushes by the gate.'

'And you've no idea what caused the noise? Was it snowing?'

'No. Just stopped. Weren't no animal, though.'

'Did you see the mackintosh the police found?'

'I'd have remembered if I had, wouldn't I? Didn't see no mackintosh. Didn't see nobody other than those two gents.

But there was someone in them bushes all right. Tell you what though, Miss Drury . . .' He leaned towards her. 'Confidentially, of course.'

'What, Jethro?'

'It weren't one of them Wychbourne ghosts.'

FIFTEEN

At least she had a breathing space for dinner preparations. *All* of them coming. That was hardly surprising, Nell supposed, as they must have been stuck on a Morton's Fork. They would be damned if they accepted (as therefore by implication they became one of the 'suspects' in Mrs Jarrett's eyes) and damned if they didn't (in which case they must be guilty).

The breathing space was cut short as Lord and Lady Ansley had asked for another brief word with her.

'At least Clarice's tribunal will be out of the way by the time they arrive,' Lady Ansley said thankfully, when Nell enquired whether any of the guests had yet come. 'And I know the dinner will be excellent. It's what happens afterwards that concerns me. Constance is so eager to have her say that she might even begin tonight. I can hardly prevent her.'

'I have good news though, Miss Drury,' Lord Ansley said, 'which might compensate for the tribunal. Gentle John is to be freed.'

'That really *is* a relief,' Nell said warmly, although the possibility of the Palmers having conspired to kill Tobias Rocke sneaked back into her mind.

'The other news is that Chief Inspector Melbray is returning tomorrow. He wishes to speak to everyone involved in these two cases together.'

Nell swallowed. 'Should I be there?'

'Yes, he specifically mentioned you, Nell. And now we should make our way to the Great Hall. The tribunal is about to begin. I'm not sure if my sister fully explained it to you. You do know that table-tipping is involved?'

'Table-tipping?' she repeated blankly. Wasn't that a form of séance?

Lord Ansley was apologetic. 'I understand that even Mr Trotter is somewhat dubious about it as he considers it most unscientific.

Clarice did ask Chief Inspector Melbray if he would like to be present; he was unable to accept but asked to be kept informed of the results. He apparently told her it could be most useful.'

Had the world gone mad? Nell wondered. Scotland Yard and Alex of all people relying on table-tipping – it was surely on a level with Ouija boards for unreliability and mischief-making. True, both sometimes produced strange results. Such as the pointer spelling out *Death*, she remembered uneasily.

'You will still take part, I hope, Nell,' Lady Ansley asked anxiously.

For a minute she wanted to shout 'No!' but she couldn't upset Lady Clarice by refusing. Instead she braced herself for the ordeal ahead as they all three walked down to the Great Hall. Arthur had already arrived and Mr Peters was busy superintending the placing of the table and chairs. These were suitably positioned near to Sir William's portrait, Nell noticed, presumably so that he could preside over the proceedings with ease and even pop down if he so chose. Mr Trotter was nervously nudging the furniture inch by inch into the places he thought best for his purposes – whatever they were.

'All looks very creepy to me, Miss Drury,' whispered Mr Peters, who was busy turning down the lamps.

Nell longed for the certainties that her work brought her instead of this weird world of spirits. Nothing certain there. She had read enough about such tables actually moving or shaking, whether by human or spiritual hand, to know that positive results were sometimes achieved where no jiggery-pokery with the table could have taken place.

Lady Clarice was beaming with anticipation; the only one here for whom there *were* any certainties in this affair, Nell thought.

'Shall we take our places, Mr Trotter? You are ready?' Lady Clarice asked.

'Why pick Sir William, Clarice?' Arthur asked as they all obeyed. 'He looks such an inoffensive fellow from his portrait.'

'It's not a question of whom we pick, Arthur,' Lady Clarice said slightly reprovingly. 'It's more who chooses us. Sir William is the leader of the Great Hall ghosts and fully deserves the honour. As you must know, Queen Elizabeth created him baronet for his help in cheering her up at times of ill fortune. He haunts this area of the hall and Sir Ralph – a mere knight then – haunts the centre of the hall, where the fire would once have been in medieval times. In his earthly life he earned the respect of the Conqueror, for pleading for the men of Kent to retain their practice of gavelkind over inheritance of property. And then there's Gilbert—'

'Shall we proceed, Clarice?' Lord Ansley asked gently. 'Sir William might be getting restless.'

'Of course. How foolish of me. This *is* a tribunal,' Lady Clarice said. 'But as to why we chose him, Arthur, it is not known whether Sir William died at another's hand or whether he himself was responsible for a death. That's makes him so ideal for a tribunal.'

In Nell's view, he should be disqualified if he couldn't make up his mind whether he was murdered or a murderer, but then dismissed such flippancy.

'It depends of course,' Lady Clarence continued, 'whether Sir William's death was a crime of fear or of passion. Consider his unfortunate position. His brother, John, was a violent man and jealous of his elder brother's title and estates. During a drinking bout John used a heavy tankard to attack Sir William, but whether in violence or in self-defence is not known. One died instantly, the other perhaps of shock, but no records survive to say which. Fortunately, John was unmarried and had no legitimate offspring and so Sir William's eldest son inherited Wychbourne.'

'Shall we proceed, Clarice?' Lord Ansley repeated firmly.

'Indeed, yes, Gerald.'

This group would itself make an excellent subject for an oil painting, Nell thought, with all her companions in evening dress and sitting around this table as though for some fascinating after-dinner game. It was far from that.

'Hands upon the table please, palms flat down,' Lady Clarice requested.

With all their hands in place, it was easier to take this as seriously as Lady Clarice and Mr Trotter could wish, easier to believe that this table beneath them was indeed a living object that might move of its own accord. Or should it be at the spirits' accord? Nell wondered.

'Close your eyes but let all thoughts dwell on Tobias Rocke and Hubert Jarrett,' was the next command.

Some minutes passed during which Nell did her best to obey, though her mind did slip to wondering if Gilbert the butler's ghost might appear to serve cocktails. No sign of him so far.

'Are you with us, Sir William?' Mr Trotter enquired. 'Rap once if you are with us.'

Apparently not for all that could be heard were her companions' deep breaths, and she felt nothing.

'Sir William,' he called again. 'Rap once if you are with us.'

Nothing.

'Perhaps the brothers are fighting again,' Arthur murmured.

'Never. John Ansley has never darkened Wychbourne again,' Lady Clarice said. 'Gerald, you try.'

Nell sensed Lord Ansley's reluctance, but knowing how fond he was of his sister, she guessed rightly that he would not let her down. Lord Ansley cleared his throat. 'William, we're still waiting for you.'

Nothing – no, she was wrong about that. Someone must be pressing really hard on the table because it did seem to quiver. And then a noise – could that be a rap? Was someone applying too much pressure?

'Thank you, Sir William.' Mr Trotter's voice had deepened – perhaps Sir William really was speaking through him? Haphazard thoughts raced through Nell's mind.

Lady Clarice took a firm hand. 'Are we to expect Tobias Rocke's murderer to dine with us this evening? Two raps for yes, one for no.'

Too far, too far, Nell thought in alarm, even though she realized she was straining to hear if anything happened. Nothing yet. Then something did change. The table definitely moved, not once but *twice.* One of them must be making this happen, surely. Nell looked around the table, but all six faces looked as scared as she felt. Especially Mr Trotter's.

The doorbell rang. The first of the guests had arrived.

Dinner, despite Nell's best efforts, was going to be far from lively, with the guests paying more attention to their plates than the demands of social conversation. Ordeal by tribunal had been spared them, but they might be facing worse to come. From her position in the serving room it was a strange assembly in other ways too. Not only Mrs Jarrett but the other guests too were in mourning black (save for Lady Helen in startling purple) and this made the ritual procession into the dining room look truly funereal. It reminded Nell of the eccentric French gourmet Grimod de la Reynière, the first ever food critic who in the late eighteenth century had given dinner parties staged as funerals, coffin and all.

Mrs Jarrett, entering on Lord Ansley's arm, was a tall, dignified figure, her still-beautiful face calm and steady. If she was torn by private grief and tension, there was no sign of it. Her stateliness made Mrs Reynolds, Lady Kencroft and Miss Maxwell look subsidiary figures in this parade.

Would this gathering further the investigations at all? Nell wondered. It was hard to imagine how it might be possible to unravel the past and disgorge its secrets to the extent Mrs Jarrett obviously hoped. Stick to the recipe before going steaming ahead, Nell warned herself.

As she entered the comfortable drawing room after dinner with the coffee, a huge fire was being stoked by chief footman Robert and Mr Peters was preparing *digestifs*. Nell's task was only to superintend, as luckily Mrs Fielding's Annie was quite capable of serving coffee alone. The gentlemen took longer than usual before joining the ladies – nervous? Nell wondered – but after they arrived, she watched everyone settling down like an audience awaiting the rising of the curtain.

What was Mrs Jarrett about to say? Would she accuse someone of being her husband's murderer? Nell was impatient, with a mix of trepidation and excitement. This was going to be no eulogy in praise of a lost husband. Instead, when Mrs Jarrett rose to her feet to begin, it did indeed seem to Nell more like a play unfolding before her. That's how she must think of it, she decided. She'd view it with detachment, not deflected by her own reactions.

Scene: drawing room and coffee. *Centre stage*: Constance Jarrett, widow of a murdered man. *Stage left and stage right:* supporting cast. *Audience*: Nell Drury observing.

Opening line: 'You've all been so kind in your condolences and in coming here to support me.' The supporting cast murmured appropriately.

'I do wonder why, however,' Mrs Jarrett added.

Nell stiffened. Not what she had expected.

'You, Neville, are opening at the Albion shortly and are in the middle of rehearsals,' Mrs Jarrett continued. 'You're so busy and yet you have come here. Too kind.'

Neville Heydock looked too taken aback to reply, and Mrs Jarrett swept on. 'Lord Kencroft, you too are here, although the state normally absorbs all your valuable time. Katie, why are you here?'

This *was* like a play. These speeches were planned, but where would they lead? Nell couldn't even guess.

'I'll answer that for both of us,' Lady Kencroft replied instantly. 'Before the Wychbourne Follies we hadn't met together for many years. We saw each other only when our paths crossed either on stage or in society. Darlings, we'd say, how wonderful to see you. But the plays closed and we'd walk offstage. And at last came Gertrude's kind invitation to Wychbourne Court but with that came obligations to support each other – which is why Charles and I are here today.'

'Thank you, Katie,' Mrs Jarrett replied. 'I am truly grateful. The reason I am here myself, however, is for other reasons than my needing support. Hubert and I were *happily* married, which might surprise you all, but we were.'

'Just a minute, Connie,' Neville Heydock began uneasily.

They were going off-script and Nell could feel tension rising.

Mrs Jarrett didn't pause, though. 'I therefore intend to find out who killed him and Tobias.'

'Isn't that a police matter, Constance?' Miss Maxwell demanded.

'Mine also, Alice.'

'That's laudable, Constance,' Lord Ansley intervened, clearly alarmed, 'but I fail to see what you can do, terrible though this has been for you. If any of us saw anything to explain how that poison was added to Hubert's food or drink we would have informed the police.'

'That I understand,' Mrs Jarrett said coolly. 'What the police cannot discover without our help is the extent of Tobias's blackmail, an issue that was raised earlier but skilfully avoided in detail.'

Bullseye! Off-script or not, Nell wasn't going to miss a minute of this. At last she might be able to confirm those links between photographs and files.

'Excellent idea, Constance.' Mrs Reynolds clapped her hands, but no one followed suit.

'Thank you,' Mrs Jarrett replied. 'I have now realized that Hubert was one of Tobias's victims, and I propose to tell you why. I hope that now Tobias is dead, that will encourage you all to speak out.'

Staggering stockfish! Nell held her breath. This might well lead nowhere, but if it did . . .

'I do fail to see how the blackmail issue is relevant now that Tobias is dead,' Lord Kencroft retorted.

'It might not be,' Mrs Jarrett rejoined, 'but I can see no other reason for Hubert's death, even though it might be an oblique one. Before he met me,' she continued, 'Hubert was a great admirer of Mary Ann Darling. Being young and very foolish he followed her around like a puppy to the extent that she was forced to complain to Mr Edwardes.'

'He was the man who persecuted Mary Ann?' Neville Heydock asked in amazement.

So that, Nell thought with relief, confirmed that the photograph of the man lurking in the bushes outside what was probably Mary Ann's home must be of Hubert Jarrett. At last theories were becoming probabilities.

'He was,' Mrs Jarrett replied steadily. 'Tobias discovered this and made that plain to Hubert, knowing that it would ruin Hubert's chances of a future major career if it was widely known that he was forcing his attentions on Mary Ann Darling. That situation intensified after her disappearance. Tobias asked for favours, small and large. Often months, even years would go by and just when Hubert presumed he was safe, Tobias would rear up again with his sickening demands.'

'Hubert had, I presume, nothing to do with Mary Ann's death?' Lord Ansley asked.

'No,' Mrs Jarrett said sharply. 'From the time of her disappearance, however, Tobias delighted in spreading the rumour that she must have been murdered in order to alarm Hubert in case his peccadilloes led to his being suspected of killing her;

he threatened to tell the police about Hubert's pursuit of Mary Ann. Once that body was identified as hers, the pressure grew worse. I now believe he did not dare to actually carry out his threats against Hubert. He had too much to lose.'

There was a silence as Nell could see her listeners taking in the implications of what she had said. *Too much to lose?*

'Was Tobias suspected of murdering Mary Ann at the time?' Mr Heydock asked. 'He had an alibi, I understand, but alibis aren't always watertight.'

'Once and for all, Tobias was no murderer, Neville,' Lady Kencroft said, exasperated. 'Nor to my knowledge a blackmailer. He wasn't suspected of anything. He was a kind man.'

'Kind?' Mrs Reynolds shrieked. 'Katie, and you too, Gertrude, you've no idea just how *kind* Tobias was not. Several of us did and have kept mum about it ever since. You want us to speak out, Constance, so I shall. That *kind* Tobias invited me, almost ordered me, to his bed, and when I laughed him out of court he pointed out I'd no compunction about hopping into other men's beds and hence my divorce from Neville.' She turned to him. 'Wasn't that the case, *darling* Neville. That's what caused our divorce, didn't it, *darling*?'

What was going on in this obviously meaningful conversation? Nell wondered. One thing was clear. The black cross on Mrs Reynolds' photograph, and therefore in all probability the other black crosses, did indeed signify that Tobias Rocke's amorous attentions had been spurned. He had been rejected not just once but several times, and that was too much for that self-important man to accept.

'Yes, that's what caused it, Lynette.' Mr Heydock was very white.

'Or was it, darling?' she replied. 'Wasn't Tobias more interested in your gentleman's gentleman and his role in your life? Wouldn't have looked good for your career as a romantic dish if he revealed you were a nancy boy.'

Battered buttercups, so that's what Arthur had been hinting at when he had talked of secrets from past and present. He'd recognized Mr Heydock's private life as being like his own, Nell realized. Her heart went out to him though; he looked completely at a loss as how to deal with this revelation.

'That's enough, Lynette,' Miss Maxwell said sharply. Unwisely.

'And how about you, Would-be Dame Alice?' Lynette asked sweetly. 'A few questions could be asked as to why you've never married and your preference for female company. Such as your devoted Doris. It's quite fashionable nowadays, but not to the general public.'

'My personal life is no concern to anyone but me,' Miss Maxwell replied quietly. 'And Tobias had no interest in that anyway. He was – I admit – applying pressure on me because I obtained my first leading role through unfair means.'

That explained the photograph at Cannes, Nell thought, wrestling with the revelation of yet another very present secret. Tobias must have intimated that a holiday there would be welcome.

'Fascinating.' Mrs Reynolds laughed. 'You should have done what I did. Told him to go to blazes and I hope he has. After he'd spread his nasty little rumours, my career was finished. Tiny character parts if I'm lucky. Thank you, *kind* Tobias.'

'You've married again, though,' Lady Kencroft pointed out.

'There was no second marriage. There is no Mr Reynolds,' Mrs Reynolds said simply. 'Does that satisfy you? I assumed I would marry again after the divorce, but amazingly Tobias ensured that that wouldn't happen. A greatly exaggerated word in the ear of any remotely prospective husband and he was away.'

Another mask falling, Nell thought, and a totally different woman emerging from it.

Mrs Jarrett nodded. 'Just as with Mary Ann. He threatened to reveal her real name. I believe her father was a very violent man. I don't know the details, but to escape him she came to London and changed her name. Tobias was very much in pursuit of Mary Ann, Hubert told me, and he rejoiced when Mary Ann very firmly rebuffed Tobias. He took his revenge by being as persistent in his pursuit of her as Hubert was, but he had the added power of being able to scare her with more than his sexual pursuit. Little wonder she needed to escape.'

Mrs Jarrett looked at her audience as though not quite certain what she was doing there. 'As it seems, many of us did, where Tobias Rocke was concerned. I too suffered his beastly advances,' she added, sitting down.

The third black cross, Nell remembered.

Lady Ansley took Mrs Jarrett a cup of coffee and sat down

beside her. 'It was I who made the mistake, Constance, not you. I thought we could recreate the past, but we've brought back the worst of it and not the best.'

'You did us a favour, Gertrude,' Miss Maxwell said warmly. 'We're here, the truth is out, masks are off and we can feel truly together again. Look at the success of the Follies. Time slipped away then and it can again.'

Nell felt stunned. Her theories were confirmed, but at the cost of her realizing how much pain these people had suffered from Tobias Rocke. Were they indeed all glad the curtain had been lifted or had it just brought back the misery? Either way the murders, whether crimes of fear or of passion, as Lady Clarice had put it, still remained to be solved. No ghosts or spirits could help there, only Chief Inspector Melbray, possibly with an ounce of help from herself.

Tomorrow Alex Melbray would be coming to Wychbourne. This couldn't be just for another information-gathering exercise; he must know, Nell realized, who the murderer or murderers were and Alex was coming for just one purpose: confirmation. That meant she should talk to him first as tonight's revelations would surely be relevant. Lord Ansley must have been of the same opinion for he caught up with her on her way back to the east wing.

'Much has been said tonight, Nell, that Chief Inspector Melbray needs to know before he arrives in Wychbourne later tomorrow. It's hard for me to speak to him as these people are friends and guests under our roof. But we need to rid ourselves of the dark god of suspicion peering over our shoulders. Could I suggest therefore that you telephone the chief inspector tomorrow morning – a Sunday of course, but I have the telephone number of his home? You should use the telephone in my study, our private line, as the general Wychbourne number is too public for such a call. You will be alone while you make the telephone call, needless to say, so that you may speak freely. Come just before we leave for the morning service.'

This is a long way from being a Spitalfields barrow girl, Nell Drury, she thought as she thanked him, but it came with responsibilities. She would cope with those tomorrow – a wonderful word that took the stress out of everything, even the tiredness that now consumed her.

* * *

Secure in her cocoon in Lord Ansley's study, she put through the trunk call next morning and was rewarded by Alex's startled voice at hearing her. Even over the telephone she could sense he was turning over what she was saying, although neither accepting nor rejecting it. That was a relief. As she finished telling him about the tribunal, though, she had an afterthought. 'Incidentally, Lady Clarice divides her ghosts' murders into crimes of fear or crimes of passion.'

A silence and then at last he spoke. 'Thank you, Nell. I'm coming down to the Coach and Horses this evening. I'll be arranging for all those involved in these cases to gather there tomorrow.'

Gather there, and not at Wychbourne Court? That sobered her. It implied he was going to make an arrest and wanted to do that on neutral ground.

'In one of the downstairs rooms or where they held the Wychbourne Follies?' she asked tentatively.

'The latter. It's time for curtain up on the last act, Nell. Where the Wychbourne Follies began and where they should end.'

SIXTEEN

Curtain up? So Chief Inspector Melbray had a very definite plan and 'curtain up' suggested he had a play of his own to stage. Nell was torn between relief that the end must be near and panic as to what that might be. Yesterday had been difficult both for the family and by extension for the servants too. After the heated exchanges on Saturday night, the guests had been subdued yesterday, either hurrying off to church or lurking in the billiard room or hiding behind newspapers in the morning room. Even in the kitchens there had been a sense of marking time because everyone knew Chief Inspector Melbray would be coming.

Mrs Jarrett had seemed the only exception to this, seemingly still intent on her role of hunting down her husband's murderer. Was she overplaying the tragedy queen? No, because she had every reason to do so, Nell reminded herself. Mrs Reynolds – as she was still being addressed – was noticeably quiet. Lady Ansley had seemed abstracted when Nell arrived for their meeting in the Velvet Room. The household still had to be run however, and the menus had been agreed in record time both yesterday and today.

The first thing Nell noticed when she arrived at the Coach and Horses shortly before eleven o'clock was two police motor cars discreetly parked in the yard and even more ominously a police van. Male voices from one of the ground-floor rooms suggested that policemen were tucked out of sight – for the moment. As she reached the upper room, she recognized Sergeant Caring, in plain clothes and carefully situated near the door. He wasn't exactly guarding it, but he wasn't far away.

Nell took a deep breath. The audience for today's drama – if that is what it was going to be – were already in their places, but the murmur of their voices was low; everyone was waiting for the curtain to rise. The chairs had been placed not in front of the stage, as they had been for the Wychbourne

Follies, but in a large semicircle facing the internal wall on her right. They were surrounding the focal point – one solitary empty chair. No doubt about who would be sitting there. She seemed to be one of the last to arrive, as the whole Ansley family, save for the dowager, was already seated and so were the guests and their servants, Mr Trotter and Arthur Fontenoy. Everyone involved, Alex Melbray had said. Even the Palmers were present and Jethro, for once looking ill at ease and not his usual cocky self.

As Nell took a place near the door, Chief Inspector Melbray slipped in almost unnoticed to take his seat. She saw Sergeant Caring edging much closer to the door and nerved herself up for what was to happen. Nothing she could do now would change the script of this drama.

'The Wychbourne Follies, happy occasion though I'm told it was,' the Chief Inspector began formally, 'was, as we all know, immediately followed by a tragic drama in which you all played a part, some small, some leading roles. And because this is a drama, I'm sure you're aware that there'll be no walking offstage and back into your private lives until it ends.'

Clever, Nell thought, after her first shock at the way he was approaching this task. He was managing to put the audience at one remove from Tobias Rocke and Hubert Jarrett's murders and yet underline the enormity of what had happened.

'We'll take it act by act,' Chief Inspector Melbray continued dispassionately. 'Lady Ansley has kindly agreed to begin with what could be called a curtain raiser.'

Lady Ansley? She had been part of this? Surely it was unfair to have involved her in this? No, she was wrong, Nell realized. It was clear that she was fully prepared and she rose to her feet with complete composure.

'I'm afraid I did indeed begin this terrible train of events. I had no intentions beyond wanting to see my old friends again. You still are our friends and I hope will remain so. But I was concerned over whether the Follies would please everyone and in worrying too much about that, I was foolish enough to mention Mary Ann Darling.'

'Act I,' the inspector said, as Lady Ansley resumed her seat. 'Enter Lord Ansley.'

Crackling crepes, where did the inspector think this stylized opening would lead? Nell held her breath. From insisting Mary Ann was little or no part of the investigation, he now seemed to be implying that she was an integral part.

Lord Ansley too was obviously prepared. 'At Miss Darling's request, Mr Heydock and I helped in what we thought was merely Mary Ann's disappearance from the Gaiety in order to have a quieter and happier life. As far as we knew, our plan had worked, although later we were told that her body had been identified. Isn't that so, Neville?'

Mr Heydock nodded. 'Yes,' he replied. 'I couldn't see who the lover waiting in the cab was, but it was highly unlikely to have been Tobias Rocke. It could, however – forgive me, Constance – have been Hubert Jarrett who replaced him in the cab.'

Mrs Jarrett must have disciplined herself for this ordeal because Nell could see no sign of distress as she spoke. 'It could indeed have been him, Neville. Hubert wasn't married at the time and had been one of Mary Ann's persistent admirers. Nevertheless, I am certain he did not murder Mary Ann. He was not a violent man. Alibi or not, I still believe Tobias killed her.'

Is this what the chief inspector wants? Nell wondered. Participation by his cast? Does he already know where it's leading?

'We can check Mr Rocke's alibi more closely,' the inspector said. 'He had a motive for killing her as we believe that she had rejected his sexual attentions. He had nothing to gain from her death though, except for revenge.'

'He most certainly did,' Miss Maxwell said indignantly. 'He was making her life a misery by threatening to reveal her whereabouts to her father, but Mary Ann was going to ask the Guv'nor to deal with him.'

'I agree with you, Alice,' Mrs Jarrett said quietly. 'Tobias was a cunning man. He would have arranged an alibi for her death, and later he identified the body, no doubt at his own suggestion. He wanted the police investigation closed.'

'That is possible,' the inspector agreed. 'But I suggest we move on to Act Two, the recent murder of Tobias Rocke. Does the motive stem back to Miss Darling or to newer causes: his blackmailing habits, both in the past and the present? Indeed, very much the present: Mr Trotter is included in our cast because he was being blackmailed by Mr Rocke.'

'Me?' squeaked Mr Trotter.

'Why should you be excluded, Mr Trotter?' Mrs Reynolds asked. 'The rest of us are undergoing scrutiny by the inspector's magnifying glass, so why not you?'

'But I was staying at Wychbourne Court. I came back with Lady Clarice,' Mr Trotter stuttered. 'I have an alibi.'

'Tobias wasn't murdered until well after eleven o'clock. An agile gentleman like you could have slipped out of a door or window again,' Mrs Reynolds mocked him.

'I'd prefer it if we kept to my script, Mrs Reynolds,' the inspector said.

'Oh, come now. I'm sure you know by now that I have no such claim to that name. Mrs Heydock will do, won't it, darling?' She turned to Neville Heydock.

'It will, my dove,' he rejoined. To her surprise, Nell thought he looked almost pleased at the idea for all his sarcasm.

'Nonetheless, as scriptwriter I must intervene,' the inspector said mildly. 'Call this Act Three. From your statements, you were all back at Wychbourne Court by about twenty to eleven, save for you, Miss Drury, who arrived shortly before the hour. All of you were seen in the supper room at least briefly, and then dispersed to either the billiard room or drawing room or retired to bed. One unidentifiable figure was seen by Jethro James to be leaving by a side door.'

'Mr Trotter,' Mrs Reynolds (as Nell had become accustomed to thinking of her) shot back.

'One of the servants perhaps?' Mr Heydock suggested.

'Possible,' the inspector conceded. 'Tobias Rocke and John Palmer were seen together by Mr Jethro James at the church lychgate at eleven fifteen or so, about the same time as he also heard odd sounds in the churchyard bushes, which were probably linked to the murder in the porch very shortly after.'

There was something that didn't add up here, Nell thought uneasily. This rustling in the bushes. Alex was right in that this was probably linked to the murder shortly after, but what about the noise she had heard when she left the Coach and Horses over half an hour earlier? Was that just the wind, or had that too been connected with the murder?

'James's testimony can't be relied on,' Mr Heydock objected.

'Why not? He wouldn't have had reason to murder poor old Tobias,' Mrs Reynolds pointed out tartly.

Neville shrugged. 'Perhaps he caught him poaching.'

'Why would he bother to kill him in the church porch?' she asked scornfully. To this she received no answer either from Neville or anyone else. Indeed, Nell thought, their audience seemed relieved that the limelight was off them – excepting Chief Inspector Melbray, who was gently pushing the dialogue onwards.

'Why indeed?' he asked. 'Shall we proceed with those whom Tobias Rocke was blackmailing, or attempting to?'

'Oh, excellent!' Mrs Reynolds drawled. 'Here I come again, gripping a knife *and* a stone to commit my murders. I always manage to overdo things.'

'Be quiet, Lynette,' Mr Heydock snapped.

'Anything to hide, my pet? I haven't.'

Chief Inspector Melbray again took over. 'We should consider whether these were crimes of passion or fear.'

He'd remembered Lady Clarice's words, Nell thought with a rush of excitement. Where was this leading?

'Would you classify Tobias Rocke's murder as one of passion?' he continued.

'Fear. He was threatening several of us,' Mr Heydock said.

'There are other motivations for murder,' Miss Maxwell pointed out. 'Hatred or greed – although both might be said to come under passion.'

'We really must be talking of two different Tobiases,' Lady Kencroft broke in angrily. 'This is not the Tobias I knew.'

'Then he was a Jekyll and Hyde,' Mrs Jarrett said matter-of-factly. 'He most certainly made my husband's life a misery, and I am of the opinion that he could well have murdered Mary Ann, if not the night of her disappearance, then later.'

'He had a motive to kill her, given that he did not seem a man who would take rejection lightly,' the inspector replied. 'Or was he blackmailing her murderer?' A pause. 'Or does the motive lie much nearer to us in time?'

No one answered. 'Consider these things,' he continued softly. 'The inter-act curtain is falling on Tobias Rocke.'

'And when it rises?' Lord Ansley asked stiffly.

'Someone will, I hope, remember my poor Hubert who was also murdered,' Mrs Jarrett intervened tartly.

'We all shall,' the inspector said soberly. 'Act Four, the death of Hubert Jarrett. The evidence points to his being poisoned here in Wychbourne, and the probability is that the poison was in a sandwich eaten here at the Coach and Horses.'

'Risky,' Mr Heydock commented.

'Indeed, yet Mr Jarrett was almost certainly the intended target,' the inspector replied. 'Different though the two methods of murder were, it also seems certain that his death was linked to that of Tobias Rocke. Both crimes had a degree of planning, given the need to have knife and poison at hand, but also an element of improvisation: the church porch would hardly be a first choice for a murder, nor would the risk attached to the sandwich option at a funeral gathering. Why, however, was Mr Jarrett killed?'

'The answer is simple,' Lord Kencroft said. 'Hubert knew who had killed Tobias.'

'Your curtain raiser implied Mary Ann was the reason for both murders,' Alice Maxwell said.

'But that excludes dear Mr Trotter,' Mrs Reynolds complained.

'And that, short though that act was, brings us to the final one,' Chief Inspector Melbray said. 'I am convinced that both Mr Rocke's and Mr Jarrett's deaths were crimes of passion, not fear.'

Both? Nell was startled. Who would kill Mr Jarrett for reasons of passion. Unless . . . A memory came back to her at last. Something he had said, something that didn't fit. Even now she couldn't pin it down.

'Passion?' Mrs Jarrett rose to her feet, trembling. 'Are you implying that I poisoned my husband, Chief Inspector? I adored Hubert. Why would I want to kill him and even if I did, would I do it here, among friends?'

'No, Mrs Jarrett. I am quite sure that you did not kill your husband. And, Mr Trotter, I am equally sure that you did not kill Tobias Rocke.'

'Thank you.' Mr Trotter looked on the verge of tears. 'I began to think I must have murdered him in a trance and that he would return to haunt me.'

'Has he done so?' Lady Clarice enquired eagerly.

'I doubt it very much, Lady Clarice,' the inspector said firmly. 'His spirit would have another mission. To seek revenge on his true murderer.'

Arthur Fontenoy broke the tense silence. 'And who is that, inspector? You said this was the final act of your drama.'

'I did. Mr Rocke's murder was a crime of passion and revenge by the only person who, I believe, had reason to kill both men for passion, not fear. Who hated Tobias Rocke so much and then turned on Hubert Jarrett. The reason was the murder of Mary Ann Darling, whom she believed had been killed by Tobias Rocke.'

Doris Paget's shriek rang out. 'I was with her, I was *with her* all the time. I swear to it. It's just not true.'

'Some of the time, Miss Paget,' Chief Inspector Melbray said gravely. 'You were with her in the church porch when you both took part in Tobias Rocke's murder. You were with her when you returned to the house that night, after which you parted, you to the servants' east wing, she to the west wing. You had not been with her when she hurried briefly back to Wychbourne Court to make her presence known at the buffet supper before slipping out again to join you. But you were most certainly with her when Mr Jarrett was poisoned.'

All this time Miss Maxwell had said nothing, her face impassive. Nell expected Chief Inspector Melbray to move forward, conscious that Sergeant Caring was on the alert, ready to move at any moment. But nothing happened. Stunned faces stared at each other, at the inspector and at Miss Maxwell herself.

At last Alice Maxwell rose to her feet. 'I would like to say a few words, Chief Inspector.' Her rich, deep voice rang out as though she were indeed on stage.

'I . . .' She hesitated for a moment, then continued, '. . . I did indeed murder Tobias Rocke. I did so alone, however. Miss Paget was not involved. As to regrets, I have none. I did poison Hubert Jarrett and for that my apologies to you, Constance, however inadequate they may appear. As regards Tobias Rocke, I killed him with pleasure and may he rot in hell.'

She paused then and Chief Inspector Melbray stood up. Perhaps he had seen, as Nell had, that Mrs Jarrett was in tears.

'One moment, if you please, Inspector, before we leave,' Alice Maxwell said calmly. 'I wish to tell you about Tobias Rocke.'

'That is not advisable, Alice,' Lord Ansley said anxiously. 'A solicitor should be present.'

'Not necessary, thank you, Gerald. I shall deliver one of the great speeches of my life – and for once it is my own. Do please let me enjoy it, Chief Inspector. The Old Bailey may not allow me such latitude. There are times when women such as Medea, St Joan and myself come to their full power, Medea having slaughtered her children, St Joan at the stake, and I, no doubt less dramatically, now. We women have our strengths and we have our weaknesses. In my case, Tobias Rocke was foolish enough to disregard the former and play to the latter. He took every opportunity over the years to remind me that my private life is not an orthodox one, however long its pedigree. Its joys were sung by the poetess Sappho in the Isle of Lesbos but have been ignored since. I have been blessed by them. One word of my private life, however, and my career would have vanished. Neville is in the same position.'

'But think of me, Alice, you killed my husband,' Constance Jarrett choked.

Nell shuddered. Alice Maxwell was pitiless, engrossed in her own life and career above all. And yet something wasn't adding up, she realized. Alex had talked of a crime of passion, but what Alice Maxwell was describing was a crime of fear, caused by the blackmail.

'There was more to it than his blackmail, wasn't there?' she heard herself blurting out.

Alice Maxwell turned the cold eyes of Medea on her. 'Yes,' she said. 'So much more.'

Nell couldn't stop now. 'You killed Mr Rocke in passion because of Mary Ann Darling.'

Alice Maxwell's impassive face changed to raw emotion. Would the inspector stop her now? Nell wondered. No. He made no move.

'Tobias Rocke constantly tormented Mary Ann,' Alice Maxwell said, 'and threatened her not only that he would reveal her true name, but that he would boast of having possessed her body. Until I came to Wychbourne, I had no idea that he had murdered her too, although I had always hated him because she was indeed scared of him. I had thought that he was also the ghoul who pursued her so fervently to and from the theatre. That was Hubert, I learned, but that made no difference.'

'But you killed him, my husband,' Mrs Jarrett screamed at her.

'I did. Between them they ruined Mary Ann's short life. Shortly after I arrived at Wychbourne Court, I accused Tobias of this and of murdering her. He jeered at me, pointing out that even if he did track her down and strangle her I could prove nothing. He took great pleasure in telling me so. I knew I had no choice then just as I had no choice over Hubert once I discovered what he had done to Mary Ann. I had to avenge her death and the great suffering she had endured.'

'Everyone has choice,' Lady Ansley said.

Alice turned on her. 'I am not everyone,' she said simply. 'And, Chief Inspector Melbray, my dear Doris played no part in this. I killed Tobias, I put the poison in Hubert Jarrett's sandwich.'

'I began this,' Lady Ansley cried, 'with my thoughtless mention of Mary Ann. Why, oh why, did you mind so much about her plight?'

Alice Maxwell smiled. 'We cannot all have the person we truly love, and that is the misfortune that many of us bear. As I did. She did not reciprocate, but Mary Ann was the great love of my life.'

'Crimes of passion, Nell.' Alex had asked her to wait until the formalities were carried out and the police motor cars had left for Sevenoaks police station. The Wychbourne party, including Mr Trotter, had departed for the Court, and Nell had been grateful to see Alex again when he at last appeared looking worn out. That empty room upstairs had been a lonely place.

'Did you know it was Alice Maxwell?' she asked.

'Yes.'

'How?'

'Many reasons. I looked at her carefully because she and Doris Paget were the last to leave, hence no risk of anyone observing them from behind. Then, so their statements said, after a brief appearance in the supper room for Miss Maxwell they retired to their beds where no guests could be asked to verify that, unlike those who adjourned to the billiard or drawing rooms. There's much stronger evidence of course, which will be presented at the trial. More importantly, Nell, you provided a fresh eye on the case; you told me about the footprints, you brought me your conclusions on the blackmail, but there was far more than that. You pointed me in the direction of what kind of crime this was. A crime of passion.'

'For Doris Paget too?'

'Oh, yes. I'm sure they acted together. Poor Miss Paget's passion was for Alice.' He paused. 'It's been a long morning, Nell. You've had to listen to all these emotions and terrible stories from the past and must have wondered how I could sit there so calmly waiting to trap my victims. So at this moment I'm sure you don't like me very much. I'm so tired I'm not even sure I care about being liked. This is the work I do, this is the life I lead. The motor cars have left for Sevenoaks now, and I have to go there too, before going back to the Yard. But Nell, before I leave Wychbourne, I just want to be sure—'

'Whether jolly Sir William is still hanging around in the Great Hall?' she interrupted flippantly. He looked solemn and that scared her.

'No. Whether passion is—'

She didn't hear whether there was more because his lips were on hers, his arms around her, and her body trembling with life within. Her arms seemed to moving without her permission and her lips responding. She'd forgotten that feeling – it had been a long time since she was in a man's arms and now she wondered why.

When he pulled away, she had to cling on to his arm to steady herself. She heard herself stammering, but the only words she could manage to say were 'Passion, Alex. I seem to have rapped twice for yes.'

She saw him swallow hard, above his stiff collar. 'Or was that me? Does it matter?'

'No.' And this time she took the lead.

SEVENTEEN

How much longer? Four days since Alice Maxwell's arrest and no more news of what was happening. Nell was tired of listening to the continuous and often inaccurate chatter on the subject both in the servants' hall and even among the Ansley family. Lady Helen tended to raise a world-weary eyebrow whenever the matter was mentioned, Rex Beringer had left for London (to Lady Sophy's disappointment, Nell suspected), but Lord Richard and Lady Sophy had had much to say about the silence that had fallen over the arrest.

'Not cricket,' Lord Richard had grumbled to Nell. 'The Follies was my idea and yet we haven't a clue as to what's going on.'

'But it was Mother's plan to invite them all in the first place,' Lady Sophy had pointed out. 'It's not cricket to blame her either. How was she to know? Imagine – suppose we all met in fifty years' time and discovered we'd secretly been murderers and blackmailers?'

'Kenelm would cast us to the dogs if he'd inherited the stately pile by then,' Lord Richard had observed. Nell had never met Sir Kenelm, the Ansleys' eldest son, because owing to his service abroad in the Colonial Office he rarely visited Wychbourne.

The unrest in the Ansley family was echoed in the servants' hall. The commotion over Alice Maxwell was bad enough, Nell thought as she finished her breakfast, but for her there was the added frustration that she was longing to hear the full story from Alex.

A new mystery in the servants' hall had arisen since Monday, however. The Strange Disappearance of Miss Smith. Like Mary Ann Darling, she had simply vanished three days ago without a word to them. Then she had reappeared yesterday morning and blithely taken up her duties as though nothing had happened.

Given the family's silence on the matter and a sheepish look on Lord Richard's face, Mrs Fielding had with great relish voiced the general opinion that 'something was up'. Mr Briggs in particular had been confused by her loss, looking round at mealtimes with a look of puzzlement. When Nell had tackled her in Pug's Parlour after curiosity reached breaking point, Miss Smith had announced cheerily that Lord Richard had 'tried it on'. On returning from a trip to the seaside in his motor car, a carefully staged flat tyre had resulted in the need to stay in a hotel overnight. Miss Smith had informed Lord Richard that he would be sleeping in the motor car while she took the hotel room that by coincidence he had already booked. She had then commented that the whole experience had been 'jolly good fun'.

At last, just before luncheon, the call Nell had been waiting for came. Lord Ansley wanted to see her in his study.

'I've heard from Chief Inspector Melbray, Miss Drury,' Lord Ansley said, and her hopes rose. News at last. Something would be happening. 'He would like you to accompany us to London tomorrow,' he continued, 'and for us all to dine at Romano's with him. An appropriate venue, he points out, even if its cuisine might not be comparable with yours.'

Real action. What should she wear? she immediately wondered, then guiltily pushed that subject to one side for later.

'He wants to tell us more about these appalling cases,' Lord Ansley explained. 'Alice Maxwell has been charged, and Doris Paget too, I'm afraid, despite Miss Maxwell's valiant efforts to take all the blame on herself. For Paget, the price of love has proved bitter.'

Nell thought back to Monday's events, after her initial glow of pleasure at the invitation had been carefully stored away. The price of love, Miss Maxwell and Doris Paget, Hubert Jarrett and Mary Ann Darling, Tobias Rocke and his obsession with power: she reflected on all these until her thoughts slid sideways. What would Scotland Yard have made of the great Chief Inspector Melbray clasping a witness in his arms? After all, she might be a witness in the case and would be seeing Alex at the Old Bailey. Then it would be back to teas and picnics.

She tried to convince herself that the problem of Alex would slowly diminish over time, but that didn't please her either. You're not usually so hen-witted, Nell Drury, she told herself. What *do* you want? The moon perhaps? Wychbourne *and* Alex Melbray? Impossible. They'd been through all that. He had his job, which he couldn't share with her and she had hers, in which she suspected Chief Inspector Melbray was not highly interested. Regrettably, she put him down as eat-to-live, not a live-to-eat man. Not that she approved of the latter either. Oh, how complicated life was.

She pulled herself together. 'Thank you, Lord Ansley. I'd be delighted to come.'

'We'll take the Rolls-Royce and stay overnight at the Waldorf Hotel if that would suit you.'

'Thank you, Lord Ansley,' she replied, her mind slipping back to what she could wear. Did she even have a dress posh enough for dining at Romano's? The old black? The blue? It would be evening dress, she remembered. Neither would suit. It would have to be the pink chiffon again.

Corking cobnuts, she thought, as she sat in state in the rear seat of the Rolls-Royce, sharing the warm rug over her knees with Lady Ansley. This was living in style. The Phantom Rolls-Royce had been a rare step last year into glamour for the Ansleys. Their family fortunes, like those of every other estate owner in the country, had been much depleted by the war and the high rates of income tax, currently swinging between four and five shillings to the pound. Nearly a quarter of everything that came in from the estate was paid in tax, though the estate was swallowing up more and more in costs.

As they motored along the Strand, Nell compared it with her earlier visit to Romano's when she had scuttled along the pavement in the rain under her umbrella. Today a doorman stepped out smartly to open the motor car door for Lady Ansley and, goodness gracious, for her, Nell Drury. The chauffeur winked at her; it was Mr Ramsay today, as he'd insisted to the regular chauffeur that this trip was *his* turn. He would be taking the Rolls-Royce to the Waldorf after this and he no doubt had his own plans for a free evening and morning in London.

At first she could see no sign of Alex, while they were handing their coats to the attendant in the entrance hall. No, she was wrong. There he was, just turning away from that magnificent flower stall and bearing two roses – yes, *roses*, at this time of year – which he presented to Lady Ansley and herself. His eyes briefly met hers, which sent a tremor through her, which she tried to ignore. It was business as usual when he spoke however.

'We have a room set aside for us on this floor so that we can talk over what has happened, and then we shall dine upstairs,' he explained.

Lord Ansley did not comment and Nell knew he must be thinking of that other night so long ago when he had dined here upstairs in a private room.

'I haven't come here since my Gaiety days,' Lady Ansley remarked, peeping into the restaurant as they were conducted to the room they were to use. 'How very sensible – just look at that gallery at the far end. That's new. And all these Arabian Nights murals. I'd quite forgotten them.'

Nell was delighted to see Signor Murano, awaiting them with a tray of cocktails when they reached the comfortable anteroom they were to use. No alcoholic cocktail for Alex Melbray, underlining the fact that he was working. But there would be a little pleasure too, she hoped. This Hanky Panky cocktail was just the sort of modern drink Peters would have disapproved of – and no doubt the ghost of Gilbert the butler would share that sentiment. It was delicious.

'You've heard that Alice Maxwell has been charged,' Alex began, 'and Doris Paget too, of course. She was eager to take all the blame. They had been lovers for many years, though publicly she retained her position as servant. Regrettably, neither devotion to one's lover nor employer guarantees immunity from the law.'

Devotion to one's employer? Is he thinking of me and Wychbourne too? Nell wondered fleetingly. Nonsense, she told herself briskly. This was business for him and must be for her too.

'You'll want to know what happened,' he continued. 'Miss Maxwell and Miss Paget made no bones about giving us the whole story. Doris Paget became Miss Maxwell's dresser some years after the Gaiety period, but she did know Tobias Rocke and was puzzled when Miss Maxwell agreed to his accompanying them on a holiday to Cannes when she knew very well that Miss Maxwell disliked him intensely. It took some time, she told us, before Miss Maxwell confided in her, perhaps the point at which they became lovers. Incidentally, a similar situation occurred with Mr Heydock and his "Jeeves", when Rocke became aware of their relationship. You may be pleased to hear, however, that Mr Heydock and Mrs Reynolds are to remarry, an arrangement that perhaps suits them both. Mrs Reynolds will regain a spouse and social acceptance and Mr Heydock a wife which given the current laws on his private life is a great advantage.'

Nell realized too late that she was staring at him, once more thinking of last Monday's astonishing end, but before she could switch her gaze he caught her eye and, dabbling damsons, she knew she was blushing.

'To continue,' the inspector said quietly, 'Alice Maxwell had realized that Tobias Rocke might well be at Wychbourne and was prepared for his playing his usual game of cat and mouse with her. As soon as she arrived he agreed to have a chat, then said he really hadn't time, or perhaps he might at some point. They did indeed meet. What she was not prepared for was Tobias Rocke's airy claim that not only was he involved in Miss Darling's disappearance but that he had killed her great love, knowing that she could do nothing about it. As you recall, she told us that he'd jeered that even if he did strangle Mary Ann, there was nothing that could be proved now. That, together with his refusal to deny murdering her, settled his fate. It was one mocking step too far. Miss Maxwell decided he was not going to ruin any more lives as he had Mary Ann's. Compared with her love for Mary Ann, Miss Paget's undying devotion to her, emotional and physical seems to have been disregarded. Now belatedly, Miss Maxwell has, I believe, realized it.

'They used the knife,' the inspector continued, 'that Alice Maxwell had brought to the Coach and Horses from the Court, intending to use it in her Medea speech at the Follies, but in the event she did not use it at the actual performance, probably because she knew by then that she had another use for it. After the attack on Tobias Rocke, it was returned to the props bag they used for the Follies and although we searched her luggage as well as that of the other guests, we missed it because Doris Paget kept that with her. Miss Maxwell and Doris had intended to be the last to return to Wychbourne after the show's end; they would begin the walk back with Tobias Rocke and attack him in the bushy area by the churchyard fence. Most of those walking, I gathered, had pocket torches to help the dim lights on the driveway. Miss Maxwell and Miss Paget duly waited for Rocke until about ten thirty – though their statements claimed they left ten minutes earlier than that. Unfortunately for them, Rocke went home with the Palmers, which meant that plans for his murder had to be hastily changed. Knowing Rocke would be returning in due course, Miss Paget made her way with the knife through the bushes to the far end so that she could see when Rocke came down Mill Lane. That's where Jethro heard her.'

And the rustling in the bushes I heard as I left, Nell thought, must have been Doris Paget beginning to make her way to the far end of the churchyard.

'Having hurried back to Wychbourne Court to establish her presence,' the inspector explained, 'Alice Maxwell left again by the side entrance, as noted by our friend Jethro, and rushed back down the drive. It would be easy enough to manufacture a reason for returning should she be unlucky enough to meet anyone. In fact, she didn't and she reached the church porch just as Tobias left the lychgate and walked past the porch, with Miss Paget unnoticed hot on his tail.

'Alice Maxwell called out to him, he looked surprised but, in turning to reply to her, he gave Miss Paget the opportunity to strike. You know what happened then. Rocke managed to stagger through the gate, which was blocked open by the snow, and collapsed on the green. Doris Paget rushed after him, picked up the stone and made sure that this time he would not be staggering anywhere. There was plenty of blood, but they had provided for that possibility, as they could not afford to leave such an ornamented and probably therefore identifiable knife in the wound. Realizing that they could not risk blood being found on either of them, Miss Paget had slipped into Sevenoaks late on Friday and, as it was she who had volunteered to stab Rocke, she acquired one of those new ultra-light mackintoshes, the one we later found in the bushes.'

'Even though they have confessed, do you have other evidence than the mackintosh?' Lord Ansley asked. 'It could surely have belonged to any of your other suspects.'

'We do. We have, for instance, traced the shop where the

mackintosh was bought. They remember Miss Paget. I have to admit, however, that motivation made us look at Mr Heydock first as a suspect.'

'Not Mr Trotter?' Nell enquired innocently.

'Not on account of murder anyway. Perhaps my colleagues investigating fraud will be active on his account.'

'Poor Mr Trotter,' Lady Ansley said. 'I feel quite affectionate towards him now. The sad thing is that I do believe he has some strange powers and certainly Clarice does. There was after all that most strange movement of the table at the Great Hall tribunal.'

Nell agreed, but strange phenomena were not evidence of Mr Trotter's integrity. 'What about Mr Jarrett, Inspector?' she asked instead. 'Have they confessed to killing him too and do you have evidence?'

'Again only their confessions. Almost eagerly given as far as Alice Maxwell is concerned. She and Jarrett were always rivals, as is generally known, and each was determined to be the first of them to be recognized by the King for their services to the stage. Imagine therefore her consternation when after she had gone to such lengths to avenge the death of Mary Ann Darling and thus rid herself of her blackmailer, Mr Jarrett then took on his mantle by threatening to reveal her relationship with Miss Paget. That might not have shaken the theatre world but would certainly have ruled out the granting of an honour. Queen Victoria might not have recognized that such relationships took place, but Queen Mary and King George are made of more practical stuff.

'That was bad enough,' he continued, 'but then, as we know, she discovered that it was not Tobias Rocke alone, but Jarrett who made Mary Ann's life miserable, in Jarrett's case by harassing her. It is true that Hubert Jarrett was then a young man but not so young that one can merely dismiss his attachment as puppy love. If I may say this of your former friend, Lady Ansley, his need for power over his wife suggests far otherwise. Mary Ann had rejected his advances and for someone of Jarrett's disposition that was no more acceptable than it had been to Tobias Rocke. When in addition to his threats Miss Maxwell discovered he was Mary Ann's stalker, that sealed her rival's fate.'

'Cheyne Gardens,' Nell exclaimed. *That* was what had stuck in her mind after the inquest on Tobias Rocke. It hadn't fitted.

'Yes, Miss Drury, Cheyne Gardens. No one, save the Gaiety Guv'nor himself, knew where Mary Ann lived,' the inspector continued. 'Not even her great friend Alice Maxwell. And yet Hubert Jarrett knew.'

'And so Alice put the arsenic in his food?' Lord Ansley asked.

'Yes. Knowing from Mrs Palmer's invitation that they would be coming to the Coach and Horses for the funeral gathering, she and Doris Paget were able to make plans; all they needed was an opportunity to poison him and to delay the death if they could, though that wasn't essential. The perfect chance arose when they received the funeral announcement about the Coach and Horses gathering and Lady Ansley then spoke to Miss Maxwell on the telephone about the arrangements; Miss Maxwell was able to offer Doris Paget's services. They brought the poison with them – a possibility you suggested, Miss Drury – which had been inserted into a sandwich of the kind of bread used locally in Wychbourne. All Miss Paget had to do was add the shrimp filling when she arrived. She went straight to the pub to get the lie of the land and realized she could just slip the sandwich on a plate and offer it to Mr Jarrett.' He paused. 'I repeat that Wychbourne was not the source of the rat poison, Lord Ansley, and your kitchens, Miss Drury, are blameless.'

'I'm most grateful,' Nell said solemnly.

'And now, Lord Ansley, Lady Ansley, shall we dine?'

'No arsenic, if you please, Chief Inspector,' Lady Ansley replied.

'Foie gras, I do assure you, and the best champagne.'

Alex politely took Lady Ansley's arm and with Nell following with Lord Ansley, they were conducted by the maitre d' up the stairs to the first floor, where he stopped by the door of a room on the right.

'By George,' Lord Ansley said, 'this is the same room, isn't it? I've often visited Romano's since but always avoided this floor. Did it have to be here, Chief Inspector?'

'I realize that it will bring back sad memories,' Alex said, 'but despite that, I hope you will enjoy it. I also hope you will not object to my having invited two other guests, one of whom worked here with Signor Murano in former years, although he now lives in southern France. The wine will be from his own vineyard, as he learned much about wine from Romano's. Lady Ansley, Miss Drury, Lord Ansley, may I introduce Madame la Marquise and Monsieur le Marquis de Vaucluse.'

What on earth was this about? Why invite strangers? Nell wondered, even such interesting guests. The Marquis was a tall man in his mid-fifties and the fair-haired Marquise with her lively eyes was about the same age. This was yet another mystery from Alex Melbray. She sensed he was holding something back but couldn't even begin to guess what it was. And then Alex Melbray told them.

'You know her better as Mary Ann Darling.'

The room spun around her and it wasn't just the cocktail. Nell was sure of that at least. Had she misheard? No, she could see Lord Ansley was smiling, advancing towards the Marquise.

'Mary Ann,' he murmured.

She hadn't misheard. This really *was* Mary Ann Darling. Not murdered, but very much alive and *here,* smiling but a little anxious too.

'You must forgive me, Lady Ansley, Gerald and Miss Drury too, for remaining silent so long,' she said.

Lady Ansley's face changed from shock to warmth. 'Madame la Marquise, I took over your part in *The Flower Shop Girl.* I'm so sorry.'

'I know you did. I read it in the magazines and was delighted. I saw your photographs and knew you were right for the part and that I would like to meet you and now I have. I longed for the opportunity to do so and to tell my friends that I was safe and happy. But I could not, while that man was alive, not even Gerald.'

'We feared you were dead, Mary Ann.' His voice was choked with emotion.

'Thanks to Louis and to you, Gerald, and dear Neville, I am not. You were the only ones I trusted. I was so sad that you believed I had met my death. The inspector tells me that it was my former landlady who reported me missing, as the Guv'nor, bless him, must have left that job to her. So it was she who was called on to identify that body and she seized the opportunity probably to enrich herself. My estate, such as it was, went to the Crown as my family could not be traced, but I suspect that my valuable jewellery could well have crept into my landlady's pockets.

'Tobias Rocke, I fear,' she continued, 'purposely misled Alice by telling her he had murdered me. When that body was found he used that dead body for his own ends. Poor woman, whoever she was. I believe that there was more to it than just his wish to infuriate Alice, however. If he could believe me dead and the investigation into my disappearance closed, he would find it easier to forget that the charms of the great Tobias Rocke had been rejected. He loved power over other people and that can be an evil thing, dear friends. It is at its worst when challenged. And love can lead to evil too. Poor Alice did indeed love me. But because of that she murdered two people and that I cannot forgive her – or myself for being its object.'

'No, Madame, she did it for herself, not you,' Lady Ansley said. 'She couldn't reach your heart and took out her rage on others.'

Mary Ann bowed her head. 'Thank you, Lady Ansley. My silence has brought unhappiness to others that I did not intend. Tobias Rocke was still active, however. He would not have forgotten the way I slighted him, as he saw it. Despite the distress I inadvertently caused, however, the plan for my disappearance worked perfectly, and dear Louis and I have been happy ever since.'

'May we know what happened after you left us that night?' Lord Ansley asked.

'The cab driver of the first cab originally intended for me was a friend of mine,' she explained. 'Louis arranged with him to draw up by Romano's door after our own cab was in place. Our friend told the truth. His cab was empty when it arrived at my lodgings. Louis's and my cab took us to the Embankment Gardens only. There I changed my coat, put on a wig and different hat, all rather shabby, and Louis too was clad in everyday clothes. We walked up Villiers Street to Charing Cross railway station, where we had left our luggage; the night service to Paris had already left, and so we took a train to Dover, stayed the night there and took the Paris connection the following day. Now we live near Avignon. We are lucky. We have three children, and one of them is a singer.'

She smiled at Lady Ansley. 'But she does not sing "Song of My Heart". I can hear the gramophone record of your singing that, but that is not the same as hearing you. Would you sing it for me, Gertrude?'

'Only if you sing it with me, Mary Ann.' There were tears in Lady Ansley's eyes and, Nell realized, in hers too.

'Shall we have a picnic lunch before you leave, Nell?' Alex had come to the Waldorf to meet her the next morning. 'We could try the gardens by the river. I heard a bird or two singing as I walked here.'

'It's February, Alex,' she protested.

'A picnic inside a restaurant then.'

Nell burst out laughing. 'Done.'

'I'm glad you're laughing. I thought I'd been crossed off your dancing programme for having pushed you away not once but twice and then unfairly steamrollering you.'

'I did cross you off.'

'Put me back on probation then.' He hesitated. 'I'll have to stay in London, Nell. There's nothing we can do about it. Scotland Yard won't move to Kent even if you plan any more crimes around Wychbourne.'

'And Wychbourne won't move to London,' Nell tried to say lightly. She looked at him and then hastened to regain ground. 'Not yet anyway.'

'What if that saucepan of ours boils over? Do we devote ourselves forever to our respective tasks of clearing the world of crime and educating its cuisine?'

'No,' she said without thinking. But what if she *did* think? Would the decision be different?

Alex sighed. 'There's a poem by Robert Browning about a loving lady at her window and her adoring knight passing by. Neither could pluck up their courage to do anything about it, so they became old and grey and had to put up statues of themselves to preserve their relationship.'

'I don't fancy that.'

'Don't leave it too long, Nell.'